I0828109

PLAYING *with* FIRE

PLAYING *with* FIRE

The Weird Tales of

ARTHUR CONAN DOYLE

Edited by Mike Ashley

THE BRITISH LIBRARY

This collection first published in 2021 by
The British Library
96 Euston Road
London NW1 2DB

Dates attributed to each story relate to first publication.

These stories are presented as they were originally published and as such contain language in common usage at the time of their writing. Neither the publisher nor the editor endorses any language which would now be considered xenophobic or offensive.

Reprinted in 2025
Represented in the EU by Authorised Rep Compliance Ltd., Ground Floor, 71 Lower Baggot Street, Dublin, D02 P593, Ireland. arccompliance.com

Cataloguing in Publication Data
A catalogue record for this publication is available from the British Library

ISBN 978 0 7123 5425 7

Cover design by Mauricio Villamayor with illustration by Mag Ruhig.

Text design and typesetting by Tetragon, London.
Printed in Malta by Gutenberg Press.

CONTENTS

INTRODUCTION

The Scientist and the Psychic

Arthur Conan Doyle's name is so inextricably linked to his creation, Sherlock Holmes, that it overshadows much of his other work. Doyle was only too aware of that, becoming tired of Holmes when the time spent on new stories stopped him writing what he preferred; mostly historical fiction but, following his interest in spiritualism, tales of the strange and supernatural. Doyle wrote almost as many of these strange stories as he did those featuring Sherlock Holmes. Once we include further stories classifiable these days as science fiction, we find that he wrote as many if not more strange stories as he did tales of the Great Detective.

This volume brings together some of his best, most unusual and diverse weird tales, many of which reflect upon aspects of his life. He wrote about some of his own spiritual experiences in a little-known essay 'Stranger Than Fiction' which is reprinted here for the first time.

Doyle was a natural storyteller. He was born in 1859 into an artistic family—his father, uncle and grandfather were all published artists and illustrators. Both his uncle, Richard Doyle, and his father, Charles Altamont Doyle, produced bizarre and often grotesque images. Richard became renowned for his pictures of fairies and elves and his reputation overshadowed that of his younger brother, Charles, whose comparative lack of success as an artist turned him to drink, and the production of even more bizarre drawings. It is hard to imagine that his father's illustrations did not have an influence on the young Arthur.

Scottish by birth, but Irish by descent, Arthur was gifted with that natural Celtic ability to spin yarns. He was further encouraged by his great uncle, Michael Conan, from whom he gained his middle name. Conan, a barrister and art journalist, lived for many years in Paris and his relationship with young Arthur was mostly by mail. He would send the boy a variety of adventure novels which sparked Doyle's imagination. His early favourite writers were Mayne Reid, R.M. Ballantyne and Sir Walter Scott. At the age of six, young Arthur had penned his first story about a hunter who meets his fate with a tiger. Even at that age, Doyle realised it was easy to get your character into a problem but less easy to help him out.

In 1868 Doyle was sent to Hodder, near Preston, Lancashire, a preparatory school for the Jesuit College at Stonyhurst which he attended from 1870 to 1875. While at Hodder, Doyle would regale his fellow pupils with heroic adventure stories and was bribed to finish the yarns with cakes and cream tarts. While at Stonyhurst, Doyle began a small magazine called *Wasp* to which he contributed poems and cartoons—he also claimed he contributed to the college magazine, though that was not until later years.

From Stonyhurst, Doyle continued his education at the Jesuit College of Feldkirch in Austria to improve his German. He was already fluent in French and was reading the novels of Jules Verne in their original language. He had also been an avid reader of the leading Scottish magazine *Blackwood's* to which a close friend of the family, John Hill Burton—a noted lawyer and historian—regularly contributed.

It is perhaps no surprise, then, that when Doyle considered submitting material for possible publication that his first choice of market was *Blackwood's*. This first story, 'The Haunted Grange of Goresthorpe', written perhaps in 1877 or 1878, is a highly gothic ghost story, rather too melodramatic and formulaic. It tells of two lads, one a medical student, who spend a night in a reputedly haunted house and witness the ghost of a murderer being pursued by his victim. It reads just as if it was one of the stories he must have told to his friends, full of exuberance and atmosphere.

Blackwood's set it aside, either to reconsider it, or return it at some stage (it is not clear that they had a return address) and forgot about it. It remained in their archives for over a century before being discovered and eventually published by the Arthur Conan Doyle Society in 2000. I have not reprinted it here because it lacks the polish of his later work, but it is of significance because it shows that his first attempt at formal publication was with a ghost story.

Doyle was himself a medical student at this time, struggling to acquire the money to pay for his scholarship, despite being helped by another family friend, Dr Waller. Doyle's father had been retired by his employers in June 1876 and the family were in need of income. As the eldest son, though only seventeen at the time, Doyle must have felt a responsibility to contribute. His elder sister, Annette, worked as a governess in Portugal and sent much of her salary home. So, despite his medical studies, until he qualified in August 1881, Doyle looked for other means of income.

Unfazed by hearing nothing from *Blackwood's*, Doyle submitted a new story, 'The Mystery of Sasassa Valley', to the rival Edinburgh magazine, *Chambers's Journal*. It is in much the same vein as his first attempt. Two young men try to seek their fortune in South Africa and learn of the legend of the haunted valley. This time the mystery is rationalised, so it is not a genuine supernatural story, but it is full of the same bravura melodrama. And this time it was accepted, appearing in the issue for 6 September 1879. Arthur Conan Doyle was a published author.

His medical studies limited his time to write, and he later admitted that most of the stories he submitted were rejected, but now and then one made it through. He was learning the writing trade at the same time he was discovering life as a doctor. He placed articles with the *British Medical Journal* and *The Lancet* as well as pursuing an interest in photography with articles in the *British Journal of Photography*.

He was also having adventures. During the spring of 1880 he served as a surgeon on the whaler *Hope* in the Arctic and after he graduated he served as a doctor on the *Mayumba* on the coast of West Africa in January 1882, both before he opened his practice in Southsea in May 1882.

He continued to write. His experiences in the Arctic led to what many regard as his first important short story, and a ghost story of considerable merit, 'The Captain of the "Polestar"', published in *Temple Bar* in January 1883 and reprinted here.

At the same time Doyle took interest in the growing fascination for spiritualism, though at this stage it was purely from a scientific perspective. In January 1881 he attended a lecture, 'Does Death End All?' given by an American preacher Joseph Cook. At the same time interested parties were discussing the need for a disciplined approach to studying spiritual and psychic matters resulting in the formation of the Society for Psychical Research (SPR) in February 1882. Though Doyle did not join the Society until January 1893 he had many dealings with leading members during the late 1880s and his early interest in psychic phenomena is evident in 'The Winning Shot', reprinted here. In the story, which had been rejected by Doyle's regular markets and eventually appeared in *Bow Bells* for 11 July 1883, Doyle discusses several examples of strange phenomena, such as those recorded by the medium Daniel Dunglas Home, and found in the writings of Catherine Crowe.

Doyle was particularly interested in the powers of the mind, such as telepathy, and the extent to which one individual can exercise power over another. He explored this idea first in 'John Barrington Cowles', which ran in two weekly editions of *Cassell's Saturday Journal* during April 1884. Set during Doyle's own days at Edinburgh University, he depicts the power that a *femme fatale* can exercise over a student.

Doyle reused the idea in his novella 'The Parasite', also included here. By now, Doyle had become a confirmed spiritualist and had also joined the Society for Psychical Research, sharing his interest in the study of mesmerism with scientist Oliver Lodge. Doyle was fascinated by whatever constituted the human soul and wondered whether mesmerism could take over not only physical control but spiritual. As Doyle wrote in 'Stranger Than Fiction', included here:

> I am always conscious of the latent powers of the human spirit, and of the direct intervention into human life of outside forces which mould and modify our actions.

At the time Doyle was writing 'The Parasite', *Harper's Monthly* was serialising George Du Maurier's *Trilby*, probably the best-known novel on the idea of mesmeric control. It has been suggested that Doyle was anxious to finish his novella by way of comparison with *Trilby*, with Doyle emphasising the study of mind-control as a possible future science. 'The Parasite' was serialised in *Harper's* companion magazine, *Harper's Weekly* during November 1894 yet the novella has never received the recognition garnered by *Trilby*.

Doyle had turned to writing full-time in June 1891 and by now he was also actively involved in spiritualism and psychic research. This may seem strange to those who know Doyle only through reading the stories featuring the highly logical and scientific Sherlock Holmes. In *The Hound of the Baskervilles,* serialised in *The Strand Magazine* in 1901, his client, a doctor, suggests that the events on Dartmoor might be caused by something not of this Earth, to which Holmes retorts: 'And you, a trained man of science, believe it to be supernatural?' Holmes allowed Doyle to retain a rational mind, while also being every bit as interested in the inexplicable.

In June 1894, along with two officials from the SPR, Doyle investigated a house in Dorset where there were reports of unexplained noises. They concluded it was a hoax, but it demonstrates Doyle's sincere interest in psychic phenomena. When he contributed a series called 'Round the Fire Stories' to *The Strand* at the end of the decade he included one, 'The Story of the Brown Hand' (1899), where one of the characters refers to his experiences with the SPR. Likewise, 'Playing With Fire' (1900) is set during a séance which gets out of hand. 'The Leather Funnel' (1902), later added to the collection *Round the Fire Stories,* shows Doyle's interest in psychometry where physical contact with an object allows its past to be investigated.

Over the next few decades Doyle found himself once again busy writing Holmes stories and struggling to return to his historical novels, but he also created a popular new character in the form of Professor Challenger. He first appeared in *The Lost World,* serialised in 1912 followed by *The Poison Belt* in 1913. These are both science fiction stories, but at times his dual interests in science and the supernatural overlapped. 'The Terror of Blue John Gap' (1910), for example, suggests a monster deep in the caves of the Peak District, whilst 'The Horror of the Heights' (1913) suggests monsters in the upper atmosphere. The supernatural, or perhaps I should call it a psychic science, would also start to intrude upon the adventures of Professor Challenger and the investigations of Sherlock Holmes. In 'The Adventure of the Creeping Man' (1923) Holmes discovers that a professor's odd behaviour is due to experimenting with monkey glands. The short novel 'The Land of Mist' (1926) has Challenger investigating spiritualism and becoming converted. 'When the World Screamed' (1928) depicts the Earth as a living organism.

Against these explorations of psychic or scientific possibilities, Doyle continued to produce the occasional more restrained ghost story including 'How it Happened' (1913) and 'The Bully of Brocas Court' (1921), both reprinted here. The latter employs Doyle's lifelong interest in boxing and allows us to bring this collection to a close with a rather unusual ghost.

Doyle's reputation was dented quite considerably because of his belief in the case of the Cottingley Fairies. In 1920 two young children took photographs of what were supposed to be fairies at the bottom of their garden. Doyle became interested in the case and used it to demonstrate what exists beyond our normal perception. Anyone today looking at those photographs can tell that they are fake—they were cut-out pictures of fairies. But Doyle was convinced, just as he had been convinced by many mediums at séances and by spirit photographs. In the eyes of many Doyle was seen as gullible, but he never swayed from his conviction and this is what is important when it came to his fiction. Doyle could produce a story that feels real because he put his heart and soul into it. You have only to read the stories included here to know that Doyle was a great storyteller, creating characters and images with which you could associate and in which you would believe. Why otherwise would so many believe that Sherlock Holmes and Dr Watson were real? Doyle's ability to convince himself of what others saw as fakery was the same ability with which he could create living and breathing characters in his fiction, and powerful and memorable imagery. The stories collected here show the gifted imagination of a master storyteller, and you will remember them for a long, long time.

Mike Ashley

A NOTE FROM THE PUBLISHER

The original short stories reprinted in the British Library's classic fiction series were written and published in a period ranging across the nineteenth and twentieth centuries. There are many elements of these stories which continue to entertain modern readers; however, in some cases there are also uses of language, instances of stereotyping and some attitudes expressed by narrators or characters which may not be endorsed by the publishing standards of today. We acknowledge therefore that some elements in the stories selected for reprinting may continue to make uncomfortable reading for some of our audience. With these new editions British Library Publishing aims to offer a new readership a chance to read some of the rare material of the British Library's collections in an affordable format, to enjoy their merits and to look back into the worlds of the past two centuries as portrayed by their writers. It is not possible to separate these stories from the history of their writing and as such the following stories are presented as they were originally published with minor edits only, made for consistency of style and sense. We welcome feedback from our readers, which can be sent to the following address:

British Library Publishing
The British Library
96 Euston Road
London, NW1 2DB
United Kingdom

STRANGER THAN FICTION

WHEN one casts one's thoughts back upon one's own life in search of things which seem particularly strange, it is not in the material events that one most clearly perceives them. I have had the good fortune to have had a fairly adventurous life and to have visited strange parts of the world under interesting conditions. I have seen something of two wars. I have practised the most dramatic profession in the world. I have travelled from North Greenland and Spitzbergen to West Africa, and my thoughts can conjure up many a recollection of storm and danger, of whales and bears and sharks and snakes, and all that used to interest me as a schoolboy. And yet whatever I could say upon such subjects someone else has said already with more authority and experience. It is rather when you look closely into the intimate workings of your own mind and spirit, the queer intuitions, the strange happenings, the inexplicable things which come suddenly to the surface and are glimpsed rather than seen, the incredible coincidences, the stories which should end one way but either end the other or else have no definite finish at all, tailing off into oblivion with ragged fringes of mystery behind them instead of the neat little knot of the tidy-minded romancer—it is these, I say, which seem to be really stranger than any fiction.

The most remarkable experiences in a man's life are those in which he feels most, and they are precisely those of which he is least disposed to talk. All the really very serious things in my life, the things which have been stamped deep into me and left their impress for ever, are things of which I could never bring myself to speak. And yet it is within the compass of just these intimate and vital things that one perceives strange forces to be moving and is conscious of vague and wonderful compulsions and directions which are, I think, the innermost facts of life. Personally, I am always conscious of the latent powers of the human spirit, and of the direct intervention into human life of outside forces which mould and modify our actions. They are usually too subtle for direct definition, but occasionally they become so crude that one cannot overlook them.

I will take a very obvious example, which I have quoted before, but which may bear re-telling, as it shows the thing in its most undeniable form. In the year 1892 I was travelling in Switzerland and had occasion to cross the Gemmi Pass. On the top of it was a lonely inn which looks down upon a populous valley on either side, but is itself entirely isolated during the winter. I supposed that it was deserted at that time, but I was told upon inquiry that this was not so. The family laid in a supply of food and remained there for some months utterly cut off from the people below them. The singularity of such a position arrested my attention, and a story began at once to form itself within my brain, in which I conceived the desperate position of a group of characters strongly antagonistic and reacting upon each other, who had no refuge from each other's company and were irresistibly impelled towards black tragedy while the golden lights of happy human life twinkled in the valleys beneath them. These ideas were still weaving themselves in my brain and building themselves up into symmetrical form in the strange semi-conscious impersonal way that such things grow, when I bought a book of Maupassant's to while away my return journey through France. It was certainly a book which I had never read before. The first story in it was called 'l'Auberge'—'The Inn'—and there was the whole of my conception already finished by a master hand! It was the same inn, the Gemmi Pass, the winter, the group of characters, all complete. There was a great dog that I had not yet come upon. The rest was what I had schemed and what I would assuredly have published as my own but for this happy chance that saved me. But was it a chance? Could it have been a chance? That Maupassant had passed that way and that his quick brain had seen the possibilities of the lonely inn—that is likely enough. But that in the few days between thinking the story and writing it I should buy the one and only book in the world which would prevent me from making a fool of myself—could that be a coincidence, or was a kindly outside influence at work to save me from such an error? Whether coincidence or guidance, it was one of those things that are stranger than fiction.

And yet I am willing to admit that without any external action at all, unless it be the malign one of some mischievous Puck, the most extraordinary coincidences do occur in life which one would certainly never dare to invent. Here is a case in point.

Since I have at various times written certain detective stories, some simple souls have been willing to identify me with my hero and to call me in to their aid when they were in distress. I have even been offered a blank cheque to take up a case. Possibly so long as it remained blank it would about represent the value which I could give in exchange. Still, I may claim with some complacency that out of half-a-dozen cases which pity or curiosity has induced me to investigate I have always reached a solution. In one notorious case I was, however, the victim of the extraordinary coincidence to which I allude. In connection with the crime I had suspicions of a certain family which I will call Wilder—not necessarily as being the direct criminals, but as knowing a good deal about the matter. One member of this family had, to my knowledge, gone to California some years before. His name was John and he was an architect by profession. Presently, from a small town in California which I will call St Anne, I began to receive papers alluding to my investigation and scribbled all round the margins with ribald blasphemy. On one of these communications was the address from which it came. I at once wrote to the Chief of the Police of that town, giving the address and asking if he could tell me whether a John Wilder, architect, late of England, was living there. He answered me that it was so. Now, surely you would think that this was final. I had actually been able to give the name and trade of a man living six thousand miles away with nothing to direct me but a line of deduction. I was convinced that the line was correct, and I notified the British police of the result. Can it be believed that the answer I received from them some weeks later was that they had investigated the matter, that it was a coincidence, and that the John Wilder in question was a different man from him whom I sought?

The insane papers sent to me were from a well-known religious maniac who lived in the same boarding-house. This man was an American and had certainly nothing to do with the crime, but I am unable to understand even now how he came to take any interest in the matter if there were not some Englishman near him to coach him in the details. However, I can, of course, only accept the police report, as correct and claim to have been the victim of a coincidence which certainly could not be used in fiction.

It is in the twilight-land, where spirit and matter meet, that the strangest happenings occur. Sometimes they are very slight and objectless, and yet point to vast issues behind them. I remember that in Rome my wife and I were walking on the Pincio. She had never been there before nor read anything about it, for it was the first day of our visit. She suddenly said, in an abstracted voice, 'There is a statue of Dante there.' A few moments later we came upon the statue, which had been concealed by bushes. I said, 'How could you possibly know that?' She answered, 'I have no idea. I simply *knew* it.' What a trivial, inconclusive episode, and yet can all science give a name or an explanation for such an incident?

I have studied the occult for thirty years, and it seems strange to me to listen to the confident opinions, generally negative ones, which are expressed upon the subject by people who have not given it really serious thought for as many minutes. This is not the time or place for me to give my views, which are still those of a student rather than of a dogmatist. But I have had one or two experiences which are a little outside the usual range of *séances* or manifestations, and also outside the range of what one could render credible in fiction. In one of these affairs I seemed to brush very close to something really remarkable, unless deception on one side and coincidence upon the other have established a strange working partnership.

I was living in the country at the time, and formed an acquaintance with a small doctor—small physically and also in professional practice—who lived hard by. He was a student of the occult, and my curiosity was aroused by learning that he had one room in his house which no one entered except himself, as it was reserved for mystic and philosophic purposes. Finding that I was interested in such subjects, Dr Brown, as I will call him, suggested one day that I should join a secret society of esoteric students. The invitation had been led up to by a good deal of preparatory inquiry. The dialogue between us ran somewhat thus:—

'What shall I get from it?'

'In time, you will get powers.'

'What sort of powers?'

'They are powers which people would call supernatural. They are perfectly natural, but they are got by knowledge of deeper forces of Nature.'

'If they are good, why should not everyone know them?'

'They would be capable of great abuse in the wrong hands.'

'How can you prevent their getting into wrong hands?'

'By carefully examining our initiates.'

'Should I be examined?'

'Certainly.'

'By whom?'

'The people would be in London.'

'Should I have to present myself?'

'No, no; they would do it without your knowledge.'

'And after that?'

'You would then have to study.'

'Study what?'

'You would have to learn by heart a considerable mass of material. That would be the first thing.'

'If this material is in print, why does it not become public property?'

'It is not in print. It is in manuscript. Each manuscript is carefully numbered and trusted to the honour of a passed initiate. We have never had a case of one going wrong.'

'Well,' said I, 'it is very interesting, and you can go ahead with the next step, whatever it may be.'

Some little time later—it may have been a week—I woke in the very early morning with a most extraordinary sensation. It was not a nightmare or any prank of a dream. It was quite different to that, for it persisted after I was wide awake. I can only describe it by saying that I was tingling all over. It was not painful, but it was queer and disagreeable, as a mild electric shock would be. I thought at once of the little doctor.

In a few days I had a visit from him. 'You have been examined and you have passed,' said he, with a smile. 'Now you must say definitely whether you will go on with it. You can't take it up and drop it. It is serious, and you must leave it alone or go forward with a whole heart.'

It began to dawn upon me that it really was serious, so serious that there seemed no possible space for it in my very crowded and preoccupied life. I said as much, and he took it in very good part. 'Very well,' said he, 'we won't talk of it any more unless you change your mind.'

There was a sequel to the story. A month or two later, on a pouring wet day, the little doctor called, bringing with him another medical man whose name was familiar to me in connection with exploration and tropical service. They sat together beside my study fire and talked. One could not but observe that the famous and much-travelled man was very deferential to the little country surgeon, who was the younger of the two.

'He is one of my initiates,' said the latter to me. 'You know,' he continued, turning to his companion, 'Doyle nearly joined us once.' The other looked at me with great interest, and then at once plunged into a conversation with his mentor as to the wonders he had seen and, as I understood, actually done. I listened amazed. It sounded like the talk of two lunatics. One phrase stuck in my memory.

'When first you took me up with you,' said he, 'and we were hovering over the town I used to live in in Central Africa, I was able for the first time to see the islands out in the lake. I always knew they were there, but they were too far off to be seen from the shore. Was it not extraordinary that I should first see them when I was living in England?'

There were other remarks as wonderful. 'A conspiracy to impress a simpleton,' says the sceptic. Well, we will leave it at that, if the sceptic so wills, but I am under the impression that I have brushed against something strange. This is one of the stories with an untidy, ragged ending such as the editor abhors.

One more queer experience which will bear telling. I volunteered once to sleep in a haunted house in Dorsetshire. Two other investigators went with me. We were a deputation from the Psychical Society—of which, by the way, I am almost an original member. It took us the whole railway journey from town to read up the evidence as to the senseless noises which had made life unendurable for the occupants, who were tied by a lease and could not get away. We sat up there two nights. On the first nothing occurred. On the second, one of our party left us and I sat up with the late Mr Podmore, a well-known student of these things. We had, of course, taken every precaution to checkmate fraud, putting worsted threads across the stairs, and so on.

In the middle of the night a fearsome uproar broke out. It was like someone belabouring a resounding table with a heavy cudgel. It was not an accidental creaking of wood or anything of that sort, but a deafening row. We had all doors open, so we rushed at once into the kitchen, from which the sound had surely come. There was nothing there—doors were all locked, windows barred, and threads unbroken. Podmore took away the light and pretended that we had both returned to our sitting-room, while I waited in the dark in the hope of a return of the disturbance. None came—or ever did come. What occasioned it we never knew. It was of the same character as all the other disturbances we had read about, but shorter in time. Here there was a sequel to the story. Some years later the house was burned down, which may or may not have had a bearing upon the sprite which seemed to haunt it, but a more suggestive thing is that the skeleton of a child about ten years old was dug up in the garden. This I give on the authority of a relation of the family who were so plagued. The suggestion was that the child had been done to death there, and that the subsequent phenomena, of which we had one small sample, were in some way a sequence to this tragedy. There is a theory that a young life cut short in sudden and unnatural fashion may leave, as it were, a store of unused vitality which may be put to strange uses. But here again we are drifting into regions which are stranger than fiction. The unknown and the marvellous press upon us from all sides. They loom above us and around us in undefined and fluctuating shapes, some dark, some shimmering, but all warning us of the limitations of what we call matter, and of the need for spirituality if we are to keep in touch with the true inner facts of life.

THE CAPTAIN OF THE 'POLESTAR'

[Being an extract from the singular journal of JOHN M'ALISTER RAY, *student of medicine.]*

SEPTEMBER *11th.*—Lat. 81° 40' N.; long. 2° E. Still lying-to amid enormous ice-fields. The one which stretches away to the north of us, and to which our ice-anchor is attached, cannot be smaller than an English county. To the right and left unbroken sheets extend to the horizon. This morning the mate reported that there were signs of pack ice to the southward. Should this form of sufficient thickness to bar our return, we shall be in a position of danger, as the food, I hear, is already running somewhat short. It is late in the season, and the nights are beginning to reappear. This morning I saw a star twinkling just over the fore-yard, the first since the beginning of May. There is considerable discontent among the crew, many of whom are anxious to get back home to be in time for the herring season, when labour always commands a high price upon the Scotch coast. As yet their displeasure is only signified by sullen countenances and black looks, but I heard from the second mate this afternoon that they contemplated sending a deputation to the captain to explain their grievance. I much doubt how he will receive it, as he is a man of fierce temper, and very sensitive about anything approaching to an infringement of his rights. I shall venture after dinner to say a few words to him upon the subject. I have always found that he will tolerate from me what he would resent from any other member of the crew. Amsterdam Island, at the north-west corner of Spitzbergen, is visible upon our starboard quarter—a rugged line of volcanic rocks, intersected by white seams, which represent glaciers. It is curious to think that at the present moment there is probably no human being nearer to us than the Danish settlements in the south of Greenland—a good nine hundred miles as the crow flies. A captain takes a great responsibility upon himself when he risks his vessel under such circumstances. No whaler has ever remained in these latitudes till so advanced a period of the year.

9 p.m.—I have spoken to Captain Craigie, and though the result has been hardly satisfactory, I am bound to say that he listened to what I had to say very quietly and even deferentially. When I had finished he put on that air of iron determination which I have frequently observed upon his face, and paced rapidly backwards and forwards across the narrow cabin for some minutes. At first I feared that I had seriously offended him, but he dispelled the idea by sitting down again, and putting his hand upon my arm with a gesture which almost amounted to a caress. There was a depth of tenderness too in his wild dark eyes which surprised me considerably. 'Look here, Doctor,' he said, 'I'm sorry I ever took you—I am indeed—and I would give fifty pounds this minute to see you standing safe upon the Dundee quay. It's hit or miss with me this time. There are fish to the north of us. How dare you shake your head, sir, when I tell you I saw them blowing from the masthead?'—this in a sudden burst of fury, though I was not conscious of having shown any signs of doubt. 'Two-and-twenty fish in as many minutes as I am a living man, and not one under ten foot.* Now, Doctor, do you think I can leave the country when there is only one infernal strip of ice between me and my fortune? If it came on to blow from the north tomorrow we could fill the ship and be away before the frost could catch us. If it came on to blow from the south—well, I suppose the men are paid for risking their lives, and as for myself it matters but little to me, for I have more to bind me to the other world than to this one. I confess that I am sorry for *you*, though. I wish I had old Angus Tait who was with me last voyage, for he was a man that would never be missed, and you—you said once that you were engaged, did you not?'

'Yes,' I answered, snapping the spring of the locket which hung from my watch-chain, and holding up the little vignette of Flora.

'Curse you!' he yelled, springing out of his seat, with his very beard bristling with passion. 'What is your happiness to me? What have I to do with her that you must dangle her photograph before my eyes?' I almost thought that he was about to strike me in the frenzy of his rage, but with another imprecation he dashed open the door of the cabin and rushed out upon deck, leaving me considerably astonished at his extraordinary violence. It is the first time that he has ever shown me anything but courtesy and kindness. I can hear him pacing excitedly up and down overhead as I write these lines.

I should like to give a sketch of the character of this man, but it seems presumptuous to attempt such a thing upon paper, when the idea in my own mind is at best a vague and uncertain one. Several times I have thought that I grasped the clue which might explain it, but only to be disappointed by his presenting himself in some new light which would upset all my conclusions. It may be that no human eye but my

* A whale is measured among whalers not by the length of its body, but by the length of its whalebone.

own shall ever rest upon these lines, yet as a psychological study I shall attempt to leave some record of Captain Nicholas Craigie.

A man's outer case generally gives some indication of the soul within. The captain is tall and well-formed, with dark, handsome face, and a curious way of twitching his limbs, which may arise from nervousness, or be simply an outcome of his excessive energy. His jaw and whole cast of countenance is manly and resolute, but the eyes are the distinctive feature of his face. They are of the very darkest hazel, bright and eager, with a singular mixture of recklessness in their expression, and of something else which I have sometimes thought was more allied with horror than any other emotion. Generally the former predominated, but on occasions, and more particularly when he was thoughtfully inclined, the look of fear would spread and deepen until it imparted a new character to his whole countenance. It is at these times that he is most subject to tempestuous fits of anger, and he seems to be aware of it, for I have known him lock himself up so that no one might approach him until his dark hour was passed. He sleeps badly, and I have heard him shouting during the night, but his cabin is some little distance from mine, and I could never distinguish the words which he said.

This is one phase of his character, and the most disagreeable one. It is only through my close association with him, thrown together as we are day after day, that I have observed it. Otherwise he is an agreeable companion, well-read and entertaining, and as gallant a seaman as ever trod a deck. I shall not easily forget the way in which he handled the ship when we were caught by a gale among the loose ice at the beginning of April. I have never seen him so cheerful, and even hilarious, as he was that night, as he paced backwards and forwards upon the bridge amid the flashing of the lightning and the howling of the wind. He has told me several times that the thought of death was a pleasant one to him, which is a sad thing for a young man to say; he cannot be much more than thirty, though his hair and moustache are already slightly grizzled. Some great sorrow must have overtaken him and blighted his whole life. Perhaps I should be the same if I lost my Flora—God knows! I think if it were not for her that I should care very little whether the wind blew from the north or the south tomorrow. There, I hear him come down the companion, and he has locked himself up in his room, which shows that he is still in an unamiable mood. And so to bed, as old Pepys would say, for the candle is burning down (we have to use them now since the nights are closing in), and the steward has turned in, so there are no hopes of another one.

September 12th.—Calm, clear day, and still lying in the same position. What wind there is comes from the south-east, but it is very slight. Captain is in a better humour, and apologised to me at breakfast for his rudeness. He still looks somewhat distrait, however, and retains that wild look in his eyes which in a Highlander would mean that he was 'fey'—at least so our chief engineer remarked to me, and he has some reputation among the Celtic portion of our crew as a seer and expounder of omens.

It is strange that superstition should have obtained such mastery over this hard-headed and practical race. I could not have believed to what an extent it is carried had I not observed it for myself. We have had a perfect epidemic of it this voyage, until I have felt inclined to serve out rations of sedatives and nerve-tonics with the Saturday allowance of grog. The first symptom of it was that shortly after leaving Shetland the men at the wheel used to complain that they heard plaintive cries and screams in the wake of the ship, as if something were following it and were unable to overtake it. This fiction has been kept up during the whole voyage, and on dark nights at the beginning of the seal-fishing it was only with great difficulty that men could be induced to do their spell. No doubt what they heard was either the creaking of the rudder-chains, or the cry of some passing sea-bird. I have been fetched out of bed several times to listen to it, but I need hardly say that I was never able to distinguish anything unnatural. The men, however, are so absurdly positive upon the subject that it is hopeless to argue with them. I mentioned the matter to the captain once, but to my surprise he took it very gravely, and indeed appeared to be considerably disturbed by what I told him. I should have thought that he at least would have been above such vulgar delusions.

All this disquisition upon superstition leads me up to the fact that Mr Manson, our second mate, saw a ghost last night—or, at least, says that he did, which of course is the same thing. It is quite refreshing to have some new topic of conversation after the eternal routine of bears and whales which has served us for so many months. Manson swears the ship is haunted, and that he would not stay in her a day if he had any other place to go to. Indeed the fellow is honestly frightened, and I had to give him some chloral and bromide of potassium this morning to steady him down. He seemed quite indignant when I suggested that he had been having an extra glass the night before, and I was obliged to pacify him by keeping as grave a countenance as possible during his story, which he certainly narrated in a very straightforward and matter-of-fact way.

'I was on the bridge,' he said, 'about four bells in the middle watch, just when the night was at its darkest. There was a bit of a moon, but the clouds were blowing across it so that you couldn't see far from the ship. John M'Leod, the harpooner, came aft from the fo'c'sle-head and reported a strange noise on the starboard bow. I went forrard and we both heard it, sometimes like a bairn crying and sometimes like a wench in pain. I've been seventeen years to the country and I never heard seal, old or young, make a sound like that. As we were standing there on the fo'c'sle-head the moon came out from behind a cloud, and we both saw a sort of white figure moving across the ice-field in the same direction that we had heard the cries. We lost sight of it for a while, but it came back on the port bow, and we could just make it out like a shadow on the ice. I sent a hand aft for the rifles, and M'Leod and I went down on to the pack, thinking that maybe it might be a bear. When we got on the ice I lost sight of M'Leod, but I pushed on in the direction where I could still hear the cries. I followed them for a mile or maybe more, and then running round a hummock I came right on to the top of it standing and waiting for me seemingly. I don't know what it was. It wasn't a bear, anyway. It was tall and white and straight, and if it wasn't a man nor a woman, I'll stake my davy it was something worse. I made for the ship as hard as I could run, and precious glad I was to find myself aboard. I signed articles to do my duty by the ship, and on the ship I'll stay, but you don't catch me on the ice again after sundown.'

That is his story, given as far as I can in his own words. I fancy what he saw must, in spite of his denial, have been a young bear erect upon its hind legs, an attitude which they often assume when alarmed. In the uncertain light this would bear a resemblance to a human figure, especially to a man whose nerves were already somewhat shaken. Whatever it may have been, the occurrence is unfortunate, for it has produced a most unpleasant effect upon the crew. Their looks are more sullen than before, and their discontent more open. The double grievance of being debarred from the herring fishing and of being detained in what they choose to call a haunted vessel, may lead them to do something rash. Even the harpooners, who are the oldest and steadiest among them, are joining in the general agitation.

Apart from this absurd outbreak of superstition, things are looking rather more cheerful. The pack which was forming to the south of us has partly cleared away, and the water is so warm as to lead me to believe that we are lying in one of those branches of the gulfstream which run up between Greenland and Spitzbergen. There are numerous small Medusæ and sea-lemons about the ship, with abundance of shrimps, so that there is every possibility of 'fish' being sighted. Indeed one was seen blowing about dinner-time, but in such a position that it was impossible for the boats to follow it.

September 13th.—Had an interesting conversation with the chief mate, Mr Milne, upon the bridge. It seems that our captain is as great an enigma to the seamen, and even to the owners of the vessel, as he has been to me. Mr Milne tells me that when the ship is paid off, upon returning from a voyage, Captain Craigie disappears, and is not seen again until the approach of another season, when he walks quietly into the office of the company, and asks whether his services will be required. He has no friend in Dundee, nor does anyone pretend to be acquainted with his early history. His position depends entirely upon his skill as a seaman, and the name for courage and coolness which he had earned in the capacity of mate, before being entrusted with a separate command. The unanimous opinion seems to be that he is not a Scotchman, and that his name is an assumed one. Mr Milne thinks that he has devoted himself to whaling simply for the reason that it is the most dangerous occupation which he could select, and that he courts death in every possible manner. He mentioned several instances of this, one of which is rather curious, if true. It seems that on one occasion he did not put in an appearance at the office, and a substitute had to be selected in his place. That was at the time of the last Russian and Turkish War. When he turned up again next spring he had a puckered wound in the side of his neck which he used to endeavour to conceal with his cravat. Whether the mate's inference that he had been engaged in the war is true or not I cannot say. It was certainly a strange coincidence.

The wind is veering round in an easterly direction, but is still very slight. I think the ice is lying closer than it did yesterday. As far as the eye can reach on every side there is one wide expanse of spotless white, only broken by an occasional rift or the dark shadow of a hummock. To the south there is the narrow lane of blue water which is our sole means of escape, and which is closing up every day. The captain is taking a heavy responsibility upon himself. I hear that the tank of potatoes has been finished, and even the biscuits are running short, but he preserves the same impassable countenance, and spends the greater part of the day at the crow's nest, sweeping the horizon with his glass. His manner is very variable, and he seems to avoid my society, but there has been no repetition of the violence which he showed the other night.

7.30 p.m.—My deliberate opinion is that we are commanded by a madman. Nothing else can account for the extraordinary vagaries of Captain Craigie. It is fortunate that I have kept this journal of our voyage, as it will serve to justify us in case we have to put him under any sort of restraint, a step which I should only consent to as a last resource. Curiously enough it was he himself who suggested lunacy and not mere eccentricity as the secret of his strange conduct. He was standing upon the bridge about an hour ago, peering as usual through his glass, while I was walking up and down the quarter-deck. The majority of the men were below at their tea, for the watches have not been regularly kept of late. Tired of walking, I leaned against the bulwarks, and admired the mellow glow cast by the sinking sun upon the great ice-fields which surround us. I was suddenly aroused from the reverie into which I had fallen by a hoarse voice at my elbow, and starting round I found that the captain had descended and was standing by my side. He was staring out over the ice with an expression in which horror, surprise, and something approaching to joy were contending for the mastery. In spite of the cold, great drops of perspiration were coursing down his forehead, and he was evidently fearfully excited. His limbs twitched like those of a man upon the verge of an epileptic fit, and the lines about his mouth were drawn and hard.

'Look!' he gasped, seizing me by the wrist, but still keeping his eyes upon the distant ice, and moving his head slowly in a horizontal direction, as if following some object which was moving across the field of vision. 'Look! There, man, there! Between the hummocks! Now coming out from behind the far one! You see her—you *must* see her! There still! Flying from me, by God, flying from me—and gone!'

He uttered the last two words in a whisper of concentrated agony which shall never fade from my remembrance. Clinging to the ratlines he endeavoured to climb up upon the top of the bulwarks as if in the hope of obtaining a last glance at the departing object. His strength was not equal to the attempt, however, and he staggered back against the saloon skylights, where he leaned panting and exhausted. His face was so livid that I expected him to become unconscious, so lost no time in leading him down the companion, and stretching him upon one of the sofas in the cabin. I then poured him out some brandy, which I held to his lips, and which had a wonderful effect upon him, bringing the blood back into his white face and steadying his poor shaking limbs. He raised himself up upon his elbow, and looking round to see that we were alone, he beckoned to me to come and sit beside him.

'You saw it, didn't you?' he asked, still in the same subdued awesome tone so foreign to the nature of the man.

'No, I saw nothing.'

His head sank back again upon the cushions. 'No, he wouldn't without the glass,' he murmured. 'He couldn't. It was the glass that showed her to me, and then the eyes of love—the eyes of love. I say, Doc, don't let the steward in! He'll think I'm mad. Just bolt the door, will you!'

I rose and did what he had commanded.

He lay quiet for a while, lost in thought apparently, and then raised himself up upon his elbow again, and asked for some more brandy.

'You don't think I am, do you, Doc?' he asked, as I was putting the bottle back into the after-locker. 'Tell me now, as man to man, do you think that I am mad?'

'I think you have something on your mind,' I answered, 'which is exciting you and doing you a good deal of harm.'

'Right there, lad!' he cried, his eyes sparkling from the effects of the brandy. 'Plenty on my mind—plenty! But I can work out the latitude and the longitude, and I can handle my sextant and manage my logarithms. You couldn't prove me mad in a court of law, could you, now?' It was curious to hear the man lying back and coolly arguing out the question of his own sanity.

'Perhaps not,' I said; 'but still I think you would be wise to get home as soon as you can, and settle down to a quiet life for a while.'

'Get home, eh?' he muttered, with a sneer upon his face. 'One word for me and two for yourself, lad. Settle down with Flora—pretty little Flora. Are bad dreams signs of madness?'

'Sometimes,' I answered.

'What else? What would be the first symptoms?'

'Pains in the head, noises in the ears, flashes before the eyes, delusions—'

'Ah! what about them?' he interrupted. 'What would you call a delusion?'

'Seeing a thing which is not there is a delusion.'

'But she *was* there!' he groaned to himself. 'She *was* there!' and rising, he unbolted the door and walked with slow and uncertain steps to his own cabin, where I have no doubt that he will remain until tomorrow morning. His system seems to have received a terrible shock, whatever it may have been that he imagined himself to have seen. The man becomes a greater mystery every day, though I fear that the solution which he has himself suggested is the correct one, and that his reason is affected. I do not think that a guilty conscience has anything to do with his behaviour. The idea is a popular one among the officers, and, I believe, the crew; but I have seen nothing to support it. He has not the air of a guilty man, but of one who has had terrible usage at the hands of fortune, and who should be regarded as a martyr rather than a criminal.

The wind is veering round to the south tonight. God help us if it blocks that narrow pass which is our only road to safety! Situated as we are on the edge of the main Arctic pack, or the 'barrier' as it is called by the whalers, any wind from the north has the effect of shredding out the ice around us and allowing our escape, while a wind from the south blows up all the loose ice behind us, and hems us in between two packs. God help us, I say again!

September 14th.—Sunday, and a day of rest. My fears have been confirmed, and the thin strip of blue water has disappeared from the southward. Nothing but the great motionless ice-fields around us, with their weird hummocks and fantastic pinnacles. There is a deathly silence over their wide expanse which is horrible. No lapping of the waves now, no cries of seagulls or straining of sails, but one deep universal silence in which the murmurs of the seamen, and the creak of their boots upon the white shining deck, seem discordant and out of place. Our only visitor was an Arctic fox, a rare animal upon the pack, though common enough upon the land. He did not come near the ship, however, but after surveying us from a distance fled rapidly across the ice. This was curious conduct, as they generally know nothing of man, and being of an inquisitive nature, become so familiar that they are easily captured. Incredible as it may seem, even this little incident produced a bad effect upon the crew. 'Yon puir beastie kens mair, ay, an' sees mair nor you nor me!' was the comment of one of the leading harpooners, and the others nodded their acquiescence. It is vain to attempt to argue against such puerile superstition. They have made up their minds that there is a curse upon the ship, and nothing will ever persuade them to the contrary.

The captain remained in seclusion all day except for about half an hour in the afternoon, when he came out upon the quarter-deck. I observed that he kept his eye fixed upon the spot where the vision of yesterday had appeared, and was quite prepared for another outburst, but none such came. He did not seem to see me, although I was standing close beside him. Divine service was read as usual, by the chief engineer. It is a curious thing that in whaling vessels the Church of England Prayer-book is always employed, although there is never a member of that Church among either officers or crew. Our men are all Roman Catholics or Presbyterians, the former predominating. Since a ritual is used which is foreign to both, neither can complain that the other is preferred to them, and they listen with all attention and devotion, so that the system has something to recommend it.

A glorious sunset, which made the great fields of ice look like a lake of blood. I have never seen a finer and at the same time more weird effect. Wind is veering round. If it will blow twenty-four hours from the north all will yet be well.

September 15th.—Today is Flora's birthday. Dear lass! it is well that she cannot see her boy, as she used to call me, shut up among the ice-fields with a crazy captain and a few weeks' provisions. No doubt she scans the shipping list in the *Scotsman* every morning to see if we are reported from Shetland. I have to set an example to the men and look cheery and unconcerned; but God knows, my heart is very heavy at times.

The thermometer is at nineteen Fahrenheit today. There is but little wind, and what there is comes from an unfavourable quarter. Captain is in an excellent humour; I think he imagines he has seen some other omen or vision, poor fellow, during the night, for he came into my room early in the morning, and stooping down over my bunk, whispered, 'It wasn't a delusion, Doc; it's all right!' After breakfast he asked me to find out how much food was left, which the second mate and I proceeded to do. It is even less than we had expected. Forward they have half a tank full of biscuits, three barrels of salt meat, and a very limited supply of coffee beans and sugar. In the after-hold and lockers there are a good many luxuries, such as tinned salmon, soups, haricot mutton, etc., but they will go a very short way among a crew of fifty men. There are two barrels of flour in the store-room, and an unlimited supply of tobacco. Altogether there is about enough to keep the men on half rations for eighteen or twenty days—certainly not more. When we reported the state of things to the captain, he ordered all hands to be piped, and addressed them from the quarter-deck. I never saw him to better advantage. With his tall, well-knit figure, and dark animated face, he seemed a man born to command, and he discussed the situation in a cool sailor-like way which showed that while appreciating the danger he had an eye for every loophole of escape.

'My lads,' he said, 'no doubt you think I brought you into this fix, if it is a fix, and maybe some of you feel bitter against me on account of it. But you must remember that for many a season no ship that comes to the country has brought in as much oil-money as the old *Polestar*, and every one of you has had his share of it. You can leave your wives behind you in comfort, while other poor fellows come back to find their lassies on the parish. If you have to thank me for the one you have to thank me for the other, and we may call it quits. We've tried a bold venture before this and succeeded, so now that we've tried one and failed we've no cause to cry out about it. If the worst comes to the worst, we can make the land across the ice, and lay in a stock of seals which will keep us alive until the spring. It won't come to that, though, for you'll see the Scotch coast again before three weeks are out. At present every man must go on half rations, share and share alike, and no favour to any. Keep up your hearts and you'll pull through this as you've pulled through many a danger before.' These few simple words of his had a wonderful effect upon the crew. His former unpopularity was forgotten, and the old harpooner whom I have already mentioned for his superstition, led off three cheers, which were heartily joined in by all hands.

September 16th.—The wind has veered round to the north during the night, and the ice shows some symptoms of opening out. The men are in a good humour in spite of the short allowance upon which they have been placed. Steam is kept up in the engine-room, that there may be no delay should an opportunity for escape present itself. The captain is in exuberant spirits, though he still retains that wild 'fey' expression which I have already remarked upon. This burst of cheerfulness puzzles me more than his former gloom. I cannot understand it. I think I mentioned in an early part of this journal that one of his oddities is that he never permits any person to enter his cabin, but insists upon making his own bed, such as it is, and performing every other office for himself. To my surprise he handed me the key today and requested me to go down there and take the time by his chronometer while he measured the altitude of the sun at noon. It is a bare little room, containing a washing-stand and a few books, but little else in the way of luxury, except some pictures upon the walls. The majority of these are small cheap oleographs, but there was one water-colour sketch of the head of a young lady which arrested my attention. It was evidently a portrait, and not one of those fancy types of female beauty which sailors particularly affect. No artist could have evolved from his own mind such a curious mixture of character and weakness. The languid, dreamy eyes, with their drooping lashes, and the broad, low brow, unruffled by thought or care, were in strong contrast with the clean-cut, prominent jaw, and the resolute set of the lower lip. Underneath it in one of the corners was written, 'M.B., æt. 19.' That anyone in the short space of nineteen years of existence could develop such strength of will as was stamped upon her face seemed to me at the time to be well-nigh incredible. She must have been an extraordinary woman. Her features have thrown such a glamour over me that, though I had but a fleeting glance at them, I could, were I a draughtsman, reproduce them line for line upon this page of the journal. I wonder what part she has played in our captain's life. He has hung her picture at the end of his berth, so that his eyes continually rest upon it. Were he a less reserved man I should make some remark upon the subject. Of the other things in his cabin there was nothing worthy of mention—uniform coats, a camp-stool, small looking-glass, tobacco-box, and numerous pipes, including an oriental hookah—which, by the by, gives some colour to Mr Milne's story about his participation in the war, though the connection may seem rather a distant one.

11.20 p.m.—Captain just gone to bed after a long and interesting conversation on general topics. When he chooses he can be a most fascinating companion, being remarkably well-read, and having the power of expressing his opinion forcibly without appearing to be dogmatic. I hate to have my intellectual toes trod upon. He spoke about the nature of the soul, and sketched out the views of Aristotle and Plato upon the subject in a masterly manner. He seems to have a leaning for metempsychosis and the doctrines of Pythagoras. In discussing them we touched upon modern spiritualism, and I made some joking allusion to the impostures of Slade, upon which, to my surprise, he warned me most impressively against confusing the innocent with the guilty, and argued that it would be as logical to brand Christianity as an error because Judas, who professed that religion, was a villain. He shortly afterwards bade me good night and retired to his room.

The wind is freshening up, and blows steadily from the north. The nights are as dark now as they are in England. I hope tomorrow may set us free from our frozen fetters.

September 17th.—The Bogie again. Thank Heaven that I have strong nerves! The superstition of these poor fellows, and the circumstantial accounts which they give, with the utmost earnestness and self-conviction, would horrify any man not accustomed to their ways. There are many versions of the matter, but the sum-total of them all is that something uncanny has been flitting round the ship all night, and that Sandie M'Donald of Peterhead and 'lang' Peter Williamson of Shetland saw it, as also did Mr Milne on the bridge—so, having three witnesses, they can make a better case of it than the second mate did. I spoke to Milne after breakfast, and told him that he should be above such nonsense, and that as an officer he ought to set the men a better example. He shook his weather-beaten head ominously, but answered with characteristic caution, 'Mebbe, aye, mebbe na, Doctor,' he said, 'I didna ca' it a ghaist. I canna' say I preen my faith in sea-bogles an' the like, though there's a mony as claims to ha' seen a' that and waur. I'm no easy feared, but maybe your ain bluid would run a bit cauld, mun, if instead o' speerin' aboot it in daylicht ye were wi' me last night, an' seed an awfu' like shape, white an' gruesome, whiles here, whiles there, an' it greetin' and ca'ing in the darkness like a bit lambie that hae lost its mither. Ye would na' be sae ready to put it a' doon to auld wives' clavers then, I'm thinkin'.' I saw it was hopeless to reason with him, so contented myself with begging him as a personal favour to call me up the next time the spectre appeared—a request to which he acceded with many ejaculations expressive of his hopes that such an opportunity might never arise.

As I had hoped, the white desert behind us has become broken by many thin streaks of water which intersect it in all directions. Our latitude today was 80° 52' N., which shows that there is a strong southerly drift upon the pack. Should the wind continue favourable it will break up as rapidly as it formed. At present we can do nothing but smoke and wait and hope for the best. I am rapidly becoming a fatalist. When dealing with such uncertain factors as wind and ice a man can be nothing else. Perhaps it was the wind and sand of the Arabian deserts which gave the minds of the original followers of Mahomet their tendency to bow to kismet.

These spectral alarms have a very bad effect upon the captain. I feared that it might excite his sensitive mind, and endeavoured to conceal the absurd story from him, but unfortunately he overheard one of the men making an allusion to it, and insisted upon being informed about it. As I had expected, it brought out all his latent lunacy in an exaggerated form. I can hardly believe that this is the same man who discoursed philosophy last night with the most critical acumen and coolest judgement. He is pacing backwards and forwards upon the quarter-deck like a caged tiger, stopping now and again to throw out his hands with a yearning gesture, and stare impatiently out over the ice. He keeps up a continual mutter to himself, and once he called out, 'But a little time, love—but a little time!' Poor fellow, it is sad to see a gallant seaman and accomplished gentleman reduced to such a pass, and to think that imagination and delusion can cow a mind to which real danger was but the salt of life. Was ever a man in such a position as I, between a demented captain and a ghost-seeing mate? I sometimes think I am the only really sane man aboard the vessel—except perhaps the second engineer, who is a kind of ruminant, and would care nothing for all the fiends in the Red Sea so long as they would leave him alone and not disarrange his tools.

The ice is still opening rapidly, and there is every probability of our being able to make a start tomorrow morning. They will think I am inventing when I tell them at home all the strange things that have befallen me.

12 p.m.—I have been a good deal startled, though I feel steadier now, thanks to a stiff glass of brandy. I am hardly myself yet, however, as this handwriting will testify. The fact is, that I have gone through a very strange experience, and am beginning to doubt whether I was justified in branding everyone on board as madmen because they professed to have seen things which did not seem reasonable to my understanding. Pshaw! I am a fool to let such a trifle unnerve me; and yet, coming as it does after all these alarms, it has an additional significance, for I cannot doubt either Mr Manson's story or that of the mate, now that I have experienced that which I used formerly to scoff at.

After all it was nothing very alarming—a mere sound, and that was all. I cannot expect that anyone reading this, if anyone ever should read it, will sympathise with my feelings, or realise the effect which it produced upon me at the time. Supper was over, and I had gone on deck to have a quiet pipe before turning in. The night was very dark—so dark that, standing under the quarter-boat, I was unable to see the officer upon the bridge. I think I have already mentioned the extraordinary silence which prevails in these frozen seas. In other parts of the world, be they ever so barren, there is some slight vibration of the air—some faint hum, be it from the distant haunts of men, or from the leaves of the trees or the wings of the birds, or even the faint rustle of the grass that covers the ground. One may not actively perceive the sound, and yet if it were withdrawn it would be missed. It is only here in these Arctic seas that stark, unfathomable stillness obtrudes itself upon you all in its gruesome reality. You find your tympanum straining to catch some little murmur, and dwelling eagerly upon every accidental sound within the vessel. In this state I was leaning against the bulwarks when there arose from the ice almost directly underneath me a cry, sharp and shrill, upon the silent air of the night, beginning, as it seemed to me, at a note such as prima donna never reached, and mounting from that ever higher and higher until it culminated in a long wail of agony, which might have been the last cry of a lost soul. The ghastly scream is still ringing in my ears. Grief, unutterable grief, seemed to be expressed in it, and a great longing, and yet through it all there was an occasional wild note of exultation. It shrilled out from close beside me, and yet as I glared into the darkness I could discern nothing. I waited some little time, but without hearing any repetition of the sound, so I came below, more shaken than I have ever been in my life before. As I came down the companion I met Mr Milne coming up to relieve the watch. 'Weel, Doctor,' he said, 'maybe that's auld wives' clavers tae? Did ye no hear it skirling? Maybe that's a supersteetion? What d'ye think o't noo?' I was obliged to apologise to the honest fellow, and acknowledge that I was as puzzled by it as he was. Perhaps tomorrow things may look different. At present I dare hardly write all that I think. Reading it again in days to come, when I have shaken off all these associations, I should despise myself for having been so weak.

September 18th.—Passed a restless and uneasy night, still haunted by that strange sound. The captain does not look as if he had had much repose either, for his face is haggard and his eyes bloodshot. I have not told him of my adventure of last night, nor shall I. He is already restless and excited, standing up, sitting down, and apparently utterly unable to keep still.

A fine lead appeared in the pack this morning, as I had expected, and we were able to cast off our ice-anchor, and steam about twelve miles in a west-sou'-westerly direction. We were then brought to a halt by a great floe as massive as any which we have left behind us. It bars our progress completely, so we can do nothing but anchor again and wait until it breaks up, which it will probably do within twenty-four hours, if the wind holds. Several bladder-nosed seals were seen swimming in the water, and one was shot, an immense creature more than eleven feet long. They are fierce, pugnacious animals, and are said to be more than a match for a bear. Fortunately they are slow and clumsy in their movements, so that there is little danger in attacking them upon the ice.

The captain evidently does not think we have seen the last of our troubles, though why he should take a gloomy view of the situation is more than I can fathom, since everyone else on board considers that we have had a miraculous escape, and are sure now to reach the open sea.

'I suppose you think it's all right now, Doctor?' he said, as we sat together after dinner.

'I hope so,' I answered.

'We mustn't be too sure—and yet no doubt you are right. We'll all be in the arms of our own true loves before long, lad, won't we? But we mustn't be too sure—we mustn't be too sure.'

He sat silent a little, swinging his leg thoughtfully backwards and forwards. 'Look here,' he continued; 'it's a dangerous place this, even at its best—a treacherous, dangerous place. I have known men cut off very suddenly in a land like this. A slip would do it sometimes—a single slip, and down you go through a crack, and only a bubble on the green water to show where it was that you sank. It's a queer thing,' he continued with a nervous laugh, 'but all the years I've been in this country I never once thought of making a will—not that I have anything to leave in particular, but still when a man is exposed to danger he should have everything arranged and ready—don't you think so?'

'Certainly,' I answered, wondering what on earth he was driving at.

'He feels better for knowing it's all settled,' he went on. 'Now if anything should ever befall me, I hope that you will look after things for me. There is very little in the cabin, but such as it is I should like it to be sold, and the money divided in the same proportion as the oil-money among the crew. The chronometer I wish you to keep yourself as some slight remembrance of our voyage. Of course all this is a mere precaution, but I thought I would take the opportunity of speaking to you about it. I suppose I might rely upon you if there were any necessity?'

'Most assuredly,' I answered; 'and since you are taking this step, I may as well—'

'You! you!' he interrupted. '*You're* all right. What the devil is the matter with *you*? There, I didn't mean to be peppery, but I don't like to hear a young fellow, that has hardly began life, speculating about death. Go up on deck and get some fresh air into your lungs instead of talking nonsense in the cabin, and encouraging me to do the same.'

The more I think of this conversation of ours the less do I like it. Why should the man be settling his affairs at the very time when we seem to be emerging from all danger? There must be some method in his madness. Can it be that he contemplates suicide? I remember that upon one occasion he spoke in a deeply reverent manner of the heinousness of the crime of self-destruction. I shall keep my eye upon him, however, and though I cannot obtrude upon the privacy of his cabin, I shall at least make a point of remaining on deck as long as he stays up.

Mr Milne pooh-poohs my fears, and says it is only the 'skipper's little way.' He himself takes a very rosy view of the situation. According to him we shall be out of the ice by the day after tomorrow, pass Jan Meyen two days after that, and sight Shetland in little more than a week. I hope he may not be too sanguine. His opinion may be fairly balanced against the gloomy precautions of the captain, for he is an old and experienced seaman, and weighs his words well before uttering them.

*

The long-impending catastrophe has come at last. I hardly know what to write about it. The captain is gone. He may come back to us again alive, but I fear me—I fear me. It is now seven o'clock of the morning of the 19th of September. I have spent the whole night traversing the great ice-floe in front of us with a party of seamen in the hope of coming upon some trace of him, but in vain. I shall try to give some account of the circumstances which attended upon his disappearance. Should anyone ever chance to read the words which I put down, I trust they will remember that I do not write from conjecture or from hearsay, but that I, a sane and educated man, am describing accurately what actually occurred before my very eyes. My inferences are my own, but I shall be answerable for the facts.

The captain remained in excellent spirits after the conversation which I have recorded. He appeared to be nervous and impatient, however, frequently changing his position, and moving his limbs in an aimless choreic way which is characteristic of him at times. In a quarter of an hour he went upon deck seven times, only to descend after a few hurried paces. I followed him each time, for there was something about his face which confirmed my resolution of not letting him out of my sight. He seemed to observe the effect which his movements had produced, for he endeavoured by an overdone hilarity, laughing boisterously at the very smallest of jokes, to quiet my apprehensions.

After supper he went on to the poop once more, and I with him. The night was dark and very still, save for the melancholy soughing of the wind among the spars. A thick cloud was coming up from the northwest, and the ragged tentacles which it threw out in front of it were drifting across the face of the moon, which only shone now and again through a rift in the wrack. The captain paced rapidly backwards and forwards, and then seeing me still dogging him, he came across and hinted that he thought I should be better below—which, I need hardly say, had the effect of strengthening my resolution to remain on deck.

I think he forgot about my presence after this, for he stood silently leaning over the taffrail and peering out across the great desert of snow, part of which lay in shadow, while part glittered mistily in the moonlight. Several times I could see by his movements that he was referring to his watch, and once he muttered a short sentence, of which I could only catch the one word 'ready.' I confess to having felt an eerie feeling creeping over me as I watched the loom of his tall figure through the darkness, and noted how completely he fulfilled the idea of a man who is keeping a tryst. A tryst with whom? Some vague perception began to dawn upon me as I pieced one fact with another, but I was utterly unprepared for the sequel.

By the sudden intensity of his attitude I felt that he saw something. I crept up behind him. He was staring with an eager questioning gaze at what seemed to be a wreath of mist, blown swiftly in a line with the ship. It was a dim nebulous body, devoid of shape, sometimes more, sometimes less apparent, as the light fell on it. The moon was dimmed in its brilliancy at the moment by a canopy of thinnest cloud, like the coating of an anemone.

'Coming, lass, coming,' cried the skipper, in a voice of unfathomable tenderness and compassion, like one who soothes a beloved one by some favour long looked for, and as pleasant to bestow as to receive.

What followed happened in an instant. I had no power to interfere. He gave one spring to the top of the bulwarks, and another which took him on to the ice, almost to the feet of the pale misty figure. He held out his hands as if to clasp it, and so ran into the darkness with outstretched arms and loving words. I still stood rigid and motionless, straining my eyes after his retreating form, until his voice died away in the distance. I never thought to see him again, but at that moment the moon shone out brilliantly through a chink in the cloudy heaven, and illuminated the great field of ice. Then I saw his dark figure already a very long way off, running with prodigious speed across the frozen plain. That was the last glimpse which we caught of him—perhaps the last we ever shall. A party was organised to follow him, and I accompanied them, but the men's hearts were not in the work, and nothing was found. Another will be formed within a few hours. I can hardly believe I have not been dreaming, or suffering from some hideous nightmare, as I write these things down.

7.30 p.m.—Just returned dead beat and utterly tired out from a second unsuccessful search for the captain. The floe is of enormous extent, for though we have traversed at least twenty miles of its surface, there has been no sign of its coming to an end. The frost has been so severe of late that the overlying snow is frozen as hard as granite, otherwise we might have had the footsteps to guide us. The crew are anxious that we should cast off and steam round the floe and so to the southward, for the ice has opened up during the night, and the sea is visible upon the horizon. They argue that Captain Craigie is certainly dead, and that we are all risking our lives to no purpose by remaining when we have an opportunity of escape. Mr Milne and I have had the greatest difficulty in persuading them to wait until tomorrow night, and have been compelled to promise that we will not under any circumstances delay our departure longer than that. We propose therefore to take a few hours' sleep, and then to start upon a final search.

September 20th, evening.—I crossed the ice this morning with a party of men exploring the southern part of the floe, while Mr Milne went off in a northerly direction. We pushed on for ten or twelve miles without seeing a trace of any living thing except a single bird, which fluttered a great way over our heads, and which by its flight I should judge to have been a falcon. The southern extremity of the ice-field tapered away into a long narrow spit which projected out into the sea. When we came to the base of this promontory, the men halted, but I begged them to continue to the extreme end of it, that we might have the satisfaction of knowing that no possible chance had been neglected.

We had hardly gone a hundred yards before M'Donald of Peterhead cried out that he saw something in front of us, and began to run. We all got a glimpse of it and ran too. At first it was only a vague darkness against the white ice, but as we raced along together it took the shape of a man, and eventually of the man of whom we were in search. He was lying face downwards upon a frozen bank. Many little crystals of ice and feathers of snow had drifted on to him as he lay, and sparkled upon his dark seaman's jacket. As we came up some wandering puff of wind caught these tiny flakes in its vortex, and they whirled up into the air, partially descended again, and then, caught once more in the current, sped rapidly away in the direction of the sea. To my eyes it seemed but a snow-drift, but many of my companions averred that it started up in the shape of a woman, stooped over the corpse and kissed it, and then hurried away across the floe. I have learned never to ridicule any man's opinion, however strange it may seem. Sure it is that Captain Nicholas Craigie had met with no painful end, for there was a bright smile upon his blue pinched features, and his hands were still outstretched as though grasping at the strange visitor which had summoned him away into the dim world that lies beyond the grave.

We buried him the same afternoon with the ship's ensign around him, and a thirty-two pound shot at his feet. I read the burial service, while the rough sailors wept like children, for there were many who owed much to his kind heart, and who showed now the affection which his strange ways had repelled during his lifetime. He went off the grating with a dull, sullen splash, and as I looked into the green water I saw him go down, down, down until he was but a little flickering patch of white hanging upon the outskirts of eternal darkness. Then even that faded away, and he was gone. There he shall lie, with his secret and his sorrows and his mystery all still buried in his breast, until that great day when the sea shall give up its dead, and Nicholas Craigie come out from among the ice with the smile upon his face, and his stiffened arms outstretched in greeting. I pray that his lot may be a happier one in that life than it has been in this.

I shall not continue my journal. Our road to home lies plain and clear before us, and the great ice-field will soon be but a remembrance of the past. It will be some time before I get over the shock produced by recent events. When I began this record of our voyage I little thought of how I should be compelled to finish it. I am writing these final words in the lonely cabin, still starting at times and fancying I hear the quick nervous step of the dead man upon the deck above me. I entered his cabin tonight, as was my duty, to make a list of his effects in order that they might be entered in the official log. All was as it had been upon my previous visit, save that the picture which I have described as having hung at the end of his bed had been cut out of its frame, as with a knife, and was gone. With this last link in a strange chain of evidence I close my diary of the voyage of the *Polestar*.

[Note by Dr John M'Alister Ray, senior.—I have read over the strange events connected with the death of the captain of the *Polestar*, as narrated in the journal of my son. That everything occurred exactly as he describes it I have the fullest confidence, and, indeed, the most positive certainty, for I know him to be a strong-nerved and unimaginative man, with the strictest regard for veracity. Still, the story is, on the face of it, so vague and so improbable, that I was long opposed to its publication. Within the last few days, however, I have had independent testimony upon the subject which throws a new light upon it. I had run down to Edinburgh to attend a meeting of the British Medical Association, when I chanced to come across Dr P——, an old college chum of mine, now practising at Saltash, in Devonshire. Upon my telling him of this experience of my son's, he declared to me that he was familiar with the man, and proceeded, to my no small surprise, to give me a description of him, which tallied remarkably well with that given in the journal, except that he depicted him as a younger man. According to his account, he had been engaged to a young lady of singular beauty residing upon the Cornish coast. During his absence at sea his betrothed had died under circumstances of peculiar horror.]

THE WINNING SHOT

'CAUTION.—The public are hereby cautioned against a man calling himself Octavius Gaster. He is to be recognised by his great height, his flaxen hair, and deep scar upon his left cheek, extending from the eye to the angle of the mouth. His predilection for bright colours—green neckties, and the like—may help to identify him. A slightly foreign accent is to be detected in his speech. This man is beyond the reach of the law, but is more dangerous than a mad dog. Shun him as you would shun the pestilence that walketh at noonday. Any communications as to his whereabouts will be thankfully acknowledged by A.C.U., Lincoln's Inn, London.'

This is a copy of an advertisement which may have been noticed by many readers in the columns of the London morning papers during the early part of the present year. It has, I believe, excited considerable curiosity in certain quarters, and many guesses have been hazarded as to the identity of Octavius Gaster and the nature of the charge brought against him. When I state that the 'caution' has been inserted by my elder brother, Arthur Cooper Underwood, barrister-at-law, upon my representations, it will be acknowledged that I am the most fitting person to enter upon an authentic explanation.

Hitherto the horror and vagueness of my suspicion, combined with my grief at the loss of my poor darling on the very eve of our wedding, have prevented me from revealing the events of last August to anyone save my brother.

Now, however, looking back, I can fit in many little facts almost unnoticed at the time, which form a chain of evidence that, though worthless in a court of law, may yet have some effect upon the mind of the public.

I shall therefore relate, without exaggeration or prejudice, all that occurred from the day upon which this man, Octavius Gaster, entered Toynby Hall up to the great rifle competition. I know that many people will always ridicule the supernatural, or what our poor intellects choose to regard as supernatural, and that the fact of my being a woman will be thought to weaken my evidence. I can only plead that I have never been weak-minded or impressionable, and that other people formed the same opinions of Octavius Gaster that I did.

Now to the story.

It was at Colonel Pillar's place at Roborough, in the pleasant county of Devon, that we spent our autumn holidays. For some months I had been engaged to his eldest son Charley, and it was hoped that the marriage might take place before the termination of the Long Vacation.

Charley was considered 'safe' for his degree, and in any case was rich enough to be practically independent, while I was by no means penniless.

The old Colonel was delighted at the prospect of the match, and so was my mother; so that look what way we would, there seemed to be no cloud above our horizon.

It was no wonder, then, that that August was a happy one. Even the most miserable of mankind would have laid his woes aside under the genial influence of the merry household at Toynby Hall.

There was Lieutenant Daseby, 'Jack,' as he was invariably called, fresh home from Japan in Her Majesty's ship *Shark*, who was on the same interesting footing with Fanny Pillar, Charley's sister, as Charley was with me, so that we were able to lend each other a certain moral support.

Then there was Harry, Charley's younger brother, and Trevor, his bosom friend at Cambridge.

Finally there was my mother, dearest of old ladies, beaming at us through her gold-rimmed spectacles, anxiously smoothing every little difficulty in the way of the two young couples, and never weary of detailing to them *her* own doubts and fears and perplexities when that gay young blood, Mr Nicholas Underwood, came a-wooing into the provinces, and forswore Crockford's and Tattersall's for the sake of the country parson's daughter.

I must not, however, forget the gallant old warrior who was our host; with his time-honoured jokes, and his gout, and his harmless affectation of ferocity.

'I don't know what's come over the governor lately,' Charley used to say. 'He has never cursed the Liberal Administration since you've been here, Lottie; and my belief is that unless he has a good blow-off, that Irish question will get into his system and finish him.'

Perhaps in the privacy of his own apartment the veteran used to make up for his self-abnegation during the day.

He seemed to have taken a special fancy to me, which he showed in a hundred little attentions.

'You're a good lass,' he remarked one evening, in a very port-winey whisper. 'Charley's a lucky dog, egad! and has more discrimination than I thought. Mark my words, Miss Underwood, you'll find that young gentleman isn't such a fool as he looks!'

With which equivocal compliment the Colonel solemnly covered his face with his handkerchief, and went off into the land of dreams.

*

How well I remember the day that was the commencement of all our miseries!

Dinner was over, and we were in the drawing-room, with the windows open to admit the balmy southern breeze.

My mother was sitting in the corner, engaged on a piece of fancy-work, and occasionally purring forth some truism which the dear old soul believed to be an entirely original remark, and founded exclusively upon her own individual experiences.

Fanny and the young lieutenant were billing and cooing upon the sofa, while Charley paced restlessly about the room.

I was sitting by the window, gazing out dreamily at the great wilderness of Dartmoor, which stretched away to the horizon, ruddy and glowing in the light of the sinking sun, save where some rugged tor stood out in bold relief against the scarlet background.

'I say,' remarked Charley, coming over to join me at the window, 'it seems a positive shame to waste an evening like this.'

'Confound the evening!' said Jack Daseby.

'You're always victimising yourself to the weather. Fan and I ar'n't going to move off this sofa—are we, Fan?'

That young lady announced her intention of remaining by nestling among the cushions, and glancing defiantly at her brother.

'Spooning is a demoralising thing—isn't it, Lottie?' said Charley, appealing laughingly to me.

'Shockingly so,' I answered.

'Why, I can remember Daseby here when he was as active a young fellow as any in Devon; and just look at him now! Fanny, Fanny, you've got a lot to answer for!'

'Never mind him, my dear,' said my mother, from the corner. 'Still, my experience has always shown me that moderation is an excellent thing for young people. Poor dear Nicholas used to think so too. He would never go to bed of a night until he had jumped the length of the hearthrug. I often told him it was dangerous; but he *would* do it, until one night he fell on the fender and snapped the muscle of his leg, which made him limp till the day of his death, for Doctor Pearson mistook it for a fracture of the bone, and put him in splints, which had the effect of stiffening his knee. They did say that the doctor was almost out of his mind at the time from anxiety, brought on by his younger daughter swallowing a halfpenny, and that that was what caused him to make the mistake.'

My mother had a curious way of drifting along in her conversation, and occasionally rushing off at a tangent, which made it rather difficult to remember her original proposition. On this occasion Charley had, however, stowed it away in his mind as likely to admit of immediate application.

'An excellent thing, as you say, Mrs Underwood,' he remarked; 'and we have not been out today. Look here, Lottie, we have an hour of daylight yet. Suppose we go down and have a try for a trout, if your mamma does not object.'

'Put something round your throat, dear,' said my mother, feeling that she had been outmanœuvred.

'All right, dear,' I answered; 'I'll just run up and put on my hat.'

'And we'll have a walk back in the gloaming,' said Charley, as I made for the door.

When I came down, I found my lover waiting impatiently with his fishing basket in the hall.

We crossed the lawn together, and passed the open drawing-room windows, where three mischievous faces were looking at us.

'Spooning is a terribly demoralising thing,' remarked Jack, reflectively staring up at the clouds.

'Shocking,' said Fan; and all three laughed until they woke the sleeping Colonel, and we could hear them endeavouring to explain the joke to that ill-used veteran, who apparently obstinately refused to appreciate it.

We passed down the winding lane together, and through the little wooden gate, which opens on to the Tavistock road.

Charley paused for a moment after we had emerged and seemed irresolute which way to turn.

Had we but known it, our fate depended upon that trivial question.

'Shall we go down to the river, dear,' he said, 'or shall we try one of the brooks upon the moor?'

'Whichever you like?' I answered.

'Well, I vote that we cross the moor. We'll have a longer walk back that way,' he added, looking down lovingly at the little white-shawled figure beside him.

The brook in question runs through a most desolate part of the country. By the path it is several miles from Toynby Hall; but we were both young and active, and struck out across the moor, regardless of rocks and furze-bushes.

Not a living creature did we meet upon our solitary walk, save a few scraggy Devonshire sheep, who looked at us wistfully, and followed us for some distance, as if curious as to what could possibly have induced us to trespass upon their domains.

It was almost dark before we reached the little stream, which comes gurgling down through a precipitous glen, and meanders away to help to form the Plymouth 'leat.'

Above us towered two great columns of rock, between which the water trickled to form a deep, still pool at the bottom. This pool had always been a favourite spot of Charley's, and was a pretty cheerful place by day; but now, with the rising moon reflected upon its glassy waters, and throwing dark shadows from the overhanging rocks, it seemed anything rather than the haunt of a pleasure-seeker.

'I don't think, darling, that I'll fish, after all,' said Charley, as we sat down together on a mossy bank. 'It's a dismal sort of place, isn't it?'

'Very,' said I, shuddering.

'We'll just have a rest, and then we will walk back by the pathway. You're shivering. You're not cold, are you?'

'No,' said I, trying to keep up my courage; 'I'm not cold, but I'm rather frightened, though it's very silly of me.'

'By Jove!' said my lover, 'I can't wonder at it, for I feel a bit depressed myself. The noise that water makes is like the gurgling in the throat of a dying man.'

'Don't, Charley; you frighten me!'

'Come, dear, we mustn't get the blues,' he said, with a laugh, trying to reassure me. 'Let's run away from this charnel-house place, and—Look!—see!—good gracious! what is that?'

Charley had staggered back, and was gazing upwards with a pallid face.

I followed the direction of his eyes, and could scarcely suppress a scream.

I have already mentioned that the pool by which we were standing lay at the foot of a rough mound of rocks. On the top of this mound, about sixty feet above our heads, a tall dark figure was standing, peering down, apparently, into the rugged hollow in which we were.

The moon was just topping the ridge behind, and the gaunt, angular outlines of the stranger stood out hard and clear against its silvery radiance.

There was something ghastly in the sudden and silent appearance of this solitary wanderer, especially when coupled with the weird nature of the scene.

I clung to my lover in speechless terror, and glared up at the dark figure above us.

'Hullo, you sir!' cried Charley, passing from fear into anger, as Englishmen generally do. 'Who are you, and what the devil are you doing?'

'Oh! I thought it, I thought it!' said the man who was overlooking us, and disappeared from the top of the hill.

We heard him scrambling about among the loose stones, and in another moment he emerged upon the banks of the brook and stood facing us.

Weird as his appearance had been when we first caught sight of him, the impression was intensified rather than removed by a closer acquaintance.

The moon shining full upon him revealed a long, thin face of ghastly pallor, the effect being increased by its contrast with the flaring green necktie which he wore.

A scar upon his cheek had healed badly and caused a nasty pucker at the side of his mouth, which gave his whole countenance a most distorted expression, more particularly when he smiled.

The knapsack on his back and stout staff in his hand announced him to be a tourist, while the easy grace with which he raised his hat on perceiving the presence of a lady showed that he could lay claim to the *savoir faire* of a man of the world.

There was something in his angular proportions and the bloodless face which, taken in conjunction with the black cloak which fluttered from his shoulders, irresistibly reminded me of a bloodsucking species of bat which Jack Daseby had brought from Japan upon his previous voyage, and which was the bugbear of the servants' hall at Toynby.

'Excuse my intrusion,' he said, with a slightly foreign lisp, which imparted a peculiar beauty to his voice. 'I should have had to sleep on the moor had I not had the good fortune to fall in with you.'

'Confound it, man!' said Charley; 'why couldn't you shout out, or give some warning? You quite frightened Miss Underwood when you suddenly appeared up there.'

The stranger once more raised his hat as he apologised to me for having given me such a start.

'I am a gentleman from Sweden,' he continued, in that peculiar intonation of his, 'and am viewing this beautiful land of yours. Allow me to introduce myself as Doctor Octavius Gaster. Perhaps you could tell me where I may sleep, and how I can get from this place, which is truly of great size?'

'You're very lucky in falling in with us,' said Charley. 'It is no easy matter to find your way upon the moor.'

'That can I well believe,' remarked our new acquaintance.

'Strangers have been found dead on it before now,' continued Charley. 'They lose themselves, and then wander in a circle until they fall from fatigue.'

'Ha, ha!' laughed the Swede; 'it is not I, who have drifted in an open boat from Cape Blanco to Canary, that will starve upon an English moor. But how may I turn to seek an inn?'

'Look here!' said Charley, whose interest was excited by the stranger's allusion, and who was at all times the most open-hearted of men. 'There's not an inn for many a mile round; and I daresay you have had a long day's walk already. Come home with us, and my father, the Colonel, will be delighted to see you and find you a spare bed.'

'For this great kindness how can I thank you?' returned the traveller. 'Truly, when I return to Sweden, I shall have strange stories to tell of the English and the hospitality!'

'Nonsense!' said Charley. 'Come, we will start at once, for Miss Underwood is cold. Wrap the shawl well round your neck, Lottie, and we will be home in no time.'

We stumbled along in silence, keeping as far as we could to the rugged pathway, sometimes losing it as a cloud drifted over the face of the moon, and then regaining it further on with the return of the light.

The stranger seemed buried in thought, but once or twice I had the impression that he was looking hard at me through the darkness as we strode along together.

'So,' said Charley at last, breaking the silence, 'you drifted about in an open boat, did you?'

'Ah, yes,' answered the stranger; 'many strange sights have I seen, and many perils undergone, but none worse than that. It is, however, too sad a subject for a lady's ears. She has been frightened once tonight.'

'Oh, you needn't be afraid of frightening me now,' said I, as I leaned on Charley's arm.

'Indeed there is but little to tell, and yet is it sorrowful.

'A friend of mine, Karl Osgood of Upsala, and myself started on a trading venture. Few white men had been among the wandering Moors at Cape Blanco, but nevertheless we went, and for some months lived well, selling this and that, and gathering much ivory and gold.

''Tis a strange country, where is neither wood nor stone, so that the huts are made from the weeds of the sea.

'At last, just as what we thought was a sufficiency, the Moors conspired to kill us, and came down against us in the night.

'Short was our warning, but we fled to the beach, launched a canoe and put out to sea, leaving everything behind.

'The Moors chased us, but lost us in the darkness; and when day dawned the land was out of sight.

'There was no country where we could hope for food nearer than Canary, and for that we made.

'I reached it alive, though very weak and mad; but poor Karl died the day before we sighted the islands.

'I gave him warning!

'I cannot blame myself in the matter.

'I said, "Karl, the strength that you might gain by eating them would be more than made up for by the blood that you would lose!"

'He laughed at my words, caught the knife from my belt, cut them off and eat them; and he died.'

'Eat what?' asked Charley.

'His ears!' said the stranger.

We both looked round at him in horror.

There was no suspicion of a smile or joke upon his ghastly face.

'He was what you call headstrong,' he continued, 'but he should have known better than to do a thing like that. Had he but used his will he would have lived as I did.'

'And you think a man's will can prevent him from feeling hungry?' said Charley.

'What can it not do?' returned Octavius Gaster, and relapsed into a silence which was not broken until our arrival in Toynby Hall.

Considerable alarm had been caused by our nonappearance, and Jack Daseby was just setting off with Charley's friend Trevor in search of us. They were delighted, therefore, when we marched in upon them, and considerably astonished at the appearance of our companion.

'Where the deuce did you pick up that second-hand corpse?' asked Jack, drawing Charley aside into the smoking-room.

'Shut up, man; he'll hear you,' growled Charley. 'He's a Swedish doctor on a tour, and a deuced good fellow. He went in an open boat from What's-it's-name to another place. I've offered him a bed for the night.'

'Well, all I can say is,' remarked Jack, 'that his face will never be his fortune.'

'Ha, ha! Very good! very good!' laughed the subject of the remark, walking calmly into the room, to the complete discomfiture of the sailor. 'No, it will never, as you say, in this country be my fortune,'—and he grinned until the hideous gash across the angle of his mouth made him look more like the reflection in a broken mirror than anything else.

'Come upstairs and have a wash; I can lend you a pair of slippers,' said Charley; and hurried the visitor out of the room to put an end to a somewhat embarrassing situation.

Colonel Pillar was the soul of hospitality, and welcomed Doctor Gaster as effusively as if he had been an old friend of the family.

'Egad, sir,' he said, 'the place is your own; and as long as you care to stop you are very welcome. We're pretty quiet down here, and a visitor is an acquisition.'

My mother was a little more distant. 'A very well informed young man, Lottie,' she remarked to me; 'but I wish he would wink his eyes more. I don't like to see people who never wink their eyes. Still, my dear, my life has taught me one great lesson, and that is that a man's looks are of very little importance compared with his actions.'

With which brand new and eminently original remark, my mother kissed me and left me to my meditations.

Whatever Doctor Octavius Gaster might be physically, he was certainly a social success.

By next day he had so completely installed himself as a member of the household that the Colonel would not hear of his departure.

He astonished everybody by the extent and variety of his knowledge. He could tell the veteran considerably more about the Crimea than he knew himself; he gave the sailor information about the coast of Japan; and even tackled my athletic lover upon the subject of rowing, discoursing about levers of the first order, and fixed points and fulcra, until the unhappy Cantab was fain to drop the subject.

Yet all this was done so modestly and even deferentially, that no one could possibly feel offended at being beaten upon their own ground. There was a quiet power about everything he said and did which was very striking.

I remember one example of this, which impressed us all at the time.

Trevor had a remarkably savage bulldog, which, however fond of its master, fiercely resented any liberties from the rest of us. This animal was, it may be imagined, rather unpopular, but as it was the pride of the student's heart it was agreed not to banish it entirely, but to lock it up in the stable and give it a wide berth.

From the first, it seemed to have taken a decided aversion to our visitor, and showed every fang in its head whenever he approached it.

On the second day of his visit we were passing the stable in a body, when the growls of the creature inside arrested Doctor Gaster's attention.

'Ha!' he said. 'There is that dog of yours, Mr Trevor, is it not?'

'Yes; that's Towzer,' assented Trevor.

'He is a bulldog, I think? What they call the national animal of England on the Continent?'

'Pure-bred,' said the student, proudly.

'They are ugly animals—very ugly! Would you come into the stable and unchain him, that I may see him to advantage. It is a pity to keep an animal so powerful and full of life in captivity.'

'He's rather a nipper,' said Trevor, with a mischievous expression in his eye; 'but I suppose you are not afraid of a dog?'

'Afraid?—no. Why should I be afraid?'

The mischievous look on Trevor's face increased as he opened the stable door. I heard Charley mutter something to him about its being past a joke, but the other's answer was drowned by the hollow growling from inside.

The rest of us retreated to a respectable distance, while Octavius Gaster stood in the open doorway with a look of mild curiosity upon his pallid face.

'And those,' he said, 'that I see so bright and red in the darkness—are those his eyes?'

'Those are they,' said the student, as he stooped down and unbuckled the strap.

'Come here!' said Octavius Gaster.

The growling of the dog suddenly subsided into a long whimper, and instead of making the furious rush that we expected, he rustled among the straw as if trying to huddle into a corner.

'What the deuce is the matter with him?' exclaimed his perplexed owner.

'Come here!' repeated Gaster, in sharp metallic accents, with an indescribable air of command in them. 'Come here!'

To our astonishment, the dog trotted out and stood at his side, but looking as unlike the usually pugnacious Towzer as is possible to conceive. His ears were drooping, his tail limp, and he altogether presented the very picture of canine humiliation.

'A very fine dog, but singularly quiet,' remarked the Swede, as he stroked him down.

'Now, sir, go back!'

The brute turned and slunk back into its corner. We heard the rattling of its chain as it was being fastened, and next moment Trevor came out of the stable-door with blood dripping from his finger.

'Confound the beast!' he said. 'I don't know what can have come over him. I've had him three years, and he never bit me before.'

I fancy—I cannot say it for certain—but I fancy that there was a spasmodic twitching of the cicatrix upon our visitor's face, which betokened an inclination to laugh.

Looking back, I think that it was from that moment that I began to have a strange indefinable fear and dislike of the man.

*

Week followed week, and the day fixed for my marriage began to draw near.

Octavius Gaster was still a guest at Toynby Hall, and, indeed, had so ingratiated himself with the proprietor that any hint at departure was laughed to scorn by that worthy soldier.

'Here you've come, sir, and here you'll stay; you shall, by Jove!'

Whereat Octavius would smile and shrug his shoulders and mutter something about the attractions of Devon, which would put the Colonel in a good humour for the whole day afterwards.

My darling and I were too much engrossed with each other to pay very much attention to the traveller's occupations. We used to come upon him sometimes in our rambles through the woods, sitting reading in the most lonely situations.

He always placed the book in his pocket when he saw us approaching. I remember on one occasion, however, that we stumbled upon him so suddenly that the volume was still lying open before him.

'Ah, Gaster,' said Charley, 'studying, as usual! What an old bookworm you are! What's the book? Ah, a foreign language; Swedish, I suppose?'

'No, it is not Swedish,' said Gaster; 'it is Arabic.'

'You don't mean to say you know Arabic?'

'Oh, very well—very well indeed!'

'And what's it about?' I asked, turning over the leaves of the musty old volume.

'Nothing that would interest one so young and fair as yourself, Miss Underwood,' he answered, looking at me in a way which had become habitual to him of late. 'It treats of the days when mind was stronger than what you call matter; when great spirits lived that were able to exist without these coarse bodies of ours, and could mould all things to their so-powerful wills.'

'Oh, I see; a kind of ghost story,' said Charley. 'Well, adieu; we won't keep you from your studies.'

We left him sitting in the little glen still absorbed in his mystical treatise. It must have been imagination which induced me, on turning suddenly round half an hour later, to think that I saw his familiar figure glide rapidly behind a tree.

I mentioned it to Charley at the time, but he laughed my idea to scorn.

*

I alluded just now to a peculiar manner which this man Gaster had of looking at me. His eyes seemed to lose their usual steely expression when he did so, and soften into something which might be almost called caressing. They seemed to influence me strangely, for I could always tell, without looking at him, when his gaze was fixed upon me.

Sometimes I fancied that this idea was simply due to a disordered nervous system or morbid imagination; but my mother dispelled that delusion from my mind.

'Do you know,' she said, coming into my bedroom one night, and carefully shutting the door behind her, 'if the idea was not so utterly preposterous, Lottie, I should say that that Doctor was madly in love with you?'

'Nonsense, 'ma!' said I, nearly dropping my candle in my consternation at the thought.

'I really think so, Lottie,' continued my mother. 'He's got a way of looking which is very like that of your poor dear father, Nicholas, before we were married. Something of this sort, you know.'

And the old lady cast an utterly heart-broken glance at the bed-post.

'Now, go to bed,' said I, 'and don't have such funny ideas. Why, poor Doctor Gaster knows that I am engaged as well as you do.'

'Time will show,' said the old lady, as she left the room; and I went to bed with the words still ringing in my ears.

Certainly, it is a strange thing that on that very night a thrill which I had come to know well ran through me, and awakened me from my slumbers.

I stole softly to the window, and peered out through the bars of the Venetian blinds, and there was the gaunt, vampire-like figure of our Swedish visitor standing upon the gravel-walk, and apparently gazing up at my window.

It may have been that he detected the movement of the blind, for, lighting a cigarette, he began pacing up and down the avenue.

I noticed that at breakfast next morning he went out of his way to explain the fact that he had been restless during the night, and had steadied his nerves by a short stroll and a smoke.

After all, when I came to consider it calmly, the aversion which I had against the man and my distrust of him were founded on very scanty grounds. A man might have a strange face, and be fond of curious literature, and even look approvingly at an engaged young lady, without being a very dangerous member of society.

I say this to show that even up to that point I was perfectly unbiased and free from prejudice in my opinion of Octavius Gaster.

*

'I say!' remarked Lieutenant Daseby, one morning; 'what do you think of having a picnic today?'

'Capital!' ejaculated everybody.

'You see, they are talking of commissioning the old *Shark* soon, and Trevor here will have to go back to the mill. We may as well compress as much fun as we can into the time.'

'What is it that you call nicpic?' asked Doctor Gaster.

'It's another of our English institutions for you to study,' said Charley. 'It's our version of a *fête champêtre*.'

'Ah, I see! That will be very jolly!' acquiesced the Swede.

'There are half a dozen places we might go to,' continued the Lieutenant. 'There's the Lover's Leap, or Black Tor, or Beer Ferris Abbey.'

'That's the best,' said Charley. 'Nothing like ruins for a picnic.'

'Well the Abbey be it. How far is it?'

'Six miles,' said Trevor.

'Seven by the road,' remarked the Colonel, with military exactness. 'Mrs Underwood and I shall stay at home, and the rest of you can fit into the waggonette. You'll all have to chaperon each other.'

I need hardly say that this motion was carried also without a division.

'Well,' said Charley, 'I'll order the trap to be round in half an hour, so you'd better all make the best of your time. We'll want salmon, and salad, and hard-boiled eggs, and liquor, and any number of things. I'll look after the liquor department. What will you do, Lottie?'

'I'll take charge of the china,' I said.

'I'll bring the fish,' said Daseby.

'And I the vegetables,' added Fan.

'What will you do, Gaster?' asked Charley.

'Truly,' said the Swede, in his strange, musical accents, 'but little is left for me to do. I can, however, wait upon the ladies, and I can make what you call a salad.'

'You'll be more popular in the latter capacity than in the former,' said I, laughingly.

'Ah, you say so,' he said, turning sharp round upon me, and flushing up to his flaxen hair. 'Yes. Ha! ha! Very good!'

And with a discordant laugh, he strode out of the room.

'I say, Lottie,' remonstrated my lover, 'you've hurt the fellow's feelings.'

'I'm sure I didn't mean to,' I answered. 'If you like I'll go after him and tell him so.'

'Oh, leave him alone,' said Daseby. 'A man with a mug like that has no right to be so touchy. He'll come round right enough.'

It was true that I had not had the slightest intention of offending Gaster, still I felt pained at having annoyed him.

After I had stowed away the knives and plates into the hamper, I found that the others were still busy at their various departments. The moment seemed a favourable one for apologising for my thoughtless remark, so without saying anything to anyone, I slipped away and ran down the corridor in the direction of our visitor's room.

I suppose I must have tripped along very lightly, or it may have been the rich thick matting of Toynby Hall—certain it is that Mr Gaster seemed unconscious of my approach.

His door was open, and as I came up to it and caught sight of him inside, there was something so strange in his appearance that I paused, literally petrified for the moment with astonishment.

He had in his hand a small slip from a newspaper which he was reading, and which seemed to afford him considerable amusement. There was something horrible too in this mirth of his, for though he writhed his body about as if with laughter, no sound was emitted from his lips.

His face, which was half-turned towards me, wore an expression upon it which I had never seen on it before; I can only describe it as one of savage exultation.

Just as I was recovering myself sufficiently to step forward and knock at the door, he suddenly, with a last convulsive spasm of merriment, dashed down the piece of paper upon the table and hurried out by the other door of his room, which led through the billiard-room to the hall.

I heard his steps dying away in the distance, and peeped once more into his room.

What could be the joke that had moved this stern man to mirth? Surely some masterpiece of humour.

Was there ever a woman whose principles were strong enough to overcome her curiosity?

Looking cautiously round to make sure that the passage was empty, I slipped into the room and examined the paper which he had been reading.

It was a cutting from an English journal, and had evidently been long carried about and frequently perused, for it was almost illegible in places. There was, however, as far as I could see, very little to provoke laughter in its contents. It ran, as well as I can remember, in this way:

> 'Sudden Death in the Docks.—The master of the bark-rigged steamer Olga, from Tromsberg, was found lying dead in his cabin on Wednesday afternoon. Deceased was, it seems, of a violent disposition, and had had frequent altercations with the surgeon of the vessel. On this particular day he had been more than usually offensive, declaring that the surgeon was a necromancer and worshipper of the devil. The latter retired on deck to avoid further persecution. Shortly afterwards the steward had occasion to enter the cabin, and found the captain lying across the table

> quite dead. Death is attributed to heart disease, accelerated by excessive passion. An inquest will be held today.'

And this was the paragraph which this strange man had regarded as the height of humour!

I hurried downstairs, astonishment, not un-mixed with repugnance, predominating in my mind. So just was I, however, that the dark inference which has so often occurred to me since never for one moment crossed my mind. I looked upon him as a curious and rather repulsive enigma—nothing more.

When I met him at the picnic, all remembrance of my unfortunate speech seemed to have vanished from his mind. He made himself as agreeable as usual, and his salad was pronounced a *chef-d'œuvre*, while his quaint little Swedish songs and his tales of all climes and countries alternately thrilled and amused us. It was after luncheon, however, that the conversation turned upon a subject which seemed to have special charms for his daring mind.

I forget who it was that broached the question of the supernatural. I think it was Trevor, by some story of a hoax which he had perpetrated at Cambridge. The story seemed to have a strange effect upon Octavius Gaster, who tossed his long arms about in impassioned invective as he ridiculed those who dared to doubt about the existence of the unseen.

'Tell me,' he said, standing up in his excitement, 'which among you has ever known what you call an instinct to fail. The wild bird has an instinct which tells it of the solitary rock upon the so boundless sea on which it may lay its egg, and is it disappointed? The swallow turns to the south when the winter is coming, and has its instinct ever led it astray? And shall this instinct which tells us of the unknown spirits around us, and which pervades every untaught child and every race so savage, be wrong? I say, never!'

'Go it, Gaster!' cried Charley.

'Take your wind and have another spell,' said the sailor.

'No, never,' repeated the Swede, disregarding our amusement. 'We can see that matter exists apart from mind; then why should not mind exist apart from matter?'

'Give it up,' said Daseby.

'Have we not proofs of it?' continued Gaster, his grey eyes gleaming with excitement. 'Who that has read Steinberg's book upon spirits, or that by the eminent American, Madame Crowe, can doubt it? Did not Gustav von Spee meet his brother Leopold in the streets of Strasbourg, the same brother having been drowned three months before in the Pacific? Did not Home, the spiritualist, in open daylight, float above the housetops of Paris? Who has not heard the voices of the dead around him? I myself—'

'Well, what of yourself?' asked half a dozen of us, in a breath.

'Bah! it matters nothing,' he said, passing his hand over his forehead, and evidently controlling himself with difficulty. 'Truly, our talk is too sad for such an occasion.' And, in spite of all our efforts, we were unable to extract from Gaster any relation of his own experiences of the supernatural.

It was a merry day. Our approaching dissolution seemed to cause each one to contribute his utmost to the general amusement. It was settled that after the coming rifle match Jack was to return to his ship and Trevor to his university. As to Charley and myself, we were to settle down into a staid respectable couple.

The match was one of our principal topics of conversation. Shooting had always been a hobby of Charley's, and he was the captain of the Roborough company of Devon volunteers, which boasted some of the crack shots of the county. The match was to be against a picked team of regulars from Plymouth, and as they were no despicable opponents, the issue was considered doubtful. Charley had evidently set his heart on winning, and descanted long and loudly on the chances.

'The range is only a mile from Toynby Hall,' he said, 'and we'll all drive over, and you shall see the fun. You'll bring me luck, Lottie,' he whispered, 'I know you will.'

Oh, my poor lost darling, to think of the luck that I brought you!

There was one dark cloud to mar the brightness of that happy day.

I could not hide from myself any longer the fact that my mother's suspicions were correct, and that Octavius Gaster loved me.

Throughout the whole of the excursion his attentions had been most assiduous, and his eyes hardly ever wandered away from me. There was a manner, too, in all that he said which spoke louder than words.

I was on thorns lest Charley should perceive it, for I knew his fiery temper; but the thought of such treachery never entered the honest heart of my lover.

He did once look up with mild surprise when the Swede insisted on relieving me of a fern which I was carrying; but the expression faded away into a smile at what he regarded as Gaster's effusive good-nature. My own feeling in the matter was pity for the unfortunate foreigner, and sorrow that I should have been the means of rendering him unhappy.

I thought of the torture it must be for a wild, fierce spirit like his to have a passion gnawing at his heart which honour and pride would alike prevent him from ever expressing in words. Alas! I had not counted upon the utter recklessness and want of principle of the man; but it was not long before I was undeceived.

There was a little arbour at the bottom of the garden, over-grown with honeysuckle and ivy, which had long been a favourite haunt of Charley and myself. It was doubly dear to us from the fact that it was here, on the occasion of my former visit, that words of love had first passed between us.

After dinner on the day following the picnic I sauntered down to this little summer-house, as was my custom. Here I used to wait until Charley, having finished his cigar with the other gentlemen, would come down and join me.

On that particular evening he seemed to be longer away than usual. I waited impatiently for his coming, going to the door every now and then to see if there were any signs of his approach.

I had just sat down again after one of those fruitless excursions, when I heard the tread of a male foot upon the gravel, and a figure emerged from among the bushes.

I sprang up with a glad smile, which changed to an expression of bewilderment, and even fear, when I saw the gaunt, pallid face of Octavius Gaster peering in at me.

There was certainly something about his actions which would have inspired distrust in the mind of anyone in my position. Instead of greeting me, he looked up and down the garden, as if to make sure that we were entirely alone. He then stealthily entered the arbour, and seated himself upon a chair, in such a position that he was between me and the doorway.

'Do not be afraid,' he said, as he noticed my scared expression. 'There is nothing to fear. I do but come that I may have talk with you.'

'Have you seen Mr Pillar?' I asked, trying hard to seem at my ease.

'Ha! Have I seen your Charley?' he answered, with a sneer upon the last words. 'Are you then so anxious that he come? Can no one speak to thee but Charley, little one?'

'Mr Gaster,' I said, 'you are forgetting yourself.'

'It is Charley, Charley, ever Charley!' continued the Swede, disregarding my interruption. 'Yes, I have seen Charley. I have told him that you wait upon the bank of the river, and he has gone thither upon the wings of love.'

'Why have you told him this lie?' I asked, still trying not to lose my self-control.

'That I might see you; that I might speak to you. Do you, then, love him so? Cannot the thought of glory, and riches, and power, above all that the mind can conceive, win you from this first maiden fancy of yours? Fly with me, Charlotte, and all this, and more, shall be yours! Come!'

And he stretched his long arms out in passionate entreaty.

Even at that moment the thought flashed through my mind of how like they were to the tentacles of some poisonous insect.

'You insult me, sir!' I cried, rising to my feet. 'You shall pay heavily for this treatment of an unprotected girl!'

'Ah, you say it,' he cried, 'but you mean it not. In your heart so tender there is pity left for the most miserable of men. Nay, you shall not pass me—you shall hear me first!'

'Let me go, sir!'

'Nay; you shall not go until you tell me if nothing that I can do may win your love.'

'How dare you speak so?' I almost screamed, losing all my fear in my indignation. 'You, who are the guest of my future husband! Let me tell you, once and for all, that I had no feeling towards you before save one of repugnance and contempt, which you have now converted into positive hatred!'

'And is it so?' he gasped, tottering backwards towards the doorway, and putting his hand up to his throat as if he found a difficulty in uttering the words. 'And has my love won hatred in return? Ha!' he continued, advancing his face within a foot of mine as I cowered away from his glassy eyes. 'I know it now. It is this—it is this!' and he struck the horrible cicatrix on his face with his clenched hand. 'Maids love not such faces as this! I am not smooth, and brown, and curly like this Charley—this brainless school-boy; this human brute who cares but for his sport and his—'

'Let me pass!' I cried, rushing at the door.

'No; you shall not go—you shall not!' he hissed, pushing me backwards.

I struggled furiously to escape from his grasp. His long arms seemed to clasp me like bars of steel. I felt my strength going, and was making one last despairing effort to shake myself loose, when some irresistible power from behind tore my persecutor away from me and hurled him backwards on to the gravel walk.

Looking up, I saw Charley's towering figure and square shoulders in the doorway.

'My poor darling!' he said, catching me in his arms. 'Sit here—here in the angle. There is no danger now. I shall be with you in a minute.'

'Don't Charley, don't!' I murmured, as he turned to leave me.

But he was deaf to my entreaties, and strode out of the arbour.

I could not see either him or his opponent from the position in which he had placed me, but I heard every word that was spoken.

'You villain!' said a voice that I could hardly recognise as my lover's. 'So this is why you put me on a wrong scent?'

'That is why,' answered the foreigner, in a tone of easy indifference.

'And this is how you repay our hospitality, you infernal scoundrel!'

'Yes; we amuse ourselves in your so beautiful summer-house.'

'We! You are still on my ground and my guest, and I would wish to keep my hands from you; but, by heavens—'

Charley was speaking very low and in gasps now.

'Why do you swear? What is it, then?' asked the languid voice of Octavius Gaster.

'If you dare to couple Miss Underwood's name with this business, and insinuate that—'

'Insinuate? I insinuate nothing. What I say I say plain for all the world to hear. I say that this so chaste maiden did herself ask—'

I heard the sound of a heavy blow, and a great rattling of the gravel.

I was too weak to rise from where I lay, and could only clasp my hands together and utter a faint scream.

'You cur!' said Charley. 'Say as much again, and I'll stop your mouth for all eternity!'

There was a silence, and then I heard Gaster speaking in a husky, strange voice.

'You have struck me!' he said; 'you have drawn my blood!'

'Yes; I'll strike you again if you show your cursed face within these grounds. Don't look at me so! You don't suppose your hankey-pankey tricks can frighten me?'

An indefinable dread came over me as my lover spoke. I staggered to my feet and looked out at them, leaning against the door-way for support.

Charley was standing erect and defiant, with his young head in the air, like one who glories in the cause for which he battles.

Octavius Gaster was opposite him, surveying him with pinched lips and a baleful look in his cruel eyes. The blood was running freely from a deep gash on his lip, and spotting the front of his green necktie and white waistcoat. He perceived me the instant I emerged from the arbour.

'Ha, ha!' he cried, with a demoniacal burst of laughter. 'She comes! The bride! She comes! Room for the bride! Oh, happy pair, happy pair!'

And with another fiendish burst of merriment he turned and disappeared over the crumbling wall of the garden with such rapidity that he was gone before we had realised what it was that he was about to do.

'Oh, Charley,' I said, as my lover came back to my side, 'you've hurt him!'

'Hurt him! I should hope I have! Come, darling, you are frightened and tired. He did not injure you, did he?'

'No; but I feel rather faint and sick.'

'Come, we'll walk slowly to the house together. The rascal! It was cunningly and deliberately planned, too. He told me he had seen you down by the river, and I was going down when I met young Stokes, the keeper's son, coming back from fishing, and he told me that there was nobody there. Somehow, when Stokes said that, a thousand little things flashed into my mind at once, and I became in a moment so convinced of Gaster's villainy that I ran as hard as I could to the arbour.'

'Charley,' I said, clinging to my lover's arm, 'I fear he will injure you in some way. Did you see the look in his eyes before he leaped the wall?'

'Pshaw!' said Charley. 'All these foreigners have a way of scowling and glaring when they are angry, but it never comes to much.'

'Still, I am afraid of him,' said I, mournfully, as we went up the steps together, 'and I wish you had not struck him.'

'So do I,' Charley answered; 'for he was our guest, you know, in spite of his rascality. However, it's done now and it can't be helped, as the cook says in "Pickwick," and really it was more than flesh and blood could stand.'

I must run rapidly over the events of the next few days. For me, at least, it was a period of absolute happiness. With Gaster's departure a cloud seemed to be lifted off my soul, and a depression which had weighed upon the whole household completely disappeared.

Once more I was the light-hearted girl that I had been before the foreigner's arrival. Even the Colonel forgot to mourn over his absence, owing to the all-absorbing interest in the coming competition in which his son was engaged.

It was our main subject of conversation and bets were freely offered by the gentlemen on the success of the Roborough team, though no one was unprincipled enough to seem to support their antagonists by taking them.

Jack Daseby ran down to Plymouth, and 'made a book on the event' with some officers of the Marines, which he did in such an extraordinary way that we reckoned that in case of Roborough winning, he would lose seventeen shillings; while, should the other contingency occur, he would be involved in hopeless liabilities.

Charley and I had tacitly agreed not to mention the name of Gaster, nor to allude in any way to what had passed.

On the morning after our scene in the garden, Charley had sent a servant up to the Swede's room with instructions to pack up any things he might find there, and leave them at the nearest inn.

It was found, however, that all Gaster's effects had been already removed, though how and when was a perfect mystery to the servants.

I know of few more attractive spots than the shooting-range at Roborough. The glen in which it is situated is about half a mile long and perfectly level, so that the targets were able to range from two to seven hundred yards, the further ones simply showing as square white dots against the green of the rising hills behind.

The glen itself is part of the great moor and its sides, sloping gradually up, lose themselves in the vast rugged expanse. Its symmetrical character suggested to the imaginative mind that some giant of old had made an excavation in the moor with a titanic cheese-scoop, but that a single trial had convinced him of the utter worthlessness of the soil.

He might even be imagined to have dropped the despised sample at the mouth of the cutting which he had made, for there was a considerable elevation there, from which the riflemen were to fire, and thither we bent our steps on that eventful afternoon.

Our opponents had arrived there before us, bringing with them a considerable number of naval and military officers, while a long line of nondescript vehicles showed that many of the good citizens of Plymouth had seized the opportunity of giving their wives and families an outing on the moor.

An enclosure for ladies and distinguished guests had been erected on the top of the hill, which, with the marquee and refreshment tents, made the scene a lively one.

The country people had turned out in force, and were excitedly staking their half-crowns upon their local champions, which were as enthusiastically taken up by the admirers of the regulars.

Through all this scene of bustle and confusion we were safely conveyed by Charley, aided by Jack and Trevor, who finally deposited us in a sort of rudimentary grandstand, from which we could look round at our ease on all that was going on.

We were soon, however, so absorbed in the glorious view, that we became utterly unconscious of the betting and pushing and chaff of the crowd in front of us.

Away to the south we could see the blue smoke of Plymouth curling up into the calm summer air, while beyond that was the great sea, stretching away to the horizon, dark and vast, save where some petulant wave dashed it with a streak of foam, as if rebelling against the great peacefulness of nature.

From the Eddystone to the Start the long rugged line of the Devonshire coast lay like a map before us.

I was still lost in admiration when Charley's voice broke half-reproachfully on my ear.

'Why, Lottie,' he said, 'you don't seem to take a bit of interest in it!'

'Oh, yes I do, dear,' I answered. 'But the scenery is so pretty, and the sea is always a weakness of mine. Come and sit here, and tell me all about the match and how we are to know whether you are winning or losing.'

'I've just been explaining it,' answered Charley. 'But I'll go over it again.'

'Do, like a darling,' said I; and settled myself down to mark, learn, and inwardly digest.

'Well,' said Charley, 'there are ten men on each side. We shoot alternately; first, one of our fellows, then one of them, and so on—you understand?'

'Yes, I understand that.'

'First we fire at the two hundred yards range—those are the targets nearest of all. We fire five shots each at those. Then we fire five shots at the ones at five hundred yards—those middle ones; and then we finish up by firing at the seven hundred yards range—you see the target far over there on the side of the hill. Whoever makes the most points wins. Do you grasp it now?'

'Oh, yes; that's very simple,' I said.

'Do you know what a bull's eye is?' asked my lover.

'Some sort of sweetmeat, isn't it?' I hazarded.

Charley seemed amazed at the extent of my ignorance. 'That's the bull's-eye,' he said; 'that dark spot in the centre of the target. If you hit that, it counts five. There is another ring, which you can't see, drawn round that, and if you get inside of it, it is called a 'centre,' and counts four. Outside that, again, is called an 'outer,' and only gives you three. You can tell where the shot has hit, for the marker puts out a coloured disc, and covers the place.'

'Oh, I understand it all now,' said I, enthusiastically. 'I'll tell you what I'll do, Charley; I'll mark the score on a bit of paper every shot that is fired, and then I'll always know how Roborough is getting on!'

'You can't do better,' he laughed as he strode off to get his men together, for a warning bell signified that the contest was about to begin.

There was a great waving of flags and shouting before the ground could be got clear, and then I saw a little cluster of red-coats lying upon the greensward, while a similar group, in grey, took up their position to the left of them.

'Pang!' went a rifle-shot, and the blue smoke came curling up from the grass.

Fanny shrieked, while I gave a cry of delight, for I saw the white disc go up, which proclaimed a 'bull,' and the shot had been fired by one of the Roborough men. My elation was, however, promptly checked by the answering shot which put down five to the credit of the regulars. The next was also a 'bull,' which was speedily cancelled by another. At the end of the competition at the short range each side had scored forty-nine out of a possible fifty, and the question of supremacy was as undecided as ever.

'It's getting exciting,' said Charley, lounging over the stand. 'We begin shooting at the five hundred yards in a few minutes.'

'Oh, Charley,' cried Fanny in high excitement, 'don't you go and miss, whatever you do!'

'I won't if I can help it,' responded Charley, cheerfully.

'You made a "bull" every time just now,' I said.

'Yes, but it's not so easy when you've got your sights up. However, we'll do our best, and we can't do more. They've got some terribly good long-range men among them. Come over here, Lottie, for a moment.'

'What is it, Charley?' I asked, as he led me away from the others. I could see by the look in his face that something was troubling him.

'It's that fellow,' growled my lover. 'What the deuce does he want to come here for? I hoped we had seen the last of him!'

'What fellow?' I gasped, with a vague apprehension at my heart.

'Why, that infernal Swedish fellow, Gaster!'

I followed the direction of Charley's glance, and there, sure enough, standing on a little knoll close to the place where the riflemen were lying, was the tall, angular figure of the foreigner.

He seemed utterly unconscious of the sensation which his singular appearance and hideous countenance excited among the burly farmers around him; but was craning his long neck about, this way and that, as if in search of somebody.

As we watched him, his eye suddenly rested upon us, and it seemed to me that, even at that distance, I could see a spasm of hatred and triumph pass over his livid features.

A strange foreboding came over me, and I seized my lover's hand in both my own.

'Oh, Charley,' I cried, 'don't—don't go back to the shooting! Say you are ill—make some excuse, and come away!'

'Nonsense, lass!' said he, laughing heartily at my terror. 'Why, what in the world are you afraid of?'

'Of him!' I answered.

'Don't be so silly, dear. One would think he was a demi-god to hear the way in which you talk of him. But there! that's the bell, and I must be off.'

'Well, promise, at least, that you will not go near him?' I cried, following Charley.

'All right—all right!' said he.

And I had to be content with that small concession.

The contest at the five hundred yards range was a close and exciting one. Roborough led by a couple of points for some time, until a series of 'bulls' by one of the crack marksmen of their opponents turned the tables upon them.

At the end of it was found that the volunteers were three points to the bad—a result which was hailed by cheers from the Plymouth contingent and by long faces and black looks among the dwellers on the moor.

During the whole of this competition Octavius Gaster had remained perfectly still and motionless upon the top of the knoll on which he had originally taken up his position.

It seemed to me that he knew little of what was going on, for his face was turned away from the marksmen, and he appeared to be gazing into the distance.

Once I caught sight of his profile, and thought that his lips were moving rapidly as if in prayer, or it may have been the shimmer of the hot air of the almost Indian summer which deceived me. It was, however, my impression at the time.

And now came the competition at the longest range of all, which was to decide the match.

The Roborough men settled down steadily to their task of making up the lost ground; while the regulars seemed determined not to throw away a chance by over-confidence.

As shot after shot was fired, the excitement of the spectators became so great that they crowded round the marksmen, cheering enthusiastically at every 'bull.'

We ourselves were so far affected by the general contagion that we left our harbour of refuge, and submitted meekly to the pushing and rough ways of the mob, in order to obtain a nearer view of the champions and their doings.

The military stood at seventeen when the volunteers were at sixteen, and great was the despondency of the rustics.

Things looked brighter, however, when the two sides tied at twenty-four, and brighter still when the steady shooting of the local team raised their score to thirty-two against thirty of their opponents.

There were still, however, the three points which had been lost at the last range to be made up for.

Slowly the score rose, and desperate were the efforts of both parties to pull off the victory.

Finally, a thrill ran through the crowd when it was known that the last red-coat had fired, while one volunteer was still left, and that the soldiers were leading by four points.

Even *our* unsportsman-like minds were worked into a state of all-absorbing excitement by the nature of the crisis which now presented itself.

If the last representative of our little town could but hit the bull's-eye the match was won.

The silver cup, the glory, the money of our adherents, all depended upon that single shot.

The reader will imagine that my interest was by no means lessened when, by dint of craning my neck and standing on tiptoe, I caught sight of my Charley coolly shoving a cartridge into his rifle, and realised that it was upon his skill that the honour of Roborough depended.

It was this, I think, which lent me strength to push my way so vigorously through the crowd that I found myself almost in the first row and commanding an excellent view of the proceedings.

There were two gigantic farmers on each side of me, and while we were waiting for the decisive shot to be fired, I could not help listening to the conversation, which they carried on in broad Devon, over my head.

'Mun's a rare ugly 'un,' said one.

'He is that,' cordially assented the other.

'See to mun's een?'

'Eh, Jock; see to mun's moo', rayther!—Blessed if he bean't foamin' like Farmer Watson's dog—t' bull pup whot died mad o' the hydropathics.'

I turned round to see the favoured object of these flattering comments, and my eyes fell upon Doctor Octavius Gaster, whose presence I had entirely forgotten in my excitement.

His face was turned towards me; but he evidently did not see me, for his eyes were bent with unswerving persistence upon a point midway apparently between the distant targets and himself.

I have never seen anything to compare with the extraordinary concentration of that stare, which had the effect of making his eyeballs appear gorged and prominent, while the pupils were contracted to the finest possible point.

Perspiration was running freely down his long, cadaverous face, and, as the farmer had remarked, there were some traces of foam at the corners of his mouth. The jaw was locked, as if with some fierce effort of the will which demanded all the energy of his soul.

To my dying day that hideous countenance shall never fade from my remembrance nor cease to haunt me in my dreams. I shuddered, and turned away my head in the vain hope that perhaps the honest farmer might be right, and mental disease be the cause of all the vagaries of this extraordinary man.

A great stillness fell upon the whole crowd as Charley, having loaded his rifle, snapped up the breech cheerily, and proceeded to lie down in his appointed place.

'That's right, Mr Charles, sir—that's right!' I heard old McIntosh, the volunteer sergeant, whisper as I passed. 'A cool head and a steady hand, that's what does the trick, sir!'

My lover smiled round at the grey-headed soldier as he lay down upon the grass, and then proceeded to look along the sight of his rifle amid a silence in which the faint rustling of the breeze among the blades of grass was distinctly audible.

For more than a minute he hung upon his aim. His finger seemed to press the trigger, and every eye was fixed upon the distant target, when suddenly, instead of firing, the rifleman staggered up to his knees, leaving his weapon upon the ground.

To the surprise of everyone, his face was deadly pale, and perspiration was standing on his brow.

'I say, McIntosh,' he said, in a strange, gasping voice, 'is there anybody standing between the target and me?'

'Between, sir? No, not a soul, sir,' answered the astonished sergeant.

'There, man, there!' cried Charley, with fierce energy, seizing him by the arm, and pointing in the direction of the target, 'Don't you see him there, standing right in the line of fire?'

'There's no one there!' shouted half a dozen voices.

'No one there? Well, it must have been my imagination,' said Charley, passing his hand slowly over his forehead. 'Yet I could have sworn—Here, give me the rifle!'

He lay down again, and having settled himself into position, raised his weapon slowly to his eye. He had hardly looked along the barrel before he sprang up again with a loud cry.

'There!' he cried; 'I tell you I see it! A man dressed in volunteer uniform, and very like myself—the image of myself. Is this a conspiracy?' he continued, turning fiercely on the crowd. 'Do you tell me none of you see a man resembling myself walking from that target, and not two hundred yards from me as I speak?'

I should have flown to Charley's side had I not known how he hated feminine interference, and anything approaching to a scene. I could only listen silently to his strange wild words.

'I protest against this!' said an officer coming forward. 'This gentleman must really either take his shot, or we shall remove our men off the field and claim the victory.'

'But I'll shoot *him*!' gasped poor Charley.

'Humbug!' 'Rubbish!' 'Shoot him, then!' growled half a score of masculine voices.

'The fact is,' lisped one of the military men in front of me to another, 'the young fellow's nerves ar'n't quite equal to the occasion, and he feels it, and is trying to back out.'

The imbecile young lieutenant little knew at this point how a feminine hand was longing to stretch forth and deal him a sounding box on the ears.

'It's Martell's three-star brandy, that's what it is,' whispered the other. 'The "devils," don't you know. I've had 'em myself, and know a case when I see it.'

This remark was too recondite for my understanding, or the speaker would have run the same risk as his predecessor.

'Well, are you going to shoot or not?' cried several voices.

'Yes, I'll shoot,' groaned Charley—'I'll shoot *him* through! It's murder—sheer *murder*!'

I shall never forget the haggard look which he cast round at the crowd. 'I'm aiming *through* him, McIntosh,' he murmured, as he lay down on the grass and raised the gun for the third time to his shoulder.

There was one moment of suspense, a spurt of flame, the crack of a rifle, and a cheer which echoed across the moor, and might have been heard in the distant village.

'Well done, lad—well done!' shouted a hundred honest Devonshire voices, as the little white disc came out from behind the marker's shield and obliterated the dark 'bull' for the moment, proclaiming that the match was won.

'Well done, lad! It's Maister Pillar, of Toynby Hall. Here, let's gie mun a lift, carry mun home, for the honour o' Roborough. Come on, lads! There mun is on the grass. Wake up, Sergeant McIntosh. What be the matter with thee? Eh? What?'

A deadly stillness came over the crowd, and then a low incredulous murmur, changing to one of pity, with whispers of 'leave her alone, poor lass—leave her to hersel'!'—and then there was silence again, save for the moaning of a woman, and her short, quick cries of despair.

For, reader, my Charley, my beautiful, brave Charley, was lying cold and dead upon the ground, with the rifle still clenched in his stiffening fingers.

I heard kind words of sympathy. I heard Lieutenant Daseby's voice, broken with grief, begging me to control my sorrow, and felt his hand, as he gently raised me from my poor boy's body. This I can remember, and nothing more, until my recovery from my illness, when I found myself in the sick-room at Toynby Hall, and learned that three restless, delirious weeks had passed since that terrible day.

Stay!—do I remember nothing else?

Sometimes I think I do. Sometimes I think I can recall a lucid interval in the midst of my wanderings. I seem to have a dim recollection of seeing my good nurse go out of the room—of seeing a gaunt, bloodless face peering in through the half-open window, and of hearing a voice which said, 'I have dealt with thy so beautiful lover, and I have yet to deal with thee.' The words come back to me with a familiar ring, as if they had sounded in my ears before, and yet it may have been but a dream.

'And this is all!' you say. 'It is for this that a hysterical woman hunts down a harmless *savant* in the advertisement columns of the newspapers! On this shallow evidence she hints at crimes of the most monstrous description!'

Well, I cannot expect that these things should strike you as they struck me. I can but say that if I were upon a bridge with Octavius Gaster standing at one end, and the most merciless tiger that ever prowled in an Indian jungle at the other, I should fly to the wild beast for protection.

For me, my life is broken and blasted. I care not how soon it may end, but if my words shall keep this man out of one honest household, I have not written in vain.

*

Within a fortnight after writing this narrative, my poor daughter disappeared. All search has failed to find her. A porter at the railway station has deposed to having seen a young lady resembling her description get into a first-class carriage with a tall, thin gentleman. It is, however, too ridiculous to suppose that she can have eloped after her recent grief, and without my having had any suspicions. The detectives are, however, working out the clue.—EMILY UNDERWOOD

JOHN BARRINGTON COWLES

I

It might seem rash of me to say that I ascribe the death of my poor friend, John Barrington Cowles, to any preternatural agency. I am aware that in the present state of public feeling a chain of evidence would require to be strong indeed before the possibility of such a conclusion could be admitted.

I shall therefore merely state the circumstances which led up to this sad event as concisely and as plainly as I can, and leave every reader to draw his own deductions. Perhaps there may be some one who can throw light upon what is dark to me.

I first met Barrington Cowles when I went up to Edinburgh University to take out medical classes there. My landlady in Northumberland Street had a large house, and, being a widow without children, she gained a livelihood by providing accommodation for several students.

Barrington Cowles happened to have taken a bedroom upon the same floor as mine, and when we came to know each other better we shared a small sitting-room, in which we took our meals. In this manner we originated a friendship which was unmarred by the slightest disagreement up to the day of his death.

Cowles' father was the colonel of a Sikh regiment and had remained in India for many years. He allowed his son a handsome income, but seldom gave any other sign of parental affection—writing irregularly and briefly.

My friend, who had himself been born in India, and whose whole disposition was an ardent tropical one, was much hurt by this neglect. His mother was dead, and he had no other relation in the world to supply the blank.

Thus he came in time to concentrate all his affection upon me, and to confide in me in a manner which is rare among men. Even when a stronger and deeper passion came upon him, it never infringed upon the old tenderness between us.

Cowles was a tall, slim young fellow, with an olive, Velasquez-like face, and dark, tender eyes. I have seldom seen a man who was more likely to excite a woman's interest, or to captivate her imagination. His expression was, as a rule, dreamy, and even languid; but if in conversation a subject arose which interested him he would be all animation in a moment. On such occasions his colour would heighten, his eyes gleam, and he could speak with an eloquence which would carry his audience with him.

In spite of these natural advantages he led a solitary life, avoiding female society, and reading with great diligence. He was one of the foremost men of his year, taking the senior medal for anatomy, and the Neil Arnott prize for physics.

How well I can recollect the first time we met her! Often and often I have recalled the circumstances, and tried to remember what the exact impression was which she produced on my mind at the time. After we came to know her my judgement was warped, so that I am curious to recollect what my unbiassed instincts were. It is hard, however, to eliminate the feelings which reason or prejudice afterwards raised in me.

It was at the opening of the Royal Scottish Academy in the spring of 1879. My poor friend was passionately attached to art in every form, and a pleasing chord in music or a delicate effect upon canvas would give exquisite pleasure to his highly-strung nature. We had gone together to see the pictures, and were standing in the grand central *salon,* when I noticed an extremely beautiful woman standing at the other side of the room. In my whole life I have never seen such a classically perfect countenance. It was the real Greek type—the forehead broad, very low, and as white as marble, with a cloudlet of delicate locks wreathing round it, the nose straight and clean cut, the lips inclined to thinness, the chin and lower jaw beautifully rounded off, and yet sufficiently developed to promise unusual strength of character.

But those eyes—those wonderful eyes! If I could but give some faint idea of their varying moods, their steely hardness, their feminine softness, their power of command, their penetrating intensity suddenly melting away into an expression of womanly weakness—but I am speaking now of future impressions!

There was a tall, yellow-haired young man with this lady, whom I at once recognised as a law student with whom I had a slight acquaintance.

Archibald Reeves—for that was his name—was a dashing, handsome young fellow, and had at one time been a ringleader in every university escapade; but of late I had seen little of him, and the report was that he was engaged to be married. His companion was, then, I presumed, his *fiancée.* I seated myself upon the velvet settee in the centre of the room, and furtively watched the couple from behind my catalogue.

The more I looked at her the more her beauty grew upon me. She was somewhat short in stature, it is true; but her figure was perfection, and she bore herself in such a fashion that it was only by actual comparison that one would have known her to be under the medium height.

As I kept my eyes upon them, Reeves was called away for some reason, and the young lady was left alone. Turning her back to the pictures, she passed the time until the return of her escort in taking a deliberate survey of the company, without paying the least heed to the fact that a dozen pair of eyes, attracted by her elegance and beauty, were bent curiously upon her. With one of her hands holding the red silk cord which railed off the pictures, she stood languidly moving her eyes from face to face with as little self-consciousness as if she were looking at the canvas creatures behind her. Suddenly, as I watched her, I saw her gaze become fixed, and, as it were, intense. I followed the direction of her looks, wondering what could have attracted her so strongly.

John Barrington Cowles was standing before a picture—one, I think, by Noel Paton—I know that the subject was a noble and ethereal one. His profile was turned towards us, and never have I seen him to such advantage. I have said that he was a strikingly handsome man, but at that moment he looked absolutely magnificent. It was evident that he had momentarily forgotten his surroundings, and that his whole soul was in sympathy with the picture before him. His eyes sparkled, and a dusky pink shone through his clear olive cheeks. She continued to watch him fixedly, with a look of interest upon her face, until he came out of his reverie with a start, and turned abruptly round, so that his gaze met hers. She glanced away at once, but his eyes remained fixed upon her for some moments. The picture was forgotten already, and his soul had come down to earth once more.

We caught sight of her once or twice before we left, and each time I noticed my friend look after her. He made no remark, however, until we got out into the open air, and were walking arm-in-arm along Princes Street.

'Did you notice that beautiful woman, in the dark dress, with the white fur?' he asked.

'Yes, I saw her,' I answered.

'Do you know her?' he asked eagerly. 'Have you any idea who she is?'

'I don't know her personally,' I replied. 'But I have no doubt I could find out all about her, for I believe she is engaged to young Archie Reeves, and he and I have a lot of mutual friends.'

'Engaged!' ejaculated Cowles.

'Why, my dear boy,' I said, laughing, 'you don't mean to say you are so susceptible that the fact that a girl to whom you never spoke in your life is engaged is enough to upset you?'

'Well, not exactly to upset me,' he answered, forcing a laugh. 'But I don't mind telling you, Armitage, that I never was so taken by any one in my life. It wasn't the mere beauty of the face—though that was perfect enough—but it was the character and the intellect upon it. I hope, if she is engaged, that it is to some man who will be worthy of her.'

'Why,' I remarked, 'you speak quite feelingly. It is a clear case of love at first sight, Jack. However, to put your perturbed spirit at rest, I'll make a point of finding out all about her whenever I meet any fellow who is likely to know.'

Barrington Cowles thanked me, and the conversation drifted off into other channels. For several days neither of us made any allusion to the subject, though my companion was perhaps a little more dreamy and distraught than usual. The incident had almost vanished from my remembrance, when one day young Brodie, who is a second cousin of mine, came up to me on the university steps with the face of a bearer of tidings.

'I say,' he began, 'you know Reeves, don't you?'

'Yes. What of him?'

'His engagement is off.'

'Off!' I cried. 'Why, I only learned the other day that it was on.'

'Oh, yes—it's all off. His brother told me so. Deucedly mean of Reeves, you know, if he has backed out of it, for she was an uncommonly nice girl.'

'I've seen her,' I said; 'but I don't know her name.'

'She is a Miss Northcott, and lives with an old aunt of hers in Abercrombie Place. Nobody knows anything about her people, or where she comes from. Anyhow, she is about the most unlucky girl in the world, poor soul!'

'Why unlucky?'

'Well, you know, this was her second engagement,' said young Brodie, who had a marvellous knack of knowing everything about everybody. 'She was engaged to Prescott—William Prescott, who died. That was a very sad affair. The wedding day was fixed, and the whole thing looked as straight as a die when the smash came.'

'What smash?' I asked, with some dim recollection of the circumstances.

'Why, Prescott's death. He came to Abercrombie Place one night, and stayed very late. No one knows exactly when he left, but about one in the morning a fellow who knew him met him walking rapidly in the direction of the Queen's Park. He bade him good night, but Prescott hurried on without heeding him, and that was the last time he was ever seen alive. Three days afterwards his body was found floating in St Margaret's Loch, under St Anthony's Chapel. No one could ever understand it, but of course the verdict brought it in as temporary insanity.'

'It was very strange,' I remarked.

'Yes, and deucedly rough on the poor girl,' said Brodie. 'Now that this other blow has come it will quite crush her. So gentle and ladylike she is too!'

'You know her personally, then!' I asked.

'Oh, yes, I know her. I have met her several times. I could easily manage that you should be introduced to her.'

'Well,' I answered, 'it's not so much for my own sake as for a friend of mine. However, I don't suppose she will go out much for some little time after this. When she does I will take advantage of your offer.'

We shook hands on this, and I thought no more of the matter for some time.

The next incident which I have to relate as bearing at all upon the question of Miss Northcott is an unpleasant one. Yet I must detail it as accurately as possible, since it may throw some light upon the sequel. One cold night, several months after the conversation with my second cousin which I have quoted above, I was walking down one of the lowest streets in the city on my way back from a case which I had been attending. It was very late, and I was picking my way among the dirty loungers who were clustering round the doors of a great gin-palace, when a man staggered out from among them, and held out his hand to me with a drunken leer. The gaslight fell full upon his face, and, to my intense astonishment, I recognised in the degraded creature before me my former acquaintance, young Archibald Reeves, who had once been famous as one of the most dressy and particular men in the whole college. I was so utterly surprised that for a moment I almost doubted the evidence of my own senses; but there was no mistaking those features, which, though bloated with drink, still retained something of their former comeliness. I was determined to rescue him, for one night at least, from the company into which he had fallen.

'Holloa, Reeves!' I said. 'Come along with me. I'm going in your direction.'

He muttered some incoherent apology for his condition, and took my arm. As I supported him towards his lodgings I could see that he was not only suffering from the effects of a recent debauch, but that a long course of intemperance had affected his nerves and his brain. His hand when I touched it was dry and feverish, and he started from every shadow which fell upon the pavement. He rambled in his speech, too, in a manner which suggested the delirium of disease rather than the talk of a drunkard.

When I got him to his lodgings I partially undressed him and laid him upon his bed. His pulse at this time was very high, and he was evidently extremely feverish. He seemed to have sunk into a doze; and I was about to steal out of the room to warn his landlady of his condition, when he started up and caught me by the sleeve of my coat.

'Don't go!' he cried. 'I feel better when you are here. I am safe from her then.'

'From her!' I said. 'From whom?'

'Her! her!' he answered peevishly. 'Ah! you don't know her. She is the devil! Beautiful—beautiful; but the devil!'

'You are feverish and excited,' I said. 'Try and get a little sleep. You will wake better.'

'Sleep!' he groaned. 'How am I to sleep when I see her sitting down yonder at the foot of the bed with her great eyes watching and watching hour after hour? I tell you it saps all the strength and manhood out of me. That's what makes me drink. God help me—I'm half drunk now!'

'You are very ill,' I said, putting some vinegar to his temples; 'and you are delirious. You don't know what you say.'

'Yes, I do,' he interrupted sharply, looking up at me. 'I know very well what I say. I brought it upon myself. It is my own choice. But I couldn't—no, by heaven, I couldn't—accept the alternative. I couldn't keep my faith to her. It was more than man could do.'

I sat by the side of the bed, holding one of his burning hands in mine, and wondering over his strange words. He lay still for some time, and then, raising his eyes to me, said in a most plaintive voice—

'Why did she not give me warning sooner? Why did she wait until I had learned to love her so?'

He repeated this question several times, rolling his feverish head from side to side, and then he dropped into a troubled sleep. I crept out of the room, and, having seen that he would be properly cared for, left the house. His words, however, rang in my ears for days afterwards, and assumed a deeper significance when taken with what was to come.

My friend, Barrington Cowles, had been away for his summer holidays, and I had heard nothing of him for several months. When the winter session came on, however, I received a telegram from him, asking me to secure the old rooms in Northumberland Street for him, and telling me the train by which he would arrive. I went down to meet him, and was delighted to find him looking wonderfully hearty and well.

'By the way,' he said suddenly, that night, as we sat in our chairs by the fire, talking over the events of the holidays, 'you have never congratulated me yet!'

'On what, my boy?' I asked.

'What! Do you mean to say you have not heard of my engagement?'

'Engagement! No!' I answered. 'However, I am delighted to hear it, and congratulate you with all my heart.'

'I wonder it didn't come to your ears,' he said. 'It was the queerest thing. You remember that girl whom we both admired so much at the Academy?'

'What!' I cried, with a vague feeling of apprehension at my heart. 'You don't mean to say that you are engaged to her?'

'I thought you would be surprised,' he answered. 'When I was staying with an old aunt of mine in Peterhead, in Aberdeenshire, the Northcotts happened to come there on a visit, and as we had mutual friends we soon met. I found out that it was a false alarm about her being engaged, and then—well, you know what it is when you are thrown into the society of such a girl in a place like Peterhead. Not, mind you,' he added, 'that I consider I did a foolish or hasty thing. I have never regretted it for a moment. The more I know Kate the more I admire her and love her. However, you must be introduced to her, and then you will form your own opinion.'

I expressed my pleasure at the prospect, and endeavoured to speak as lightly as I could to Cowles upon the subject, but I felt depressed and anxious at heart. The words of Reeves and the unhappy fate of young Prescott recurred to my recollection, and though I could assign no tangible reason for it, a vague, dim fear and distrust of the woman took possession of me. It may be that this was foolish prejudice and superstition upon my part, and that I involuntarily contorted her future doings and sayings to fit into some half-formed wild theory of my own. This has been suggested to me by others as an explanation of my narrative. They are welcome to their opinion if they can reconcile it with the facts which I have to tell.

I went round with my friend a few days afterwards to call upon Miss Northcott. I remember that, as we went down Abercrombie Place, our attention was attracted by the shrill yelping of a dog—which noise proved eventually to come from the house to which we were bound. We were shown upstairs, where I was introduced to old Mrs Merton, Miss Northcott's aunt, and to the young lady herself. She looked as beautiful as ever, and I could not wonder at my friend's infatuation. Her face was a little more flushed than usual, and she held in her hand a heavy dog-whip, with which she had been chastising a small Scotch terrier, whose cries we had heard in the street. The poor brute was cringing up against the wall, whining piteously, and evidently completely cowed.

'So Kate,' said my friend, after we had taken our seats, 'you have been falling out with Carlo again.'

'Only a very little quarrel this time,' she said, smiling charmingly. 'He is a dear, good old fellow, but he needs correction now and then.' Then, turning to me, 'We all do that, Mr Armitage, don't we? What a capital thing if, instead of receiving a collective punishment at the end of our lives, we were to have one at once, as the dogs do, when we did anything wicked. It would make us more careful, wouldn't it?'

I acknowledged that it would.

'Supposing that every time a man misbehaved himself a gigantic hand were to seize him, and he were lashed with a whip until he fainted'—she clenched her white fingers as she spoke, and cut out viciously with the dog-whip—'it would do more to keep him good than any number of high-minded theories of morality.'

'Why, Kate,' said my friend, 'you are quite savage today.'

'No, Jack,' she laughed. 'I'm only propounding a theory for Mr Armitage's consideration.'

The two began to chat together about some Aberdeenshire reminiscence, and I had time to observe Mrs Merton, who had remained silent during our short conversation. She was a very strange-looking old lady. What attracted attention most in her appearance was the utter want of colour which she exhibited. Her hair was snow-white, and her face extremely pale. Her lips were bloodless, and even her eyes were of such a light tinge of blue that they hardly relieved the general pallor. Her dress was a grey silk, which harmonised with her general appearance.

She had a peculiar expression of countenance, which I was unable at the moment to refer to its proper cause.

She was working at some old-fashioned piece of ornamental needlework, and as she moved her arms her dress gave forth a dry, melancholy rustling, like the sound of leaves in the autumn. There was something mournful and depressing in the sight of her. I moved my chair a little nearer, and asked her how she liked Edinburgh, and whether she had been there long.

When I spoke to her she started and looked up at me with a scared look on her face. Then I saw in a moment what the expression was which I had observed there. It was one of fear—intense and overpowering fear. It was so marked that I could have staked my life on the woman before me having at some period of her life been subjected to some terrible experience or dreadful misfortune.

'Oh, yes, I like it,' she said, in a soft, timid voice; 'and we have been here long—that is, not very long. We move about a great deal.' She spoke with hesitation, as if afraid of committing herself.

'You are a native of Scotland, I presume?' I said.

'No—that is, not entirely. We are not natives of any place. We are cosmopolitan, you know.' She glanced round in the direction of Miss Northcott as she spoke, but the two were still chatting together near the window. Then she suddenly bent forward to me, with a look of intense earnestness upon her face, and said—

'Don't talk to me any more, please. She does not like it, and I shall suffer for it afterwards. Please, don't do it.'

I was about to ask her the reason for this strange request, but when she saw I was going to address her, she rose and walked slowly out of the room. As she did so I perceived that the lovers had ceased to talk, and that Miss Northcott was looking at me with her keen, grey eyes.

'You must excuse my aunt, Mr Armitage,' she said; 'she is odd, and easily fatigued. Come over and look at my album.'

We spent some time examining the portraits. Miss Northcott's father and mother were apparently ordinary mortals enough, and I could not detect in either of them any traces of the character which showed itself in their daughter's face. There was one old daguerreotype, however, which arrested my attention. It represented a man of about the age of forty, and strikingly handsome. He was clean shaven, and extraordinary power was expressed upon his prominent lower jaw and firm, straight mouth. His eyes were somewhat deeply set in his head, however, and there was a snake-like flattening at the upper part of his forehead, which detracted from his appearance. I almost involuntarily, when I saw the head, pointed to it, and exclaimed—

'There is your prototype in your family, Miss Northcott.'

'Do you think so?' she said. 'I am afraid you are paying me a very bad compliment. Uncle Anthony was always considered the black sheep of the family.'

'Indeed,' I answered; 'my remark was an unfortunate one, then.'

'Oh, don't mind that,' she said; 'I always thought myself that he was worth all of them put together. He was an officer in the Forty-first Regiment, and he was killed in action during the Persian War—so he died nobly, at any rate.'

'That's the sort of death I should like to die,' said Cowles, his dark eyes flashing, as they would when he was excited; 'I often wish I had taken to my father's profession instead of this vile pill-compounding drudgery.'

'Come, Jack, you are not going to die any sort of death yet,' she said, tenderly taking his hand in hers.

I could not understand the woman. There was such an extraordinary mixture of masculine decision and womanly tenderness about her, with the consciousness of something all her own in the background, that she fairly puzzled me. I hardly knew, therefore, how to answer Cowles when, as we walked down the street together, he asked the comprehensive question—

'Well, what do you think of her?'

'I think she is wonderfully beautiful,' I answered guardedly.

'That, of course,' he replied irritably. 'You knew that before you came!'

'I think she is very clever too,' I remarked.

Barrington Cowles walked on for some time, and then he suddenly turned on me with the strange question—

'Do you think she is cruel? Do you think she is the sort of girl who would take a pleasure in inflicting pain?'

'Well, really,' I answered, 'I have hardly had time to form an opinion.'

We then walked on for some time in silence.

'She is an old fool,' at length muttered Cowles. 'She is mad.'

'Who is?' I asked.

'Why, that old woman—that aunt of Kate's—Mrs Merton, or whatever her name is.'

Then I knew that my poor colourless friend had been speaking to Cowles, but he never said anything more as to the nature of her communication.

My companion went to bed early that night, and I sat up a long time by the fire, thinking over all that I had seen and heard. I felt that there was some mystery about the girl—some dark fatality so strange as to defy conjecture. I thought of Prescott's interview with her before their marriage, and the fatal termination of it. I coupled it with poor drunken Reeves' plaintive cry, 'Why did she not tell me sooner?' and with the other words he had spoken. Then my mind ran over Mrs Merton's warning to me, Cowles' reference to her, and even the episode of the whip and the cringing dog.

The whole effect of my recollections was unpleasant to a degree, and yet there was no tangible charge which I could bring against the woman. It would be worse than useless to attempt to warn my friend until I had definitely made up my mind what I was to warn him against. He would treat any charge against her with scorn. What could I do? How could I get at some tangible conclusion as to her character and antecedents? No one in Edinburgh knew them except as recent acquaintances. She was an orphan, and as far as I knew she had never disclosed where her former home had been. Suddenly an idea struck me. Among my father's friends there was a Colonel Joyce, who had served a long time in India upon the staff, and who would be likely to know most of the officers who had been out there since the Mutiny. I sat down at once, and, having trimmed the lamp, proceeded to write a letter to the Colonel. I told him that I was very curious to gain some particulars about a certain Captain Northcott, who had served in the Forty-first Foot, and who had fallen in the Persian War. I described the man as well as I could from my recollection of the daguerreotype, and then, having directed the letter, posted it that very night, after which, feeling that I had done all that could be done, I retired to bed, with a mind too anxious to allow me to sleep.

II

I got an answer from Leicester, where the Colonel resided, within two days. I have it before me as I write, and copy it verbatim.

> 'Dear Bob,' it said, 'I remember the man well. I was with him at Calcutta, and afterwards at Hyderabad. He was a curious, solitary sort of mortal; but a gallant soldier enough, for he distinguished himself at

Sobraon, and was wounded, if I remember right. He was not popular in his corps—they said he was a pitiless, cold-blooded fellow, with no geniality in him. There was a rumour, too, that he was a devil-worshipper, or something of that sort, and also that he had the evil eye, which, of course, was all nonsense. He had some strange theories, I remember, about the power of the human will and the effects of mind upon matter.

'How are you getting on with your medical studies? Never forget, my boy, that your father's son has every claim upon me, and that if I can serve you in any way I am always at your command.—Ever affectionately yours,

EDWARD JOYCE.

'*P.S.*—By the way, Northcott did not fall in action. He was killed after peace was declared in a crazy attempt to get some of the eternal fire from the sun-worshippers' temple. There was considerable mystery about his death.'

I read this epistle over several times—at first with a feeling of satisfaction, and then with one of disappointment. I had come on some curious information, and yet hardly what I wanted. He was an eccentric man, a devil-worshipper, and rumoured to have the power of the evil eye. I could believe the young lady's eyes, when endowed with that cold, grey shimmer which I had noticed in them once or twice, to be capable of any evil which human eye ever wrought; but still the superstition was an effete one. Was there not more meaning in that sentence which followed—'He had theories of the power of the human will and of the effect of mind upon matter'? I remember having once read a quaint treatise, which I had imagined to be mere charlatanism at the time, of the power of certain human minds, and of effects produced by them at a distance. Was Miss Northcott endowed with some exceptional power of the sort? The idea grew upon me, and very shortly I had evidence which convinced me of the truth of the supposition.

It happened that at the very time when my mind was dwelling upon this subject, I saw a notice in the paper that our town was to be visited by Dr Messinger, the well-known medium and mesmerist. Messinger was a man whose performance, such as it was, had been again and again pronounced to be genuine by competent judges. He was far above trickery, and had the reputation of being the soundest living authority upon the strange pseudo-sciences of animal magnetism and electro-biology. Determined, therefore, to see what the human will could do, even against all the disadvantages of glaring footlights and a public platform, I took a ticket for the first night of the performance, and went with several student friends.

We had secured one of the side boxes, and did not arrive until after the performance had begun. I had hardly taken my seat before I recognised Barrington Cowles, with his *fiancée* and old Mrs Merton, sitting in the third or fourth row of the stalls. They caught sight of me at almost the same moment, and we bowed to each other. The first portion of the lecture was somewhat commonplace, the lecturer giving tricks of pure legerdemain, with one or two manifestations of mesmerism, performed upon a subject whom he had brought with him. He gave us an exhibition of clairvoyance too, throwing his subject into a trance, and then demanding particulars as to the movements of absent friends, and the whereabouts of hidden objects, all of which appeared to be answered satisfactorily. I had seen all this before, however. What I wanted to see now was the effect of the lecturer's will when exerted upon some independent member of the audience.

He came round to that as the concluding exhibition in his performance. 'I have shown you,' he said, 'that a mesmerised subject is entirely dominated by the will of the mesmeriser. He loses all power of volition, and his very thoughts are such as are suggested to him by the master-mind. The same end may be attained without any preliminary process. A strong will can, simply by virtue of its strength, take possession of a weaker one, even at a distance, and can regulate the impulses and the actions of the owner of it. If there was one man in the world who had a very much more highly-developed will than any of the rest of the human family, there is no reason why he should not be able to rule over them all, and to reduce his fellow-creatures to the condition of automatons. Happily there is such a dead level of mental power, or rather of mental weakness, among us that such a catastrophe is not likely to occur; but still within our small compass there are variations which produce surprising effects. I shall now single out one of the audience, and endeavour 'by the mere power of will' to compel him to come upon the platform, and do and say what I wish. Let me assure you that there is no collusion, and that the subject whom I may select is at perfect liberty to resent to the uttermost any impulse which I may communicate to him.'

With these words the lecturer came to the front of the platform, and glanced over the first few rows of the stalls. No doubt Cowles' dark skin and bright eyes marked him out as a man of a highly nervous temperament, for the mesmerist picked him out in a moment, and fixed his eyes upon him. I saw my friend give a start of surprise, and then settle down in his chair, as if to express his determination not to yield to the influence of the operator. Messinger was not a man whose head denoted any great brain-power, but his gaze was singularly intense and penetrating. Under the influence of it Cowles made one or two spasmodic motions of his hands, as if to grasp the sides of his seat, and then half rose, but only to sink down again, though with an evident effort. I was watching the scene with intense interest, when I happened to catch a glimpse of Miss Northcott's face. She was sitting with her eyes fixed intently upon the mesmerist, and with such an expression of concentrated power upon her features as I have never seen on any other human countenance. Her jaw was firmly set, her lips compressed, and her face as hard as if it were a beautiful sculpture cut out of the whitest marble. Her eyebrows were drawn down, however, and from beneath them her grey eyes seemed to sparkle and gleam with a cold light.

I looked at Cowles again, expecting every moment to see him rise and obey the mesmerist's wishes, when there came from the platform a short, gasping cry as of a man utterly worn out and prostrated by a prolonged struggle. Messinger was leaning against the table, his hand to his forehead, and the perspiration pouring down his face. 'I won't go on,' he cried, addressing the audience. 'There is a stronger will than mine acting against me. You must excuse me for tonight.' The man was evidently ill, and utterly unable to proceed, so the curtain was lowered, and the audience dispersed, with many comments upon the lecturer's sudden indisposition.

I waited outside the hall until my friend and the ladies came out. Cowles was laughing over his recent experience.

'He didn't succeed with me, Bob,' he cried triumphantly, as he shook my hand. 'I think he caught a Tartar that time.'

'Yes,' said Miss Northcott, 'I think that Jack ought to be very proud of his strength of mind; don't you, Mr Armitage?'

'It took me all my time, though,' my friend said seriously. 'You can't conceive what a strange feeling I had once or twice. All the strength seemed to have gone out of me—especially just before he collapsed himself.'

I walked round with Cowles in order to see the ladies home. He walked in front with Mrs Merton, and I found myself behind with the young lady. For a minute or so I walked beside her without making any remark, and then I suddenly blurted out, in a manner which must have seemed somewhat brusque to her—

'You did that, Miss Northcott.'

'Did what?' she asked sharply.

'Why, mesmerised the mesmeriser—I suppose that is the best way of describing the transaction.'

'What a strange idea!' she said, laughing. 'You give me credit for a strong will then?'

'Yes,' I said. 'For a dangerously strong one.'

'Why dangerous?' she asked, in a tone of surprise.

'I think,' I answered, 'that any will which can exercise such power is dangerous—for there is always a chance of its being turned to bad uses.'

'You would make me out a very dreadful individual, Mr Armitage,' she said; and then looking up suddenly in my face—'You have never liked me. You are suspicious of me and distrust me, though I have never given you cause.'

The accusation was so sudden and so true that I was unable to find any reply to it. She paused for a moment, and then said in a voice which was hard and cold—

'Don't let your prejudice lead you to interfere with me, however, or say anything to your friend, Mr Cowles, which might lead to a difference between us. You would find that to be very bad policy.'

There was something in the way she spoke which gave an indescribable air of a threat to these few words.

'I have no power,' I said, 'to interfere with your plans for the future. I cannot help, however, from what I have seen and heard, having fears for my friend.'

'Fears!' she repeated scornfully. 'Pray what have you seen and heard. Something from Mr Reeves, perhaps—I believe he is another of your friends?'

'He never mentioned your name to me,' I answered, truthfully enough. 'You will be sorry to hear that he is dying.' As I said it we passed by a lighted window, and I glanced down to see what effect my words had upon her. She was laughing—there was no doubt of it; she was laughing quietly to herself. I could see merriment in every feature of her face. I feared and mistrusted the woman from that moment more than ever.

We said little more that night. When we parted she gave me a quick, warning glance, as if to remind me of what she had said about the danger of interference. Her cautions would have made little difference to me could I have seen my way to benefiting Barrington Cowles by anything which I might say. But what could I say? I might say that her former suitors had been unfortunate. I might say that I believed her to be a cruel-hearted woman. I might say that I considered her to possess wonderful, and almost preternatural powers. What impression would any of these accusations make upon an ardent lover—a man with my friend's enthusiastic temperament? I felt that it would be useless to advance them, so I was silent.

And now I come to the beginning of the end. Hitherto much has been surmise and inference and hearsay. It is my painful task to relate now, as dispassionately and as accurately as I can, what actually occurred under my own notice, and to reduce to writing the events which preceded the death of my friend.

Towards the end of the winter Cowles remarked to me that he intended to marry Miss Northcott as soon as possible—probably some time in the spring. He was, as I have already remarked, fairly well off, and the young lady had some money of her own, so that there was no pecuniary reason for a long engagement. 'We are going to take a little house out at Corstorphine,' he said, 'and we hope to see your face at our table, Bob, as often as you can possibly come.' I thanked him, and tried to shake off my apprehensions, and persuade myself that all would yet be well.

It was about three weeks before the time fixed for the marriage, that Cowles remarked to me one evening that he feared he would be late that night. 'I have had a note from Kate,' he said, 'asking me to call about eleven o'clock tonight, which seems rather a late hour, but perhaps she wants to talk over something quietly after old Mrs Merton retires.'

It was not until after my friend's departure that I suddenly recollected the mysterious interview which I had been told of as preceding the suicide of young Prescott. Then I thought of the ravings of poor Reeves, rendered more tragic by the fact that I had heard that very day of his death. What was the meaning of it all? Had this woman some baleful secret to disclose which must be known before her marriage? Was it some reason which forbade her to marry? Or was it some reason which forbade others to marry her? I felt so uneasy that I would have followed Cowles, even at the risk of offending him, and endeavoured to dissuade him from keeping his appointment, but a glance at the clock showed me that I was too late.

I was determined to wait up for his return, so I piled some coals upon the fire and took down a novel from the shelf. My thoughts proved more interesting than the book, however, and I threw it on one side. An indefinable feeling of anxiety and depression weighed upon me. Twelve o'clock came, and then half-past, without any sign of my friend. It was nearly one when I heard a step in the street outside, and then a knocking at the door. I was surprised, as I knew that my friend always carried a key—however, I hurried down and undid the latch. As the door flew open I knew in a moment that my worst apprehensions had been fulfilled. Barrington Cowles was leaning against the railings outside with his face sunk upon his breast, and his whole attitude expressive of the most intense despondency. As he passed in he gave a stagger, and would have fallen had I not thrown my left arm around him. Supporting him with this, and holding the lamp in my other hand, I led him slowly upstairs into our sitting-room. He sank down upon the sofa without a word. Now that I could get a good view of him, I was horrified to see the change which had come over him. His face was deadly pale, and his very lips were bloodless. His cheeks and forehead were clammy, his eyes glazed, and his whole expression altered. He looked like a man who had gone through some terrible ordeal, and was thoroughly unnerved.

'My dear fellow, what is the matter?' I asked, breaking the silence. 'Nothing amiss, I trust? Are you unwell?'

'Brandy!' he gasped. 'Give me some brandy!'

I took out the decanter, and was about to help him, when he snatched it from me with a trembling hand, and poured out nearly half a tumbler of the spirit. He was usually a most abstemious man, but he took this off at a gulp without adding any water to it. It seemed to do him good, for the colour began to come back to his face, and he leaned upon his elbow.

'My engagement is off, Bob,' he said, trying to speak calmly, but with a tremor in his voice which he could not conceal. 'It is all over.'

'Cheer up!' I answered, trying to encourage him. 'Don't get down on your luck. How was it? What was it all about?'

'About?' he groaned, covering his face with his hands. 'If I did tell you, Bob, you would not believe it. It is too dreadful—too horrible—unutterably awful and incredible! O Kate, Kate!' and he rocked himself to and fro in his grief; 'I pictured you an angel and I find you a—'

'A what?' I asked, for he had paused.

He looked at me with a vacant stare, and then suddenly burst out, waving his arms: 'A fiend!' he cried. 'A ghoul from the pit! A vampire soul behind a lovely face! Now, God forgive me!' he went on in a lower tone, turning his face to the wall; 'I have said more than I should. I have loved her too much to speak of her as she is. I love her too much now.'

He lay still for some time, and I had hoped that the brandy had had the effect of sending him to sleep, when he suddenly turned his face towards me.

'Did you ever read of wehr-wolves?' he asked.

I answered that I had.

'There is a story,' he said thoughtfully, 'in one of Marryat's books, about a beautiful woman who took the form of a wolf at night and devoured her own children. I wonder what put that idea into Marryat's head?'

He pondered for some minutes, and then he cried out for some more brandy. There was a small bottle of laudanum upon the table, and I managed, by insisting upon helping him myself, to mix about half a drachm with the spirits. He drank it off, and sank his head once more upon the pillow. 'Anything better than that,' he groaned. 'Death is better than that. Crime and cruelty; cruelty and crime. Anything is better than that,' and so on, with the monotonous refrain, until at last the words became indistinct, his eyelids closed over his weary eyes, and he sank into a profound slumber. I carried him into his bedroom without arousing him; and making a couch for myself out of the chairs, I remained by his side all night.

In the morning Barrington Cowles was in a high fever. For weeks he lingered between life and death. The highest medical skill of Edinburgh was called in, and his vigorous constitution slowly got the better of his disease. I nursed him during this anxious time; but through all his wild delirium and ravings he never let a word escape him which explained the mystery connected with Miss Northcott. Sometimes he spoke of her in the tenderest words and most loving voice. At others he screamed out that she was a fiend, and stretched out his arms, as if to keep her off. Several times he cried that he would not sell his soul for a beautiful face, and then he would moan in a most piteous voice, 'But I love her—I love her for all that; I shall never cease to love her.'

When he came to himself he was an altered man. His severe illness had emaciated him greatly, but his dark eyes had lost none of their brightness. They shone out with startling brilliancy from under his dark, overhanging brows. His manner was eccentric and variable—sometimes irritable, sometimes recklessly mirthful, but never natural. He would glance about him in a strange, suspicious manner, like one who feared something, and yet hardly knew what it was he dreaded. He never mentioned Miss Northcott's name—never until that fatal evening of which I have now to speak.

In an endeavour to break the current of his thoughts by frequent change of scene, I travelled with him through the highlands of Scotland, and afterwards down the east coast. In one of these peregrinations of ours we visited the Isle of May, an island near the mouth of the Firth of Forth, which, except in the tourist season, is singularly barren and desolate. Beyond the keeper of the lighthouse there are only one or two families of poor fisher-folk, who sustain a precarious existence by their nets, and by the capture of cormorants and solan geese. This grim spot seemed to have such a fascination for Cowles that we engaged a room in one of the fishermen's huts, with the intention of passing a week or two there. I found it very dull, but the loneliness appeared to be a relief to my friend's mind. He lost the look of apprehension which had become habitual to him, and became something like his old self. He would wander round the island all day, looking down from the summit of the great cliffs which gird it round, and watching the long green waves as they came booming in and burst in a shower of spray over the rocks beneath.

One night—I think it was our third or fourth on the island—Barrington Cowles and I went outside the cottage before retiring to rest, to enjoy a little fresh air, for our room was small, and the rough lamp caused an unpleasant odour. How well I remember every little circumstance in connection with that night! It promised to be tempestuous, for the clouds were piling up in the north-west, and the dark wrack was drifting across the face of the moon, throwing alternate belts of light and shade upon the rugged surface of the island and the restless sea beyond.

We were standing talking close by the door of the cottage, and I was thinking to myself that my friend was more cheerful than he had been since his illness, when he gave a sudden, sharp cry, and looking round at him I saw, by the light of the moon, an expression of unutterable horror come over his features. His eyes became fixed and staring, as if riveted upon some approaching object, and he extended his long thin forefinger, which quivered as he pointed.

'Look there!' he cried. 'It is she! It is she! You see her there coming down the side of the brae.' He gripped me convulsively by the wrist as he spoke. 'There she is, coming towards us!'

'Who?' I cried, straining my eyes into the darkness.

'She—Kate—Kate Northcott!' he screamed. 'She has come for me. Hold me fast, old friend. Don't let me go!'

'Hold up, old man,' I said, clapping him on the shoulder. 'Pull yourself together; you are dreaming; there is nothing to fear.'

'She is gone!' he cried, with a gasp of relief. 'No, by heaven! there she is again, and nearer—coming nearer. She told me she would come for me, and she keeps her word.'

'Come into the house,' I said. His hand, as I grasped it, was as cold as ice.

'Ah, I knew it!' he shouted. 'There she is, waving her arms. She is beckoning to me. It is the signal. I must go. I am coming, Kate; I am coming!'

I threw my arms around him, but he burst from me with superhuman strength, and dashed into the darkness of the night. I followed him, calling to him to stop, but he ran the more swiftly. When the moon shone out between the clouds I could catch a glimpse of his dark figure, running rapidly in a straight line, as if to reach some definite goal. It may have been imagination, but it seemed to me that in the flickering light I could distinguish a vague something in front of him—a shimmering form which eluded his grasp and led him onwards. I saw his outlines stand out hard against the sky behind him as he surmounted the brow of a little hill, then he disappeared, and that was the last ever seen by mortal eye of Barrington Cowles.

The fishermen and I walked round the island all that night with lanterns, and examined every nook and corner without seeing a trace of my poor lost friend. The direction in which he had been running terminated in a rugged line of jagged cliffs overhanging the sea. At one place here the edge was somewhat crumbled, and there appeared marks upon the turf which might have been left by human feet. We lay upon our faces at this spot, and peered with our lanterns over the edge, looking down on the boiling surge two hundred feet below. As we lay there, suddenly, above the beating of the waves and the howling of the wind, there rose a strange wild screech from the abyss below. The fishermen—a naturally superstitious race—averred that it was the sound of a woman's laughter, and I could hardly persuade them to continue the search. For my own part I think it may have been the cry of some sea-fowl startled from its nest by the flash of the lantern. However that may be, I never wish to hear such a sound again.

And now I have come to the end of the painful duty which I have undertaken. I have told as plainly and as accurately as I could the story of the death of John Barrington Cowles, and the train of events which preceded it. I am aware that to others the sad episode seemed commonplace enough. Here is the prosaic account which appeared in the *Scotsman* a couple of days afterwards:—

> '*Sad Occurrence on the Isle of May.*—The Isle of May has been the scene of a sad disaster. Mr John Barrington Cowles, a gentleman well known in University circles as a most distinguished student, and the present holder of the Neil Arnott prize for physics, has been recruiting his health in this quiet retreat. The night before last he suddenly left his friend, Mr Robert Armitage, and he has not since been heard of. It is almost certain that he has met his death by falling over the cliffs which surround the island. Mr Cowles' health has been failing for some time, partly from over-study and partly from worry connected with family affairs. By his death the University loses one of her most promising alumni.'

I have nothing more to add to my statement. I have unburdened my mind of all that I know. I can well conceive that many, after weighing all that I have said, will see no ground for an accusation against Miss Northcott. They will say that, because a man of a naturally excitable disposition says and does wild things, and even eventually commits self-murder after a sudden and heavy disappointment, there is no reason why vague charges should be advanced against a young lady. To this, I answer that they are welcome to their opinion. For my own part, I ascribe the death of William Prescott, of Archibald Reeves, and of

John Barrington Cowles to this woman with as much confidence as if I had seen her drive a dagger into their hearts.

You ask me, no doubt, what my own theory is which will explain all these strange facts. I have none, or, at best, a dim and vague one. That Miss Northcott possessed extraordinary powers over the minds, and through the minds over the bodies, of others, I am convinced, as well as that her instincts were to use this power for base and cruel purposes. That some even more fiendish and terrible phase of character lay behind this—some horrible trait which it was necessary for her to reveal before marriage—is to be inferred from the experience of her three lovers, while the dreadful nature of the mystery thus revealed can only be surmised from the fact that the very mention of it drove from her those who had loved her so passionately. Their subsequent fate was, in my opinion, the result of her vindictive remembrance of their desertion of her, and that they were forewarned of it at the time was shown by the words of both Reeves and Cowles. Above this, I can say nothing. I lay the facts soberly before the public as they came under my notice. I have never seen Miss Northcott since, nor do I wish to do so. If by the words I have written I can save any one human being from the snare of those bright eyes and that beautiful face, then I can lay down my pen with the assurance that my poor friend has not died altogether in vain.

DE PROFUNDIS

So long as the oceans are the ligaments which bind together the great, broadcast British Empire, so long will there be a dash of romance in our minds. For the soul is swayed by the waters, as the waters are by the moon, and when the great highways of an empire are along such roads as these, so full of strange sights and sounds, with danger ever running like a hedge on either side of the course, it is a dull mind indeed which does not bear away with it some trace of such a passage. And now, Britain lies far beyond herself, for the three-mile limit of every seaboard is her frontier, which has been won by hammer and loom and pick rather than by arts of war. For it is written in history that neither king nor army can bar the path to the man who, having twopence in his strong box, and knowing well where he can turn it to threepence, sets his mind to that one end. And as the frontier has broadened, the mind of Britain has broadened, too, spreading out until all men can see that the ways of the island are continental, even as those of the Continent are insular.

But for this a price must be paid, and the price is a grievous one. As the beast of old must have one young, human life as a tribute every year, so to our Empire we throw from day to day the pick and flower of our youth. The engine is world-wide and strong, but the only fuel that will drive it is the lives of British men. Thus it is that in the grey, old cathedrals as we look round upon the brasses on the walls, we see strange names, such names as they who reared those walls had never heard, for it is in Peshawur, and Umballah, and Korti, and Fort Pearson that the youngsters die, leaving only a precedent and a brass behind them. But if every man had his obelisk, even where he lay, then no frontier line need be drawn, for a cordon of British graves would ever show how high the Anglo-Celtic tide had lapped.

This, then, as well as the waters which join us to the world, has done something to tinge us with romance. For when so many have their loved ones over the seas, walking amid hillmen's bullets, or swamp malaria, where death is sudden and distance great, then mind communes with mind, and strange stories arise of dream, presentiment, or vision, where the mother sees her dying son, and is past the first bitterness of her grief ere the message comes which should have broken the news. The learned have of late looked into the matter and have even labelled it with a name; but what can we know more of it save that a poor, stricken soul, when hard-pressed and driven, can shoot across the earth some ten-thousand-mile-distant picture of its trouble to the mind which is most akin to it. Far be it from me to say that there lies no such power within us, for of all things which the brain will grasp the last will be itself; but yet it is well to be very cautious over such matters, for once at least I have known that which was within the laws of Nature seem to be far upon the further side of them.

John Vansittart was the younger partner of the firm of Hudson and Vansittart, coffee exporters of the Island of Ceylon, three-quarters Dutchman by descent, but wholly English in his sympathies. For years I had been his agent in London, and when in '72 he came over to England for a three months' holiday, he turned to me for the introductions which would enable him to see something of town and country life. Armed with seven letters he left my offices, and for many weeks scrappy notes from different parts of the country let me know that he had found favour in the eyes of my friends. Then came word of his engagement to Emily Lawson, of a cadet branch of the Hereford Lawsons, and at the very tail of the first flying rumour the news of his absolute marriage, for the wooing of a wanderer must be short, and the days were already crowding on towards the date when he must be upon his homeward journey. They were to return together to Colombo in one of the firm's own thousand-ton, barque-rigged sailing ships, and this was to be their princely honeymoon, at once a necessity and a delight.

Those were the royal days of coffee-planting in Ceylon, before a single season and a rotting fungus drove a whole community through years of despair to one of the greatest commercial victories which pluck and ingenuity ever won. Not often is it that men have the heart when their one great industry is withered to rear up, in a few years, another as rich to take its place, and the tea-fields of Ceylon are as true a monument to courage as is the lion at Waterloo. But in '72 there was no cloud yet above the skyline, and the hopes of the planters were as high and as bright as the hill-sides on which they reared their crops. Vansittart came down to London with his young and beautiful wife. I was introduced, dined with them, and it was finally arranged that I, since business called me also to Ceylon, should be a fellow-passenger with them on the *Eastern Star*, which was timed to sail on the following Monday.

It was on the Sunday evening that I saw him again. He was shown up into my rooms about nine o'clock at night, with the air of a man who is bothered and out of sorts. His hand, as I shook it, was hot and dry.

'I wish, Atkinson,' said he, 'that you could give me a little lime-juice and water. I have a beastly thirst upon me, and the more I take the more I seem to want.'

I rang and ordered a carafe and glasses. 'You are flushed,' said I. 'You don't look the thing.'

'No, I'm clean off colour. Got a touch of rheumatism in my back, and don't seem to taste my food. It is this vile London that is choking me. I'm not used to breathing air which has been used up by four million lungs all sucking away on every side of you.' He flapped his crooked hands before his face, like a man who really struggles for his breath.

'A touch of the sea will soon set you right.'

'Yes, I'm of one mind with you there. That's the thing for me. I want no other doctor. If I don't get to sea tomorrow I'll have an illness. There are no two ways about it.' He drank off a tumbler of lime-juice, and clapped his two hands with his knuckles doubled up into the small of his back.

'That seems to ease me,' said he, looking at me with a filmy eye. 'Now I want your help, Atkinson, for I am rather awkwardly placed.'

'As how?'

'This way. My wife's mother got ill and wired for her. I couldn't go—you know best yourself how tied I have been—so she had to go alone. Now I've had another wire to say that she can't come tomorrow, but that she will pick up the ship at Falmouth on Wednesday. We put in there, you know, though I count it hard, Atkinson, that a man should be asked to believe in a mystery, and cursed if he can't do it. Cursed, mind you, no less.' He leaned forward and began to draw a catchy breath like a man who is poised on the very edge of a sob.

Then first it came into my mind that I had heard much of the hard-drinking life of the island, and that from brandy came these wild words and fevered hands. The flushed cheek and the glazing eye were those of one whose drink is strong upon him. Sad it was to see so noble a young man in the grip of that most bestial of all the devils.

'You should lie down,' I said, with some severity.

He screwed up his eyes like a man who is striving to wake himself, and looked up with an air of surprise.

'So I shall presently,' said he, quite rationally. 'I felt quite swimmy just now, but I am my own man again now. Let me see, what was I talking about? Oh ah, of course, about the wife. She joins the ship at Falmouth. Now I want to go round by water. I believe my health depends upon it. I just want a little clean, first-lung air to set me on my feet again. I ask you, like a good fellow, to go to Falmouth by rail, so that in case we should be late you may be there to look after the wife. Put up at the Royal Hotel, and I will wire her that you are there. Her sister will bring her down, so that it will be all plain sailing.'

'I'll do it with pleasure,' said I. 'In fact, I would rather go by rail, for we shall have enough and to spare of the sea before we reach Colombo. I believe, too, that you badly need a change. Now, I should go and turn in, if I were you.'

'Yes, I will. I sleep aboard tonight. You know,' he continued, as the film settled down again over his eyes, 'I've not slept well the last few nights. I've been troubled with theolololog—that is to say, theolological—hang it,' with a desperate effort, 'with the doubts of theolologicians. Wondering why the Almighty made us, you know, and why He made our heads swimmy, and fixed little pains into the small of our backs. Maybe I'll do better tonight.' He rose and steadied himself with an effort against the corner of the chair back.

'Look here, Vansittart,' said I gravely, stepping up to him, and laying my hand upon his sleeve, 'I can give you a shakedown here. You are not fit to go out. You are all over the place. You've been mixing your drinks.'

'Drinks!' He stared at me stupidly.

'You used to carry your liquor better than this.'

'I give you my word, Atkinson, that I have not had a drain for two days. It's not drink. I don't know what it is. I suppose you think this is drink.' He took up my hand in his burning grasp, and passed it over his own forehead.

'Great Lord!' said I.

His skin felt like a thin sheet of velvet beneath which lies a close-packed layer of small shot. It was smooth to the touch at any one place, but to a finger passed along it, rough as a nutmeg-grater.

'It's all right,' said he, smiling at my startled face. 'I've had the prickly heat nearly as bad.'

'But this is never prickly heat.'

'No, it's London. It's breathing bad air. But tomorrow it'll be all right. There's a surgeon aboard, so I shall be in safe hands. I must be off now.'

'Not you,' said I, pushing him back into a chair. 'This is past a joke. You don't move from here until a doctor sees you. Just stay where you are.'

I caught up my hat, and rushing round to the house of a neighbouring physician, I brought him back with me. The room was empty and Vansittart gone. I rang the bell. The servant said that the gentleman had ordered a cab the instant that I had left, and had gone off in it. He had told the cabman to drive to the docks.

'Did the gentleman seem ill?' I asked.

'Ill!' The man smiled. 'No, sir, he was singin' his 'ardest all the time.'

The information was not as reassuring as my servant seemed to think, but I reflected that he was going straight back to the *Eastern Star*, and that there was a doctor aboard of her, so that there was nothing which I could do in the matter. None the less, when I thought of his thirst, his burning hands, his heavy eye, his tripping speech, and lastly, of that leprous forehead, I carried with me to bed an unpleasant memory of my visitor and his visit.

At eleven o'clock next day I was at the docks, but the *Eastern Star* had already moved down the river, and was nearly at Gravesend. To Gravesend I went by train, but only to see her topmasts far off, with a plume of smoke from a tug in front of her. I would hear no more of my friend until I rejoined him at Falmouth. When I got back to my offices, a telegram was awaiting me from Mrs Vansittart, asking me to meet her; and next evening found us both at the Royal Hotel, Falmouth, where we were to wait for the *Eastern Star*. Ten days passed, and there came no news of her.

They were ten days which I am not likely to forget. On the very day that the *Eastern Star* had cleared from the Thames, a furious, easterly gale had sprung up, and blew on from day to day for the greater part of a week without the sign of a lull. Such a screaming, raving, long-drawn storm has never been known on the southern coast. From our hotel windows the sea view was all banked in haze, with a little rain-swept half-circle under our very eyes, churned and lashed into one tossing stretch of foam. So heavy was the wind upon the waves that little sea could rise, for the crest of each billow was torn shrieking from it, and lashed broadcast over the bay. Clouds, wind, sea, all were rushing to the west, and there, looking down at this mad jumble of elements, I waited on day after day, my sole companion a white, silent woman, with terror in her eyes, her forehead pressed ever against the window, her gaze from early morning to the fall of night fixed upon that wall of grey haze through which the loom of a vessel might come. She said nothing, but that face of hers was one long wail of fear.

On the fifth day I took counsel with an old seaman. I should have preferred to have done so alone, but she saw me speak with him, and was at our side in an instant, with parted lips and a prayer in her eyes.

'Seven days out from London,' said he, 'and five in the gale. Well, the Channel's swept clear by this wind. There's three things for it. She may have popped into port on the French side. That's like enough.'

'No, no; he knew we were here. He would have telegraphed.'

'Ah, yes, so he would. Well, then, he might have run for it, and if he did that he won't be very far from Madeira by now. That'll be it, marm, you may depend.'

'Or else? You said there was a third chance.'

'Did I, marm. No, only two, I think. I don't think I said anything of a third. Your ship's out there, depend upon it, away out in the Atlantic, and you'll hear of it time enough, for the weather is breaking. Now don't you fret, marm, and wait quiet and you'll find a real blue Cornish sky tomorrow.'

The old seaman was right in his surmise, for the next day broke calm and bright, with only a low, dwindling cloud in the west to mark the last trailing wreaths of the storm-wrack. But still there came no word from the sea, and no sign of the ship. Three more weary days had passed, the weariest that I have ever spent, when there came a seafaring man to the hotel with a letter. I gave a shout of joy. It was from the captain of the *Eastern Star*. As I read the first lines of it I whisked my hand over it, but she laid her own upon it and drew it away. 'I have seen it,' said she, in a cold, quiet voice. 'I may as well see the rest, too.'

'Dear Sir,' said the letter,

'Mr Vansittart is down with the small-pox, and we are blown so far on our course that we don't know what to do, he being off his head and unfit to tell us. By dead reckoning we are but three hundred miles from Funchal, so I take it that it is best that we should push on there, get Mr V. into hospital, and wait in the Bay until you come. There's a sailing-ship due from Falmouth to Funchal in a few days' time, as I understand.

This goes by the brig *Marian* of Falmouth, and five pounds is due to the master,

'Yours respectfully,

'JNO. HINES.'

She was a wonderful woman that, only a chit of a girl fresh from school, but as quiet and strong as a man. She said nothing—only pressed her lips together tight, and put on her bonnet.

'You are going out?' I asked.

'Yes.'

'Can I be of use?'

'No; I am going to the doctor's.'

'To the doctor's?'

'Yes. To learn how to nurse a small-pox case.'

She was busy at that all the evening, and next morning we were off with a fine ten-knot breeze in the barque *Rose of Sharon* for Madeira. For five days we made good time, and were no great way from the island; but on the sixth there fell a calm, and we lay without motion on a sea of oil, heaving slowly, but making not a foot of way.

At ten o'clock that night Emily Vansittart and I stood leaning on the starboard railing of the poop, with a full moon shining at our backs, and casting a black shadow of the barque, and of our own two heads, upon the shining water. From the shadow a broadening path of moonshine stretched away to the lonely skyline, flickering and shimmering in the gentle heave of the swell. We were talking with bent heads, chatting of the calm, of the chances of wind, of the look of the sky, when there came a sudden plop, like a rising salmon, and there, in the clear light, John Vansittart sprang out of the water and looked up at us.

I never saw anything clearer in my life than I saw that man. The moon shone full upon him, and he was but three oars' length away.

His face was more puffed than when I had seen him last, mottled here and there with dark scabs, his mouth and eyes open as one who is struck with some overpowering surprise. He had some white stuff streaming from his shoulders, and one hand was raised to his ear, the other crooked across his breast. I saw him leap from the water into the air, and in the dead calm the waves of his coming lapped up against the sides of the vessel. Then his figure sank back into the water again, and I heard a rending, crackling sound like a bundle of brushwood snapping in the fire on a frosty night. There were no signs of him when I looked again, but a swift swirl and eddy on the still sea still marked the spot where he had been. How long I stood there, tingling to my finger-tips, holding up an unconscious woman with one hand, clutching at the rail of the vessel with the other, was more than I could afterwards tell. I had been noted as a man of slow and unresponsive emotions, but this time at least I was shaken to the core. Once and twice I struck my foot upon the deck to be certain that I was indeed the master of my own senses, and that this was not some mad prank of an unruly brain. As I stood, still marvelling, the woman shivered, opened her eyes, gasped, and then standing erect with her hands upon the rail, looked out over the moonlit sea with a face which had aged ten years in a summer night.

'You saw his vision?' she murmured.

'I saw something.'

'It was he! It was John! He is dead!'

I muttered some lame words of doubt.

'Doubtless he died at this hour,' she whispered. 'In hospital at Madeira. I have read of such things. His thoughts were with me. His vision came to me. Oh, my John, my dear, dear, lost John!'

She broke out suddenly into a storm of weeping, and I led her down into her cabin, where I left her with her sorrow. That night a brisk breeze blew up from the east, and in the evening of the next day we passed the two islets of Los Desertos, and dropped anchor at sundown in the Bay of Funchal. The *Eastern Star* lay no great distance from us, with the quarantine flag flying from her main, and her Jack half-way up her peak.

'You see,' said Mrs Vansittart quickly. She was dry-eyed now, for she had known how it would be.

That night we received permission from the authorities to move on board the *Eastern Star*. The captain, Hines, was waiting upon deck with confusion and grief contending upon his bluff face as he sought for words with which to break this heavy tidings, but she took the story from his lips.

'I know that my husband is dead,' she said. 'He died yesterday night, about ten o'clock, in hospital at Madeira, did he not?'

The seaman stared aghast. 'No, marm, he died eight days ago at sea, and we had to bury him out there, for we lay in a belt of calm, and could not say when we might make the land.'

Well, those are the main facts about the death of John Vansittart, and his appearance to his wife somewhere about lat. 35 N. and long. 15 W. A clearer case of a wraith has seldom been made out, and since then it has been told as such, and put into print as such, and endorsed by a learned society as such, and so floated off with many others to support the recent theory of telepathy. For myself, I hold telepathy to be proved, but I would snatch this one case from amid the evidence, and say that I do not think that it was the wraith of John Vansittart, but John Vansittart himself whom we saw that night leaping into the moonlight out of the depths of the Atlantic. It has ever been my belief that some strange chance—one of those chances which seem so improbable and yet so constantly occur—had becalmed us over the very spot where the man had been buried a week before. For the rest, the surgeon tells me that the leaden weight was not too firmly fixed, and that seven days bring about changes which fetch a body to the surface. Coming from the depth to which the weight would have sunk it, he explains that it might well attain such a velocity as to carry it clear of the water. Such is my own explanation of the matter, and if you ask me what then became of the body, I must recall to you that snapping, crackling sound, with the swirl in the water. The shark is a surface feeder and is plentiful in those parts.

THE PARASITE

I

MARCH 24. The spring is fairly with us now. Outside my laboratory window the great chestnut-tree is all covered with the big, glutinous, gummy buds, some of which have already begun to break into little green shuttlecocks. As you walk down the lanes you are conscious of the rich, silent forces of nature working all around you. The wet earth smells fruitful and luscious. Green shoots are peeping out everywhere. The twigs are stiff with their sap; and the moist, heavy English air is laden with a faintly resinous perfume. Buds in the hedges, lambs beneath them—everywhere the work of reproduction going forward!

I can see it without, and I can feel it within. We also have our spring when the little arterioles dilate, the lymph flows in a brisker stream, the glands work harder, winnowing and straining. Every year nature readjusts the whole machine. I can feel the ferment in my blood at this very moment, and as the cool sunshine pours through my window I could dance about in it like a gnat. So I should, only that Charles Sadler would rush upstairs to know what was the matter. Besides,

I must remember that I am Professor Gilroy. An old professor may afford to be natural, but when fortune has given one of the first chairs in the university to a man of four-and-thirty he must try and act the part consistently.

What a fellow Wilson is! If I could only throw the same enthusiasm into physiology that he does into psychology, I should become a Claude Bernard at the least. His whole life and soul and energy work to one end. He drops to sleep collating his results of the past day, and he wakes to plan his researches for the coming one. And yet, outside the narrow circle who follow his proceedings, he gets so little credit for it. Physiology is a recognised science. If I add even a brick to the edifice, every one sees and applauds it. But Wilson is trying to dig the foundations for a science of the future. His work is underground and does not show. Yet he goes on uncomplainingly, corresponding with a hundred semi-maniacs in the hope of finding one reliable witness, sifting a hundred lies on the chance of gaining one little speck of truth, collating old books, devouring new ones, experimenting, lecturing, trying to light up in others the fiery interest which is consuming him. I am filled with wonder and admiration when I think of him, and yet, when he asks me to associate myself with his researches, I am compelled to tell him that, in their present state, they offer little attraction to a man who is devoted to exact science. If he could show me something positive and objective, I might then be tempted to approach the question from its physiological side. So long as half his subjects are tainted with *charlatanerie* and the other half with hysteria we physiologists must content ourselves with the body and leave the mind to our descendants.

No doubt I am a materialist. Agatha says that I am a rank one. I tell her that is an excellent reason for shortening our engagement, since I am in such urgent need of her spirituality. And yet I may claim to be a curious example of the effect of education upon temperament, for by nature I am, unless I deceive myself, a highly psychic man. I was a nervous, sensitive boy, a dreamer, a somnambulist, full of impressions and intuitions. My black hair, my dark eyes, my thin, olive face, my tapering fingers, are all characteristic of my real temperament, and cause experts like Wilson to claim me as their own. But my brain is soaked with exact knowledge. I have trained myself to deal only with fact and with proof. Surmise and fancy have no place in my scheme of thought. Show me what I can see with my microscope, cut with my scalpel, weigh in my balance, and I will devote a lifetime to its investigation. But when you ask me to study feelings, impressions, suggestions, you ask me to do what is distasteful and even demoralising. A departure from pure reason affects me like an evil smell or a musical discord.

Which is a very sufficient reason why I am a little loath to go to Professor Wilson's tonight. Still I feel that I could hardly get out of the invitation without positive rudeness; and, now that Mrs Marden and Agatha are going, of course I would not if I could. But I had rather meet them anywhere else. I know that Wilson would draw me into this nebulous semi-science of his if he could. In his enthusiasm he is perfectly impervious to hints or remonstrances. Nothing short of a positive quarrel will make him realise my aversion to the whole business. I have no doubt that he has some new mesmerist or clairvoyant or medium or trickster of some sort whom he is going to exhibit to us, for even his entertainments bear upon his hobby. Well, it will be a treat for Agatha, at any rate. She is interested in it, as woman usually is in whatever is vague and mystical and indefinite.

10.50 p.m. This diary-keeping of mine is, I fancy, the outcome of that scientific habit of mind about which I wrote this morning. I like to register impressions while they are fresh. Once a day at least I endeavour to define my own mental position. It is a useful piece of self-analysis, and has, I fancy, a steadying effect upon the character. Frankly,

I must confess that my own needs what stiffening I can give it. I fear that, after all, much of my neurotic temperament survives, and that I am far from that cool, calm precision which characterises Murdoch or Pratt-Haldane. Otherwise, why should the tomfoolery which I have witnessed this evening have set my nerves thrilling so that even now I am all unstrung? My only comfort is that neither Wilson nor Miss Penclosa nor even Agatha could have possibly known my weakness.

And what in the world was there to excite me? Nothing, or so little that it will seem ludicrous when I set it down.

The Mardens got to Wilson's before me. In fact, I was one of the last to arrive and found the room crowded. I had hardly time to say a word to Mrs Marden and to Agatha, who was looking charming in white and pink, with glittering wheat-ears in her hair, when Wilson came twitching at my sleeve.

'You want something positive, Gilroy,' said he, drawing me apart into a corner. 'My dear fellow, I have a phenomenon—a phenomenon!'

I should have been more impressed had I not heard the same before. His sanguine spirit turns every fire-fly into a star.

'No possible question about the *bona fides* this time,' said he, in answer, perhaps, to some little gleam of amusement in my eyes. 'My wife has known her for many years. They both come from Trinidad, you know. Miss Penclosa has only been in England a month or two, and knows no one outside the university circle, but I assure you that the things she has told us suffice in themselves to establish clairvoyance upon an absolutely scientific basis. There is nothing like her, amateur or professional. Come and be introduced!'

I like none of these mystery-mongers, but the amateur least of all. With the paid performer you may pounce upon him and expose him the instant that you have seen through his trick. He is there to deceive you, and you are there to find him out. But what are you to do with the friend of your host's wife? Are you to turn on a light suddenly and expose her slapping a surreptitious banjo? Or are you to hurl cochineal over her evening frock when she steals round with her phosphorus bottle and her supernatural platitude? There would be a scene, and you would be looked upon as a brute. So you have your choice of being that or a dupe. I was in no very good humour as I followed Wilson to the lady.

Any one less like my idea of a West Indian could not be imagined. She was a small, frail creature, well over forty, I should say, with a pale, peaky face, and hair of a very light shade of chestnut. Her presence was insignificant and her manner retiring. In any group of ten women she would have been the last whom one would have picked out. Her eyes were perhaps her most remarkable, and also, I am compelled to say, her least pleasant, feature. They were grey in colour,—grey with a shade of green,—and their expression struck me as being decidedly furtive. I wonder if furtive is the word, or should I have said fierce? On second thoughts, feline would have expressed it better. A crutch leaning against the wall told me what was painfully evident when she rose: that one of her legs was crippled.

So I was introduced to Miss Penclosa, and it did not escape me that as my name was mentioned she glanced across at Agatha. Wilson had evidently been talking. And presently, no doubt, thought I, she will inform me by occult means that I am engaged to a young lady with wheat-ears in her hair. I wondered how much more Wilson had been telling her about me.

'Professor Gilroy is a terrible sceptic,' said he; 'I hope, Miss Penclosa, that you will be able to convert him.'

She looked keenly up at me.

'Professor Gilroy is quite right to be sceptical if he has not seen any thing convincing,' said she. 'I should have thought,' she added, 'that you would yourself have been an excellent subject.'

'For what, may I ask?' said I.

'Well, for mesmerism, for example.'

'My experience has been that mesmerists go for their subjects to those who are mentally unsound. All their results are vitiated, as it seems to me, by the fact that they are dealing with abnormal organisms.'

'Which of these ladies would you say possessed a normal organism?' she asked. 'I should like you to select the one who seems to you to have the best balanced mind. Should we say the girl in pink and white?—Miss Agatha Marden, I think the name is.'

'Yes, I should attach weight to any results from her.'

'I have never tried how far she is impressionable. Of course some people respond much more rapidly than others. May I ask how far your scepticism extends? I suppose that you admit the mesmeric sleep and the power of suggestion.'

'I admit nothing, Miss Penclosa.'

'Dear me, I thought science had got further than that. Of course I know nothing about the scientific side of it. I only know what I can do. You see the girl in red, for example, over near the Japanese jar. I shall will that she come across to us.'

She bent forward as she spoke and dropped her fan upon the floor. The girl whisked round and came straight toward us, with an enquiring look upon her face, as if some one had called her.

'What do you think of that, Gilroy?' cried Wilson, in a kind of ecstasy.

I did not dare to tell him what I thought of it. To me it was the most barefaced, shameless piece of imposture that I had ever witnessed. The collusion and the signal had really been too obvious.

'Professor Gilroy is not satisfied,' said she, glancing up at me with her strange little eyes. 'My poor fan is to get the credit of that experiment. Well, we must try something else. Miss Marden, would you have any objection to my putting you off?'

'Oh, I should love it!' cried Agatha.

By this time all the company had gathered round us in a circle, the shirt-fronted men, and the white-throated women, some awed, some critical, as though it were something between a religious ceremony and a conjurer's entertainment. A red velvet arm-chair had been pushed into the centre, and Agatha lay back in it, a little flushed and trembling slightly from excitement. I could see it from the vibration of the wheat-ears. Miss Penclosa rose from her seat and stood over her, leaning upon her crutch.

And there was a change in the woman. She no longer seemed small or insignificant. Twenty years were gone from her age. Her eyes were shining, a tinge of colour had come into her sallow cheeks, her whole figure had expanded. So I have seen a dull-eyed, listless lad change in an instant into briskness and life when given a task of which he felt himself master. She looked down at Agatha with an expression which I resented from the bottom of my soul—the expression with which a Roman empress might have looked at her kneeling slave. Then with a quick, commanding gesture she tossed up her arms and swept them slowly down in front of her.

I was watching Agatha narrowly. During three passes she seemed to be simply amused. At the fourth I observed a slight glazing of her eyes, accompanied by some dilation of her pupils. At the sixth there was a momentary rigour. At the seventh her lids began to droop. At the tenth her eyes were closed, and her breathing was slower and fuller than usual. I tried as I watched to preserve my scientific calm, but a foolish, causeless agitation convulsed me. I trust that I hid it, but I felt as a child feels in the dark. I could not have believed that I was still open to such weakness.

'She is in the trance,' said Miss Penclosa.

'She is sleeping!' I cried.

'Wake her, then!'

I pulled her by the arm and shouted in her ear. She might have been dead for all the impression that I could make. Her body was there on the velvet chair. Her organs were acting—her heart, her lungs. But her soul! It had slipped from beyond our ken. Whither had it gone? What power had dispossessed it? I was puzzled and disconcerted.

'So much for the mesmeric sleep,' said Miss Penclosa. 'As regards suggestion, whatever I may suggest Miss Marden will infallibly do, whether it be now or after she has awakened from her trance. Do you demand proof of it?'

'Certainly,' said I.

'You shall have it.' I saw a smile pass over her face, as though an amusing thought had struck her. She stooped and whispered earnestly into her subject's ear. Agatha, who had been so deaf to me, nodded her head as she listened.

'Awake!' cried Miss Penclosa, with a sharp tap of her crutch upon the floor. The eyes opened, the glazing cleared slowly away, and the soul looked out once more after its strange eclipse.

We went away early. Agatha was none the worse for her strange excursion, but I was nervous and unstrung, unable to listen to or answer the stream of comments which Wilson was pouring out for my benefit. As I bade her good-night Miss Penclosa slipped a piece of paper into my hand.

'Pray forgive me,' said she, 'if I take means to overcome your scepticism. Open this note at ten o'clock tomorrow morning. It is a little private test.'

I can't imagine what she means, but there is the note, and it shall be opened as she directs. My head is aching, and I have written enough for tonight. Tomorrow I dare say that what seems so inexplicable will take quite another complexion. I shall not surrender my convictions without a struggle.

March 25. I am amazed, confounded. It is clear that I must reconsider my opinion upon this matter. But first let me place on record what has occurred.

I had finished breakfast, and was looking over some diagrams with which my lecture is to be illustrated, when my housekeeper entered to tell me that Agatha was in my study and wished to see me immediately. I glanced at the clock and saw with surprise that it was only half-past nine.

When I entered the room, she was standing on the hearth-rug facing me. Something in her pose chilled me and checked the words which were rising to my lips. Her veil was half down, but I could see that she was pale and that her expression was constrained.

'Austin,' she said, 'I have come to tell you that our engagement is at an end.'

I staggered. I believe that I literally did stagger. I know that I found myself leaning against the bookcase for support.

'But—but—' I stammered. 'This is very sudden, Agatha.'

'Yes, Austin, I have come here to tell you that our engagement is at an end.'

'But surely,' I cried, 'you will give me some reason! This is unlike you, Agatha. Tell me how I have been unfortunate enough to offend you.'

'It is all over, Austin.'

'But why? You must be under some delusion, Agatha. Perhaps you have been told some falsehood about me. Or you may have misunderstood something that I have said to you. Only let me know what it is, and a word may set it all right.'

'We must consider it all at an end.'

'But you left me last night without a hint at any disagreement. What could have occurred in the interval to change you so? It must have been something that happened last night. You have been thinking it over and you have disapproved of my conduct. Was it the mesmerism? Did you blame me for letting that woman exercise her power over you? You know that at the least sign I should have interfered.'

'It is useless, Austin. All is over.'

Her voice was cold and measured; her manner strangely formal and hard. It seemed to me that she was absolutely resolved not to be drawn into any argument or explanation. As for me, I was shaking with agitation, and I turned my face aside, so ashamed was I that she should see my want of control.

'You must know what this means to me!' I cried. 'It is the blasting of all my hopes and the ruin of my life! You surely will not inflict such a punishment upon me unheard. You will let me know what is the matter. Consider how impossible it would be for me, under any circumstances, to treat you so. For God's sake, Agatha, let me know what I have done!'

She walked past me without a word and opened the door.

'It is quite useless, Austin,' said she. 'You must consider our engagement at an end.' An instant later she was gone, and, before I could recover myself sufficiently to follow her, I heard the hall-door close behind her.

I rushed into my room to change my coat, with the idea of hurrying round to Mrs Marden's to learn from her what the cause of my misfortune might be. So shaken was I that I could hardly lace my boots. Never shall I forget those horrible ten minutes. I had just pulled on my overcoat when the clock upon the mantel-piece struck ten.

Ten! I associated the idea with Miss Penclosa's note. It was lying before me on the table, and I tore it open. It was scribbled in pencil in a peculiarly angular handwriting.

'My Dear Professor Gilroy [it said]: Pray excuse the personal nature of the test which I am giving you. Professor Wilson happened to mention the relations between you and my subject of this evening, and it struck me that nothing could be more convincing to you than if I were to suggest to Miss Marden that she should call upon you at half-past nine tomorrow morning and suspend your engagement for half an hour or so. Science is so exacting that it is difficult to give a satisfying test, but I am convinced that this at least will be an action which she would be most unlikely to do of her own free will. Forget any thing that she may have said, as she has really nothing whatever to do with it, and will certainly not recollect any thing about it. I write this note to shorten your anxiety, and to beg you to forgive me for the momentary unhappiness which my suggestion must have caused you.

'Yours faithfully,

'Helen Penclosa.'

Really, when I had read the note, I was too relieved to be angry. It was a liberty. Certainly it was a very great liberty indeed on the part of a lady whom I had only met once. But, after all, I had challenged her by my scepticism. It may have been, as she said, a little difficult to devise a test which would satisfy me.

And she had done that. There could be no question at all upon the point. For me hypnotic suggestion was finally established. It took its place from now onward as one of the facts of life. That Agatha, who of all women of my acquaintance has the best balanced mind, had been reduced to a condition of automatism appeared to be certain. A person at a distance had worked her as an engineer on the shore might guide a Brennan torpedo. A second soul had stepped in, as it were, had pushed her own aside, and had seized her nervous mechanism, saying: 'I will work this for half an hour.' And Agatha must have been unconscious as she came and as she returned. Could she make her way in safety through the streets in such a state? I put on my hat and hurried round to see if all was well with her.

Yes. She was at home. I was shown into the drawing-room and found her sitting with a book upon her lap.

'You are an early visitor, Austin,' said she, smiling.

'And you have been an even earlier one,' I answered.

She looked puzzled. 'What do you mean?' she asked.

'You have not been out today?'

'No, certainly not.'

'Agatha,' said I seriously, 'would you mind telling me exactly what you have done this morning?'

She laughed at my earnestness.

'You've got on your professional look, Austin. See what comes of being engaged to a man of science. However, I will tell you, though I can't imagine what you want to know for. I got up at eight. I breakfasted at half-past. I came into this room at ten minutes past nine and began to read the "Memoirs of Mme. de Rémusat." In a few minutes I did the French lady the bad compliment of dropping to sleep over her pages, and I did you, sir, the very flattering one of dreaming about you. It is only a few minutes since I woke up.'

'And found yourself where you had been before?'

'Why, where else should I find myself?'

'Would you mind telling me, Agatha, what it was that you dreamed about me? It really is not mere curiosity on my part.'

'I merely had a vague impression that you came into it. I cannot recall any thing definite.'

'If you have not been out today, Agatha, how is it that your shoes are dusty?'

A pained look came over her face.

'Really, Austin, I do not know what is the matter with you this morning. One would almost think that you doubted my word. If my boots are dusty, it must be, of course, that I have put on a pair which the maid had not cleaned.'

It was perfectly evident that she knew nothing whatever about the matter, and I reflected that, after all, perhaps it was better that I should not enlighten her. It might frighten her, and could serve no good purpose that I could see. I said no more about it, therefore, and left shortly afterward to give my lecture.

But I am immensely impressed. My horizon of scientific possibilities has suddenly been enormously extended. I no longer wonder at Wilson's demonic energy and enthusiasm. Who would not work hard who had a vast virgin field ready to his hand? Why, I have known the novel shape of a nucleolus, or a trifling peculiarity of striped muscular fibre seen under a 300-diameter lens, fill me with exultation. How petty do such researches seem when compared with this one which strikes at the very roots of life and the nature of the soul! I had always looked upon spirit as a product of matter. The brain, I thought, secreted the mind, as the liver does the bile. But how can this be when I see mind working from a distance and playing upon matter as a musician might upon a violin? The body does not give rise to the soul, then, but is rather the rough instrument by which the spirit manifests itself. The windmill does not give rise to the wind, but only indicates it. It was opposed to my whole habit of thought, and yet it was undeniably possible and worthy of investigation.

And why should I not investigate it? I see that under yesterday's date I said: 'If I could see something positive and objective, I might be tempted to approach it from the physiological aspect.' Well, I have got my test. I shall be as good as my word. The investigation would, I am sure, be of immense interest. Some of my colleagues might look askance at it, for science is full of unreasoning prejudices, but if Wilson has the courage of his convictions, I can afford to have it also. I shall go to him tomorrow morning—to him and to Miss Penclosa. If she can show us so much, it is probable that she can show us more.

II

March 26. Wilson was, as I had anticipated, very exultant over my conversion, and Miss Penclosa was also demurely pleased at the result of her experiment. Strange what a silent, colourless creature she is save only when she exercises her power! Even talking about it gives her colour and life. She seems to take a singular interest in me. I cannot help observing how her eyes follow me about the room.

We had the most interesting conversation about her own powers. It is just as well to put her views on record, though they cannot, of course, claim any scientific weight.

'You are on the very fringe of the subject,' said she, when I had expressed wonder at the remarkable instance of suggestion which she had shown me. 'I had no direct influence upon Miss Marden when she came round to you. I was not even thinking of her that morning. What I did was to set her mind as I might set the alarum of a clock so that at the hour named it would go off of its own accord. If six months instead of twelve hours had been suggested, it would have been the same.'

'And if the suggestion had been to assassinate me?'

'She would most inevitably have done so.'

'But this is a terrible power!' I cried.

'It is, as you say, a terrible power,' she answered gravely, 'and the more you know of it the more terrible will it seem to you.'

'May I ask,' said I, 'what you meant when you said that this matter of suggestion is only at the fringe of it? What do you consider the essential?'

'I had rather not tell you.'

I was surprised at the decision of her answer.

'You understand,' said I, 'that it is not out of curiosity I ask, but in the hope that I may find some scientific explanation for the facts with which you furnish me.'

'Frankly, Professor Gilroy,' said she, 'I am not at all interested in science, nor do I care whether it can or cannot classify these powers.'

'But I was hoping—'

'Ah, that is quite another thing. If you make it a personal matter,' said she, with the pleasantest of smiles, 'I shall be only too happy to tell you any thing you wish to know. Let me see; what was it you asked me? Oh, about the further powers. Professor Wilson won't believe in them, but they are quite true all the same. For example, it is possible for an operator to gain complete command over his subject—presuming that the latter is a good one. Without any previous suggestion he may make him do whatever he likes.'

'Without the subject's knowledge?'

'That depends. If the force were strongly exerted, he would know no more about it than Miss Marden did when she came round and frightened you so. Or, if the influence was less powerful, he might be conscious of what he was doing, but be quite unable to prevent himself from doing it.'

'Would he have lost his own will power, then?'

'It would be over-ridden by another stronger one.'

'Have you ever exercised this power yourself?'

'Several times.'

'Is your own will so strong, then?'

'Well, it does not entirely depend upon that. Many have strong wills which are not detachable from themselves. The thing is to have the gift of projecting it into another person and superseding his own. I find that the power varies with my own strength and health.'

'Practically, you send your soul into another person's body.'

'Well, you might put it that way.'

'And what does your own body do?'

'It merely feels lethargic.'

'Well, but is there no danger to your own health?' I asked.

'There might be a little. You have to be careful never to let your own consciousness absolutely go; otherwise, you might experience some difficulty in finding your way back again. You must always preserve the connection, as it were. I am afraid I express myself very badly, Professor Gilroy, but of course I don't know how to put these things in a scientific way. I am just giving you my own experiences and my own explanations.'

Well, I read this over now at my leisure, and I marvel at myself! Is this Austin Gilroy, the man who has won his way to the front by his hard reasoning power and by his devotion to fact? Here I am gravely retailing the gossip of a woman who tells me how her soul may be projected from her body, and how, while she lies in a lethargy, she can control the actions of people at a distance. Do I accept it? Certainly not. She must prove and re-prove before I yield a point. But if I am still a sceptic, I have at least ceased to be a scoffer. We are to have a sitting this evening, and she is to try if she can produce any mesmeric effect upon me. If she can, it will make an excellent starting-point for our investigation. No one can accuse *me*, at any rate, of complicity. If she cannot, we must try and find some subject who will be like Cæsar's wife. Wilson is perfectly impervious.

10 p.m. I believe that I am on the threshold of an epoch-making investigation. To have the power of examining these phenomena from inside—to have an organism which will respond, and at the same time a brain which will appreciate and criticise—that is surely a unique advantage. I am quite sure that Wilson would give five years of his life to be as susceptible as I have proved myself to be.

There was no one present except Wilson and his wife. I was seated with my head leaning back, and Miss Penclosa, standing in front and a little to the left, used the same long, sweeping strokes as with Agatha. At each of them a warm current of air seemed to strike me, and to suffuse a thrill and glow all through me from head to foot. My eyes were fixed upon Miss Penclosa's face, but as I gazed the features seemed to blur and to fade away. I was conscious only of her own eyes looking down at me, grey, deep, inscrutable. Larger they grew and larger, until they changed suddenly into two mountain lakes toward which I seemed to be falling with horrible rapidity. I shuddered, and as I did so some deeper stratum of thought told me that the shudder represented the rigour which I had observed in Agatha. An instant later I struck the surface of the lakes, now joined into one, and down I went beneath the water with a fulness in my head and a buzzing in my ears. Down I went, down, down, and then with a swoop up again until I could see the light streaming brightly through the green water. I was almost at the surface when the word 'Awake!' rang through my head, and, with a start, I found myself back in the arm-chair, with Miss Penclosa leaning on her crutch, and Wilson, his note-book in his hand, peeping over her shoulder. No heaviness or weariness was left behind. On the contrary, though it is only an hour or so since the experiment, I feel so wakeful that I am more inclined for my study than my bedroom. I see quite a vista of interesting experiments extending before us, and am all impatience to begin upon them.

March 27. A blank day, as Miss Penclosa goes with Wilson and his wife to the Suttons'. Have begun Binet and Ferré's 'Animal Magnetism.'

What strange, deep waters these are! Results, results, results—and the cause an absolute mystery. It is stimulating to the imagination, but I must be on my guard against that. Let us have no inferences nor deductions, and nothing but solid facts. I *know* that the mesmeric trance is true; I *know* that mesmeric suggestion is true; I *know* that I am myself sensitive to this force. That is my present position. I have a large new note-book which shall be devoted entirely to scientific detail.

Long talk with Agatha and Mrs Marden in the evening about our marriage. We think that the summer vac. (the beginning of it) would be the best time for the wedding. Why should we delay? I grudge even those few months. Still, as Mrs Marden says, there are a good many things to be arranged.

March 28. Mesmerised again by Miss Penclosa. Experience much the same as before, save that insensibility came on more quickly. See Note-book A for temperature of room, barometric pressure, pulse, and respiration as taken by Professor Wilson.

March 29. Mesmerised again. Details in Note-book A.

March 30. Sunday, and a blank day. I grudge any interruption of our experiments. At present they merely embrace the physical signs which go with slight, with complete, and with extreme insensibility. Afterward we hope to pass on to the phenomena of suggestion and of lucidity. Professors have demonstrated these things upon women at Nancy and at the Salpêtrière. It will be more convincing when a woman demonstrates it upon a professor, with a second professor as a witness. And that I should be the subject—I, the sceptic, the materialist! At least, I have shown that my devotion to science is greater than to my own personal consistency. The eating of our own words is the greatest sacrifice which truth ever requires of us.

My neighbour, Charles Sadler, the handsome young demonstrator of anatomy, came in this evening to return a volume of Virchow's

'Archives' which I had lent him. I call him young, but, as a matter of fact, he is a year older than I am.

'I understand, Gilroy,' said he, 'that you are being experimented upon by Miss Penclosa.

'Well,' he went on, when I had acknowledged it, 'if I were you, I should not let it go any further. You will think me very impertinent, no doubt, but, none the less, I feel it to be my duty to advise you to have no more to do with her.'

Of course I asked him why.

'I am so placed that I cannot enter into particulars as freely as I could wish,' said he. 'Miss Penclosa is the friend of my friend, and my position is a delicate one. I can only say this: that I have myself been the subject of some of the woman's experiments, and that they have left a most unpleasant impression upon my mind.'

He could hardly expect me to be satisfied with that, and I tried hard to get something more definite out of him, but without success. Is it conceivable that he could be jealous at my having superseded him? Or is he one of those men of science who feel personally injured when facts run counter to their preconceived opinions? He cannot seriously suppose that because he has some vague grievance I am, therefore, to abandon a series of experiments which promise to be so fruitful of results. He appeared to be annoyed at the light way in which I treated his shadowy warnings, and we parted with some little coldness on both sides.

March 31. Mesmerised by Miss P.

April 1. Mesmerised by Miss P. (Note-book A.)

April 2. Mesmerised by Miss P. (Sphygmographic chart taken by Professor Wilson.)

April 3. It is possible that this course of mesmerism may be a little trying to the general constitution. Agatha says that I am thinner and darker under the eyes. I am conscious of a nervous irritability which I had not observed in myself before. The least noise, for example, makes me start, and the stupidity of a student causes me exasperation instead of amusement. Agatha wishes me to stop, but I tell her that every course of study is trying, and that one can never attain a result without paying some price for it. When she sees the sensation which my forthcoming paper on 'The Relation between Mind and Matter' may make, she will understand that it is worth a little nervous wear and tear. I should not be surprised if I got my F. R. S. over it.

Mesmerised again in the evening. The effect is produced more rapidly now, and the subjective visions are less marked. I keep full notes of each sitting. Wilson is leaving for town for a week or ten days, but we shall not interrupt the experiments, which depend for their value as much upon my sensations as on his observations.

April 4. I must be carefully on my guard. A complication has crept into our experiments which I had not reckoned upon. In my eagerness for scientific facts I have been foolishly blind to the human relations between Miss Penclosa and myself. I can write here what I would not breathe to a living soul. The unhappy woman appears to have formed an attachment for me.

I should not say such a thing, even in the privacy of my own intimate journal, if it had not come to such a pass that it is impossible to ignore it. For some time,—that is, for the last week,—there have been signs which I have brushed aside and refused to think of. Her brightness when I come, her dejection when I go, her eagerness that I should come often, the expression of her eyes, the tone of her voice—I tried to think that they meant nothing, and were, perhaps, only her ardent West Indian manner. But last night, as I awoke from the mesmeric sleep, I put out my hand, unconsciously, involuntarily, and clasped hers. When I came fully to myself, we were sitting with them locked, she looking up at me with an expectant smile, And the horrible thing was that I felt impelled to say what she expected me to say. What a false wretch I should have been! How I should have loathed myself today had I yielded to the temptation of that moment! But, thank God, I was strong enough to spring up and hurry from the room. I was rude, I fear, but I could not, no, I *could* not, trust myself another moment. I, a gentleman, a man of honour, engaged to one of the sweetest girls in England—and yet in a moment of reasonless passion I nearly professed love for this woman whom I hardly know. She is far older than myself and a cripple. It is monstrous, odious; and yet the impulse was so strong that, had I stayed another minute in her presence, I should have committed myself. What was it? I have to teach others the workings of our organism, and what do I know of it myself? Was it the sudden upcropping of some lower stratum in my nature—a brutal primitive instinct suddenly asserting itself? I could almost believe the tales of obsession by evil spirits, so overmastering was the feeling.

Well, the incident places me in a most unfortunate position. On the one hand, I am very loath to abandon a series of experiments which have already gone so far, and which promise such brilliant results. On the other, if this unhappy woman has conceived a passion for me— But surely even now I must have made some hideous mistake. She, with her age and her deformity! It is impossible. And then she knew about Agatha. She understood how I was placed. She only smiled out of amusement, perhaps, when in my dazed state I seized her hand. It was my half-mesmerised brain which gave it a meaning, and sprang with such bestial swiftness to meet it. I wish I could persuade myself that it was indeed so. On the whole, perhaps, my wisest plan would be to postpone our other experiments until Wilson's return. I have written a note to Miss Penclosa, therefore, making no allusion to last night, but saying that a press of work would cause me to interrupt our sittings for a few days. She has answered, formally enough, to say that if I should change my mind I should find her at home at the usual hour.

10 p.m. Well, well, what a thing of straw I am! I am coming to know myself better of late, and the more I know the lower I fall in my own estimation. Surely I was not always so weak as this. At four o'clock I should have smiled had any one told me that I should go to Miss Penclosa's tonight, and yet, at eight, I was at Wilson's door as usual. I don't know how it occurred. The influence of habit, I suppose. Perhaps there is a mesmeric craze as there is an opium craze, and I am a victim to it. I only know that as I worked in my study I became more and more uneasy. I fidgeted. I worried. I could not concentrate my mind upon the papers in front of me. And then, at last, almost before I knew what I was doing, I seized my hat and hurried round to keep my usual appointment.

We had an interesting evening. Mrs Wilson was present during most of the time, which prevented the embarrassment which one at least of us must have felt. Miss Penclosa's manner was quite the same as usual, and she expressed no surprise at my having come in spite of my note. There was nothing in her bearing to show that yesterday's incident had made any impression upon her, and so I am inclined to hope that I overrated it.

April 6 (evening). No, no, no, I did not overrate it. I can no longer attempt to conceal from myself that this woman has conceived a passion for me. It is monstrous, but it is true. Again, tonight, I awoke from the mesmeric trance to find my hand in hers, and to suffer that odious feeling which urges me to throw away my honour, my career, every thing, for the sake of this creature who, as I can plainly see when I am away from her influence, possesses no single charm upon earth. But when I am near her, I do not feel this. She rouses something in me, something evil, something I had rather not think of. She paralyses my better nature, too, at the moment when she stimulates my worse. Decidedly it is not good for me to be near her.

Last night was worse than before. Instead of flying I actually sat for some time with my hand in hers talking over the most intimate subjects with her. We spoke of Agatha, among other things. What could I have been dreaming of? Miss Penclosa said that she was conventional, and I agreed with her. She spoke once or twice in a disparaging way of her, and I did not protest. What a creature I have been!

Weak as I have proved myself to be, I am still strong enough to bring this sort of thing to an end. It shall not happen again. I have sense enough to fly when I cannot fight. From this Sunday night onward I shall never sit with Miss Penclosa again. Never! Let the experiments go, let the research come to an end; any thing is better than facing this monstrous temptation which drags me so low. I have said nothing to Miss Penclosa, but I shall simply stay away. She can tell the reason without any words of mine.

April 7. Have stayed away as I said. It is a pity to ruin such an interesting investigation, but it would be a greater pity still to ruin my life, and I *know* that I cannot trust myself with that woman.

11 p.m. God help me! What is the matter with me? Am I going mad? Let me try and be calm and reason with myself. First of all I shall set down exactly what occurred.

It was nearly eight when I wrote the lines with which this day begins. Feeling strangely restless and uneasy, I left my rooms and walked round to spend the evening with Agatha and her mother. They both remarked that I was pale and haggard. About nine Professor Pratt-Haldane came in, and we played a game of whist. I tried hard to concentrate my attention upon the cards, but the feeling of restlessness grew and grew until I found it impossible to struggle against it. I simply *could* not sit still at the table. At last, in the very middle of a hand, I threw my cards down and, with some sort of an incoherent apology about having an appointment, I rushed from the room. As if in a dream I have a vague recollection of tearing through the hall, snatching my hat from the stand, and slamming the door behind me. As in a dream, too, I have the impression of the double line of gas-lamps, and my bespattered boots tell me that I must have run down the middle of the road. It was all misty and strange and unnatural. I came to Wilson's house; I saw Mrs Wilson and I saw Miss Penclosa. I hardly recall what we talked about, but I do remember that Miss P. shook the head of her crutch at me in a playful way, and accused me of being late and of losing interest in our experiments. There was no mesmerism, but I stayed some time and have only just returned.

My brain is quite clear again now, and I can think over what has occurred. It is absurd to suppose that it is merely weakness and force of habit. I tried to explain it in that way the other night, but it will no longer suffice. It is something much deeper and more terrible than that. Why, when I was at the Mardens' whist-table, I was dragged away as if the noose of a rope had been cast round me. I can no longer disguise it from myself. The woman has her grip upon me. I am in her clutch. But I must keep my head and reason it out and see what is best to be done.

But what a blind fool I have been! In my enthusiasm over my research I have walked straight into the pit, although it lay gaping before me. Did she not herself warn me? Did she not tell me, as I can read in my own journal, that when she has acquired power over a subject she can make him do her will? And she has acquired that power over me. I am for the moment at the beck and call of this creature with the crutch. I must come when she wills it. I must do as she wills. Worst of all, I must feel as she wills. I loathe her and fear her, yet, while I am under the spell, she can doubtless make me love her.

There is some consolation in the thought, then, that those odious impulses for which I have blamed myself do not really come from me at all. They are all transferred from her, little as I could have guessed it at the time. I feel cleaner and lighter for the thought.

April 8. Yes, now, in broad daylight, writing coolly and with time for reflection, I am compelled to confirm every thing which I wrote in my journal last night. I am in a horrible position, but, above all, I must not lose my head. I must pit my intellect against her powers. After all, I am no silly puppet, to dance at the end of a string. I have energy, brains, courage. For all her devil's tricks I may beat her yet. May! I *must*, or what is to become of me?

Let me try to reason it out! This woman, by her own explanation, can dominate my nervous organism. She can project herself into my body and take command of it. She has a parasite soul; yes, she is a parasite, a monstrous parasite. She creeps into my frame as the hermit crab does into the whelk's shell. I am powerless. What can I do? I am dealing with forces of which I know nothing. And I can tell no one of my trouble. They would set me down as a madman. Certainly, if it got noised abroad, the university would say that they had no need of a devil-ridden professor. And Agatha! No, no, I must face it alone.

III

I read over my notes of what the woman said when she spoke about her powers. There is one point which fills me with dismay. She implies that when the influence is slight the subject knows what he is doing, but cannot control himself, whereas when it is strongly exerted he is absolutely unconscious. Now, I have always known what I did, though less so last night than on the previous occasions. That seems to mean that she has never yet exerted her full powers upon me. Was ever a man so placed before?

Yes, perhaps there was, and very near me, too. Charles Sadler must know something of this! His vague words of warning take a meaning now. Oh, if I had only listened to him then, before I helped by these repeated sittings to forge the links of the chain which binds me! But I will see him today. I will apologise to him for having treated his warning so lightly. I will see if he can advise me.

4 p.m. No, he cannot. I have talked with him, and he showed such surprise at the first words in which I tried to express my unspeakable secret that I went no further. As far as I can gather (by hints and inferences rather than by any statement), his own experience was limited to some words or looks such as I have myself endured. His abandonment of Miss Penclosa is in itself a sign that he was never really in her toils. Oh, if he only knew his escape! He has to thank his phlegmatic Saxon temperament for it. I am black and Celtic, and this hag's clutch is deep in my nerves. Shall I ever get it out? Shall I ever be the same man that I was just one short fortnight ago?

Let me consider what I had better do. I cannot leave the university in the middle of the term. If I were free, my course would be obvious. I should start at once and travel in Persia. But would she allow me to start? And could her influence not reach me in Persia, and bring me back to within touch of her crutch? I can only find out the limits of this hellish power by my own bitter experience. I will fight and fight and fight—and what can I do more?

I know very well that about eight o'clock tonight that craving for her society, that irresistible restlessness, will come upon me. How shall I overcome it? What shall I do? I must make it impossible for me to leave the room. I shall lock the door and throw the key out of the window.

But, then, what am I to do in the morning? Never mind about the morning. I must at all costs break this chain which holds me.

April 9. Victory! I have done splendidly! At seven o'clock last night I took a hasty dinner, and then locked myself up in my bedroom and dropped the key into the garden. I chose a cheery novel, and lay in bed for three hours trying to read it, but really in a horrible state of trepidation, expecting every instant that I should become conscious of the impulse. Nothing of the sort occurred, however, and I awoke this morning with the feeling that a black nightmare had been lifted off me. Perhaps the creature realised what I had done, and understood that it was useless to try to influence me. At any rate, I have beaten her once, and if I can do it once, I can do it again.

It was most awkward about the key in the morning. Luckily, there was an under-gardener below, and I asked him to throw it up. No doubt he thought I had just dropped it. I will have doors and windows screwed up and six stout men to hold me down in my bed before I will surrender myself to be hag-ridden in this way.

I had a note from Mrs Marden this afternoon asking me to go round and see her. I intended to do so in any case, but had not excepted to find bad news waiting for me. It seems that the Armstrongs, from whom Agatha has expectations, are due home from Adelaide in the *Aurora*, and that they have written to Mrs Marden and her to meet them in town. They will probably be away for a month or six weeks, and, as the *Aurora* is due on Wednesday, they must go at once—tomorrow, if they are ready in time. My consolation is that when we meet again there will be no more parting between Agatha and me.

'I want you to do one thing, Agatha,' said I, when we were alone together. 'If you should happen to meet Miss Penclosa, either in town or here, you must promise me never again to allow her to mesmerise you.'

Agatha opened her eyes.

'Why, it was only the other day that you were saying how interesting it all was, and how determined you were to finish your experiments.'

'I know, but I have changed my mind since then.'

'And you won't have it any more?'

'No.'

'I am so glad, Austin. You can't think how pale and worn you have been lately. It was really our principal objection to going to London now that we did not wish to leave you when you were so pulled down. And your manner has been so strange occasionally—especially that night when you left poor Professor Pratt-Haldane to play dummy. I am convinced that these experiments are very bad for your nerves.'

'I think so, too, dear.'

'And for Miss Penclosa's nerves as well. You have heard that she is ill?'

'No.'

'Mrs Wilson told us so last night. She described it as a nervous fever. Professor Wilson is coming back this week, and of course Mrs Wilson is very anxious that Miss Penclosa should be well again then, for he has quite a programme of experiments which he is anxious to carry out.'

I was glad to have Agatha's promise, for it was enough that this woman should have one of us in her clutch. On the other hand, I was disturbed to hear about Miss Penclosa's illness. It rather discounts the victory which I appeared to win last night. I remember that she said that loss of health interfered with her power. That may be why I was able to hold my own so easily. Well, well, I must take the same precautions tonight and see what comes of it. I am childishly frightened when I think of her.

April 10. All went very well last night. I was amused at the gardener's face when I had again to hail him this morning and to ask him to throw up my key. I shall get a name among the servants if this sort of thing goes on. But the great point is that I stayed in my room without the slightest inclination to leave it. I do believe that I am shaking myself clear of this incredible bond—or is it only that the woman's power is in abeyance until she recovers her strength? I can but pray for the best.

The Mardens left this morning, and the brightness seems to have gone out of the spring sunshine. And yet it is very beautiful also as it gleams on the green chestnuts opposite my windows, and gives a touch of gaiety to the heavy, lichen-mottled walls of the old colleges. How sweet and gentle and soothing is Nature! Who would think that there lurked in her also such vile forces, such odious possibilities! For of course I understand that this dreadful thing which has sprung out at me is neither supernatural nor even preternatural. No, it is a natural force which this woman can use and society is ignorant of. The mere fact that it ebbs with her strength shows how entirely it is subject to physical laws. If I had time, I might probe it to the bottom and lay my hands upon its antidote. But you cannot tame the tiger when you are beneath his claws. You can but try to writhe away from him. Ah, when I look in the glass and see my own dark eyes and clear-cut Spanish face, I long for a vitriol splash or a bout of the small-pox. One or the other might have saved me from this calamity.

I am inclined to think that I may have trouble tonight. There are two things which make me fear so. One is that I met Mrs Wilson in the street, and that she tells me that Miss Penclosa is better, though still weak. I find myself wishing in my heart that the illness had been her last. The other is that Professor Wilson comes back in a day or two, and his presence would act as a constraint upon her. I should not fear our interviews if a third person were present. For both these reasons I have a presentiment of trouble tonight, and I shall take the same precautions as before.

April 10. No, thank God, all went well last night. I really could not face the gardener again. I locked my door and thrust the key underneath it, so that I had to ask the maid to let me out in the morning. But the precaution was really not needed, for I never had any inclination to go out at all. Three evenings in succession at home! I am surely near the end of my troubles, for Wilson will be home again either today or tomorrow. Shall I tell him of what I have gone through or not? I am convinced that I should not have the slightest sympathy from him. He would look upon me as an interesting case, and read a paper about me at the next meeting of the Psychical Society, in which he would gravely discuss the possibility of my being a deliberate liar, and weigh it against the chances of my being in an early stage of lunacy. No, I shall get no comfort out of Wilson.

I am feeling wonderfully fit and well. I don't think I ever lectured with greater spirit. Oh, if I could only get this shadow off my life, how happy I should be! Young, fairly wealthy, in the front rank of my profession, engaged to a beautiful and charming girl—have I not every thing which a man could ask for? Only one thing to trouble me, but what a thing it is!

Midnight. I shall go mad. Yes, that will be the end of it. I shall go mad. I am not far from it now. My head throbs as I rest it on my hot hand. I am quivering all over like a scared horse. Oh, what a night I have had! And yet I have some cause to be satisfied also.

At the risk of becoming the laughing-stock of my own servant, I again slipped my key under the door, imprisoning myself for the night. Then, finding it too early to go to bed, I lay down with my clothes on and began to read one of Dumas's novels. Suddenly I was gripped—gripped and dragged from the couch. It is only thus that I can describe the overpowering nature of the force which pounced upon me. I clawed at the coverlet. I clung to the wood-work. I believe that I screamed out in my frenzy. It was all useless, hopeless. I *must* go. There was no way out of it. It was only at the outset that I resisted. The force soon became too overmastering for that. I thank goodness that there were no watchers there to interfere with me. I could not have answered for myself if there had been. And, besides the determination to get out, there came to me, also, the keenest and coolest judgement in choosing my means. I lit a candle and endeavoured, kneeling in front of the door, to pull the key through with the feather-end of a quill pen. It was just too short and pushed it further away. Then with quiet persistence I got a paper-knife out of one of the drawers, and with that I managed to draw the key back. I opened the door, stepped into my study, took a photograph of myself from the bureau, wrote something across it, placed it in the inside pocket of my coat, and then started off for Wilson's.

It was all wonderfully clear, and yet disassociated from the rest of my life, as the incidents of even the most vivid dream might be. A peculiar double consciousness possessed me. There was the predominant alien will, which was bent upon drawing me to the side of its owner, and there was the feebler protesting personality, which I recognised as being myself, tugging feebly at the overmastering impulse as a led terrier might at its chain. I can remember recognising these two conflicting forces, but I recall nothing of my walk, nor of how I was admitted to the house.

Very vivid, however, is my recollection of how I met Miss Penclosa. She was reclining on the sofa in the little boudoir in which our experiments had usually been carried out. Her head was rested on her hand, and a tiger-skin rug had been partly drawn over her. She looked up expectantly as I entered, and, as the lamp-light fell upon her face, I could see that she was very pale and thin, with dark hollows under her eyes. She smiled at me, and pointed to a stool beside her. It was with her left hand that she pointed, and I, running eagerly forward, seized it,—I loathe myself as I think of it,—and pressed it passionately to my lips. Then, seating myself upon the stool, and still retaining her hand, I gave her the photograph which I had brought with me, and talked and talked and talked—of my love for her, of my grief over her illness, of my joy at her recovery, of the misery it was to me to be absent a single evening from her side. She lay quietly looking down at me with imperious eyes and her provocative smile. Once I remember that she passed her hand over my hair as one caresses a dog; and it gave me pleasure—the caress. I thrilled under it. I was her slave, body and soul, and for the moment I rejoiced in my slavery.

And then came the blessed change. Never tell me that there is not a Providence! I was on the brink of perdition. My feet were on the edge. Was it a coincidence that at that very instant help should come? No, no, no; there is a Providence, and its hand has drawn me back. There is something in the universe stronger than this devil woman with her tricks. Ah, what a balm to my heart it is to think so!

As I looked up at her I was conscious of a change in her. Her face, which had been pale before, was now ghastly. Her eyes were dull, and the lids drooped heavily over them. Above all, the look of serene confidence had gone from her features. Her mouth had weakened. Her forehead had puckered. She was frightened and undecided. And as I watched the change my own spirit fluttered and struggled, trying hard to tear itself from the grip which held it—a grip which, from moment to moment, grew less secure.

'Austin,' she whispered, 'I have tried to do too much. I was not strong enough. I have not recovered yet from my illness. But I could not live longer without seeing you. You won't leave me, Austin? This is only a passing weakness. If you will only give me five minutes, I shall be myself again. Give me the small decanter from the table in the window.'

But I had regained my soul. With her waning strength the influence had cleared away from me and left me free. And I was aggressive—bitterly, fiercely aggressive. For once at least I could make this woman understand what my real feelings toward her were. My soul was filled with a hatred as bestial as the love against which it was a reaction. It was the savage, murderous passion of the revolted serf. I could have taken the crutch from her side and beaten her face in with it. She threw her hands up, as if to avoid a blow, and cowered away from me into the corner of the settee.

'The brandy!' she gasped. 'The brandy!'

I took the decanter and poured it over the roots of a palm in the window. Then I snatched the photograph from her hand and tore it into a hundred pieces.

'You vile woman,' I said, 'if I did my duty to society, you would never leave this room alive!'

'I love you, Austin; I love you!' she wailed.

'Yes,' I cried, 'and Charles Sadler before. And how many others before that?'

'Charles Sadler!' she gasped. 'He has spoken to you? So, Charles Sadler, Charles Sadler!' Her voice came through her white lips like a snake's hiss.

'Yes, I know you, and others shall know you, too. You shameless creature! You knew how I stood. And yet you used your vile power to bring me to your side. You may, perhaps, do so again, but at least you will remember that you have heard me say that I love Miss Marden from the bottom of my soul, and that I loathe you, abhor you! The very sight of you and the sound of your voice fill me with horror and disgust. The thought of you is repulsive. That is how I feel toward you, and if it pleases you by your tricks to draw me again to your side as you have done tonight, you will at least, I should think, have little satisfaction in trying to make a lover out of a man who has told you his real opinion of you. You may put what words you will into my mouth, but you cannot help remembering—'

I stopped, for the woman's head had fallen back, and she had fainted. She could not bear to hear what I had to say to her! What a glow of satisfaction it gives me to think that, come what may, in the future she can never misunderstand my true feelings toward her. But what will occur in the future? What will she do next? I dare not think of it. Oh, if only I could hope that she will leave me alone! But when I think of what I said to her—Never mind; I have been stronger than she for once.

April 11. I hardly slept last night, and found myself in the morning so unstrung and feverish that I was compelled to ask Pratt-Haldane to do my lecture for me. It is the first that I have ever missed. I rose at mid-day, but my head is aching, my hands quivering, and my nerves in a pitiable state.

Who should come round this evening but Wilson. He has just come back from London, where he has lectured, read papers, convened meetings, exposed a medium, conducted a series of experiments on thought transference, entertained Professor Richet of Paris, spent hours gazing into a crystal, and obtained some evidence as to the passage of matter through matter. All this he poured into my ears in a single gust.

'But you!' he cried at last. 'You are not looking well. And Miss Penclosa is quite prostrated today. How about the experiments?'

'I have abandoned them.'

'Tut, tut! Why?'

'The subject seems to me to be a dangerous one.'

Out came his big brown note-book.

'This is of great interest,' said he. 'What are your grounds for saying that it is a dangerous one? Please give your facts in chronological order, with approximate dates and names of reliable witnesses with their permanent addresses.'

'First of all,' I asked, 'would you tell me whether you have collected any cases where the mesmerist has gained a command over the subject and has used it for evil purposes?'

'Dozens!' he cried exultantly. 'Crime by suggestion—'

'I don't mean suggestion. I mean where a sudden impulse comes from a person at a distance—an uncontrollable impulse.'

'Obsession!' he shrieked, in an ecstasy of delight. 'It is the rarest condition. We have eight cases, five well attested. You don't mean to say—' His exultation made him hardly articulate.

'No, I don't,' said I. 'Good-evening! You will excuse me, but I am not very well tonight.' And so at last I got rid of him, still brandishing his pencil and his note-book. My troubles may be bad to bear, but at least it is better to hug them to myself than to have myself exhibited by Wilson, like a freak at a fair. He has lost sight of human beings. Every thing to him is a case and a phenomenon. I will die before I speak to him again upon the matter.

April 12. Yesterday was a blessed day of quiet, and I enjoyed an uneventful night. Wilson's presence is a great consolation. What can the woman do now? Surely, when she has heard me say what I have said, she will conceive the same disgust for me which I have for her. She could not, no, she *could* not, desire to have a lover who had insulted her so. No, I believe I am free from her love—but how about her hate? Might she not use these powers of hers for revenge? Tut! why should I frighten myself over shadows? She will forget about me, and I shall forget about her, and all will be well.

April 13. My nerves have quite recovered their tone. I really believe that I have conquered the creature. But I must confess to living in some suspense. She is well again, for I hear that she was driving with Mrs Wilson in the High Street in the afternoon.

April 14. I do wish I could get away from the place altogether. I shall fly to Agatha's side the very day that the term closes. I suppose it is pitiably weak of me, but this woman gets upon my nerves most terribly. I have seen her again, and I have spoken with her.

It was just after lunch, and I was smoking a cigarette in my study, when I heard the step of my servant Murray in the passage. I was languidly conscious that a second step was audible behind, and had hardly troubled myself to speculate who it might be, when suddenly a slight noise brought me out of my chair with my skin creeping with apprehension. I had never particularly observed before what sort of sound the tapping of a crutch was, but my quivering nerves told me that I heard it now in the sharp wooden clack which alternated with the muffled thud of the footfall. Another instant and my servant had shown her in.

I did not attempt the usual conventions of society, nor did she. I simply stood with the smouldering cigarette in my hand, and gazed at her. She in her turn looked silently at me, and at her look I remembered how in these very pages I had tried to define the expression of her eyes, whether they were furtive or fierce. Today they were fierce—coldly and inexorably so.

'Well,' said she at last, 'are you still of the same mind as when I saw you last?'

'I have always been of the same mind.'

'Let us understand each other, Professor Gilroy,' said she slowly. 'I am not a very safe person to trifle with, as you should realise by now. It was you who asked me to enter into a series of experiments with you, it was you who won my affections, it was you who professed your love for me, it was you who brought me your own photograph with words of affection upon it, and, finally, it was you who on the very same evening thought fit to insult me most outrageously, addressing me as no man has ever dared to speak to me yet. Tell me that those words came from you in a moment of passion and I am prepared to forget and to forgive them. You did not mean what you said, Austin? You do not really hate me?'

I might have pitied this deformed woman—such a longing for love broke suddenly through the menace of her eyes. But then I thought of what I had gone through, and my heart set like flint.

'If ever you heard me speak of love,' said I, 'you know very well that it was your voice which spoke, and not mine. The only words of truth which I have ever been able to say to you are those which you heard when last we met.'

'I know. Some one has set you against me. It was he!' She tapped with her crutch upon the floor. 'Well, you know very well that I could bring you this instant crouching like a spaniel to my feet. You will not find me again in my hour of weakness, when you can insult me with impunity. Have a care what you are doing, Professor Gilroy. You stand in a terrible position. You have not yet realised the hold which I have upon you.'

I shrugged my shoulders and turned away.

'Well,' said she, after a pause, 'if you despise my love, I must see what can be done with fear. You smile, but the day will come when you will come screaming to me for pardon. Yes, you will grovel on the ground before me, proud as you are, and you will curse the day that ever you turned me from your best friend into your most bitter enemy. Have a care, Professor Gilroy!' I saw a white hand shaking in the air, and a face which was scarcely human, so convulsed was it with passion. An instant later she was gone, and I heard the quick hobble and tap receding down the passage.

But she has left a weight upon my heart. Vague presentiments of coming misfortune lie heavy upon me. I try in vain to persuade myself that these are only words of empty anger. I can remember those relentless eyes too clearly to think so. What shall I do—ah, what shall I do? I am no longer master of my own soul. At any moment this loathsome parasite may creep into me, and then—I must tell some one my hideous secret—I must tell it or go mad. If I had some one to sympathise and advise! Wilson is out of the question. Charles Sadler would understand me only so far as his own experience carries him. Pratt-Haldane! He is a well-balanced man, a man of great common-sense and resource. I will go to him. I will tell him every thing. God grant that he may be able to advise me!

IV

6.45 p.m. No, it is useless. There is no human help for me; I must fight this out single-handed. Two courses lie before me. I might become this woman's lover. Or I must endure such persecutions as she can inflict upon me. Even if none come, I shall live in a hell of apprehension. But she may torture me, she may drive me mad, she may kill me: I will never, never, never give in. What can she inflict which would be worse than the loss of Agatha, and the knowledge that I am a perjured liar, and have forfeited the name of gentleman?

Pratt-Haldane was most amiable, and listened with all politeness to my story. But when I looked at his heavy set features, his slow eyes, and the ponderous study furniture which surrounded him, I could hardly tell him what I had come to say. It was all so substantial, so material.

And, besides, what would I myself have said a short month ago if one of my colleagues had come to me with a story of demonic possession? Perhaps I should have been less patient than he was. As it was, he took notes of my statement, asked me how much tea I drank, how many hours I slept, whether I had been overworking much, had I had sudden pains in the head, evil dreams, singing in the ears, flashes before the eyes—all questions which pointed to his belief that brain congestion was at the bottom of my trouble. Finally he dismissed me with a great many platitudes about open-air exercise, and avoidance of nervous excitement. His prescription, which was for chloral and bromide, I rolled up and threw into the gutter.

No, I can look for no help from any human being. If I consult any more, they may put their heads together and I may find myself in an asylum. I can but grip my courage with both hands, and pray that an honest man may not be abandoned.

April 15. It is the sweetest spring within the memory of man. So green, so mild, so beautiful! Ah, what a contrast between nature without and my own soul so torn with doubt and terror! It has been an uneventful day, but I know that I am on the edge of an abyss. I know it, and yet I go on with the routine of my life. The one bright spot is that Agatha is happy and well and out of all danger. If this creature had a hand on each of us, what might she not do?

April 16. The woman is ingenious in her torments. She knows how fond I am of my work, and how highly my lectures are thought of. So it is from that point that she now attacks me. It will end, I can see, in my losing my professorship, but I will fight to the finish. She shall not drive me out of it without a struggle.

I was not conscious of any change during my lecture this morning save that for a minute or two I had a dizziness and swimminess which rapidly passed away. On the contrary, I congratulated myself upon having made my subject (the functions of the red corpuscles) both interesting and clear. I was surprised, therefore, when a student came into my laboratory immediately after the lecture, and complained of being puzzled by the discrepancy between my statements and those in the text-books. He showed me his note-book, in which I was reported as having in one portion of the lecture championed the most outrageous and unscientific heresies. Of course I denied it, and declared that he had misunderstood me, but on comparing his notes with those of his companions, it became clear that he was right, and that I really had made some most preposterous statements. Of course I shall explain it away as being the result of a moment of aberration, but I feel only too sure that it will be the first of a series. It is but a month now to the end of the session, and I pray that I may be able to hold out until then.

April 26. Ten days have elapsed since I have had the heart to make any entry in my journal. Why should I record my own humiliation and degradation? I had vowed never to open it again. And yet the force of habit is strong, and here I find myself taking up once more the record of my own dreadful experiences—in much the same spirit in which a suicide has been known to take notes of the effects of the poison which killed him.

Well, the crash which I had foreseen has come—and that no further back than yesterday. The university authorities have taken my lectureship from me. It has been done in the most delicate way, purporting to be a temporary measure to relieve me from the effects of overwork, and to give me the opportunity of recovering my health. None the less, it has been done, and I am no longer Professor Gilroy. The laboratory is still in my charge, but I have little doubt that that also will soon go.

The fact is that my lectures had become the laughing-stock of the university. My class was crowded with students who came to see and hear what the eccentric professor would do or say next. I cannot go into the detail of my humiliation. Oh, that devilish woman! There is no depth of buffoonery and imbecility to which she has not forced me. I would begin my lecture clearly and well, but always with the sense of a coming eclipse. Then as I felt the influence I would struggle against it, striving with clenched hands and beads of sweat upon my brow to get the better of it, while the students, hearing my incoherent words and watching my contortions, would roar with laughter at the antics of their professor. And then, when she had once fairly mastered me, out would come the most outrageous things—silly jokes, sentiments as though I were proposing a toast, snatches of ballads, personal abuse even against some member of my class. And then in a moment my brain would clear again, and my lecture would proceed decorously to the end. No wonder that my conduct has been the talk of the colleges. No wonder that the University Senate has been compelled to take official notice of such a scandal. Oh, that devilish woman!

And the most dreadful part of it all is my own loneliness. Here I sit in a commonplace English bow-window, looking out upon a commonplace English street with its garish 'buses and its lounging policeman, and behind me there hangs a shadow which is out of all keeping with the age and place. In the home of knowledge I am weighed down and tortured by a power of which science knows nothing. No magistrate would listen to me. No paper would discuss my case. No doctor would believe my symptoms. My own most intimate friends would only look upon it as a sign of brain derangement. I am out of all touch with my kind. Oh, that devilish woman! Let her have a care! She may push me too far. When the law cannot help a man, he may make a law for himself.

She met me in the High Street yesterday evening and spoke to me. It was as well for her, perhaps, that it was not between the hedges of a lonely country road. She asked me with her cold smile whether I had been chastened yet. I did not deign to answer her. 'We must try another turn of the screw,' said she. Have a care, my lady, have a care! I had her at my mercy once. Perhaps another chance may come.

April 28. The suspension of my lectureship has had the effect also of taking away her means of annoying me, and so I have enjoyed two blessed days of peace. After all, there is no reason to despair. Sympathy pours in to me from all sides, and every one agrees that it is my devotion to science and the arduous nature of my researches which have shaken my nervous system. I have had the kindest message from the council advising me to travel abroad, and expressing the confident hope that I may be able to resume all my duties by the beginning of the summer term. Nothing could be more flattering than their allusions to my career and to my services to the university. It is only in misfortune that one can test one's own popularity. This creature may weary of tormenting me, and then all may yet be well. May God grant it!

April 29. Our sleepy little town has had a small sensation. The only knowledge of crime which we ever have is when a rowdy undergraduate breaks a few lamps or comes to blows with a policeman. Last night, however, there was an attempt made to break into the branch of the Bank of England, and we are all in a flutter in consequence.

Parkenson, the manager, is an intimate friend of mine, and I found him very much excited when I walked round there after breakfast. Had the thieves broken into the counting-house, they would still have had the safes to reckon with, so that the defence was considerably stronger than the attack. Indeed, the latter does not appear to have ever been very formidable. Two of the lower windows have marks as if a chisel or some such instrument had been pushed under them to force them open. The police should have a good clue, for the wood-work had been done with green paint only the day before, and from the smears it is evident that some of it has found its way on to the criminal's hands or clothes.

4.30 p.m. Ah, that accursed woman! That thrice accursed woman! Never mind! She shall not beat me! No, she shall not! But, oh, the she-devil! She has taken my professorship. Now she would take my honour. Is there nothing I can do against her, nothing save— Ah, but, hard pushed as I am, I cannot bring myself to think of that!

It was about an hour ago that I went into my bedroom, and was brushing my hair before the glass, when suddenly my eyes lit upon something which left me so sick and cold that I sat down upon the edge of the bed and began to cry. It is many a long year since I shed tears, but all my nerve was gone, and I could but sob and sob in impotent grief and anger. There was my house jacket, the coat I usually wear after dinner, hanging on its peg by the wardrobe, with the right sleeve thickly crusted from wrist to elbow with daubs of green paint.

So this was what she meant by another turn of the screw! She had made a public imbecile of me. Now she would brand me as a criminal. This time she has failed. But how about the next? I dare not think of it—and of Agatha and my poor old mother! I wish that I were dead!

Yes, this is the other turn of the screw. And this is also what she meant, no doubt, when she said that I had not realised yet the power she has over me. I look back at my account of my conversation with her, and I see how she declared that with a slight exertion of her will her subject would be conscious, and with a stronger one unconscious. Last night I was unconscious. I could have sworn that I slept soundly in my bed without so much as a dream. And yet those stains tell me that I dressed, made my way out, attempted to open the bank windows, and returned. Was I observed? Is it possible that some one saw me do it and followed me home? Ah, what a hell my life has become! I have no peace, no rest. But my patience is nearing its end.

10 p.m. I have cleaned my coat with turpentine. I do not think that any one could have seen me. It was with my screw-driver that I made the marks. I found it all crusted with paint, and I have cleaned it. My head aches as if it would burst, and I have taken five grains of antipyrine. If it were not for Agatha, I should have taken fifty and had an end of it.

May 3. Three quiet days. This hell fiend is like a cat with a mouse. She lets me loose only to pounce upon me again. I am never so frightened as when every thing is still. My physical state is deplorable—perpetual hiccough and ptosis of the left eyelid.

I have heard from the Mardens that they will be back the day after tomorrow. I do not know whether I am glad or sorry. They were safe in London. Once here they may be drawn into the miserable network in which I am myself struggling. And I must tell them of it. I cannot marry Agatha so long as I know that I am not responsible for my own actions. Yes, I must tell them, even if it brings every thing to an end between us.

Tonight is the university ball, and I must go. God knows I never felt less in the humour for festivity, but I must not have it said that I am unfit to appear in public. If I am seen there, and have speech with some of the elders of the university it will go a long way toward showing them that it would be unjust to take my chair away from me.

11.30 p.m. I have been to the ball. Charles Sadler and I went together, but I have come away before him. I shall wait up for him, however, for, indeed, I fear to go to sleep these nights. He is a cheery, practical fellow, and a chat with him will steady my nerves. On the whole, the evening was a great success. I talked to every one who has influence, and I think that I made them realise that my chair is not vacant quite yet. The creature was at the ball—unable to dance, of course, but sitting with Mrs Wilson. Again and again her eyes rested upon me. They were almost the last things I saw before I left the room. Once, as I sat sideways to her, I watched her, and saw that her gaze was following some one else. It was Sadler, who was dancing at the time with the second Miss Thurston. To judge by her expression, it is well for him that he is not in her grip as I am. He does not know the escape he has had. I think I hear his step in the street now, and I will go down and let him in. If he will—

May 4. Why did I break off in this way last night? I never went down stairs, after all—at least, I have no recollection of doing so. But, on the other hand, I cannot remember going to bed. One of my hands is greatly swollen this morning, and yet I have no remembrance of injuring it yesterday. Otherwise, I am feeling all the better for last night's festivity. But I cannot understand how it is that I did not meet Charles Sadler when I so fully intended to do so. Is it possible— My God, it is only too probable! Has she been leading me some devil's dance again? I will go down to Sadler and ask him.

Mid-day. The thing has come to a crisis. My life is not worth living. But, if I am to die, then she shall come also. I will not leave her behind, to drive some other man mad as she has me. No, I have come to the limit of my endurance. She has made me as desperate and dangerous a man as walks the earth. God knows I have never had the heart to hurt a fly, and yet, if I had my hands now upon that woman, she should never leave this room alive. I shall see her this very day, and she shall learn what she has to expect from me.

I went to Sadler and found him, to my surprise, in bed. As I entered he sat up and turned a face toward me which sickened me as I looked at it.

'Why, Sadler, what has happened?' I cried, but my heart turned cold as I said it.

'Gilroy,' he answered, mumbling with his swollen lips, 'I have for some weeks been under the impression that you are a madman. Now

I know it, and that you are a dangerous one as well. If it were not that I am unwilling to make a scandal in the college, you would now be in the hands of the police.'

'Do you mean—' I cried.

'I mean that as I opened the door last night you rushed out upon me, struck me with both your fists in the face, knocked me down, kicked me furiously in the side, and left me lying almost unconscious in the street. Look at your own hand bearing witness against you.'

Yes, there it was, puffed up, with sponge-like knuckles, as after some terrific blow. What could I do? Though he put me down as a madman, I must tell him all. I sat by his bed and went over all my troubles from the beginning. I poured them out with quivering hands and burning words which might have carried conviction to the most sceptical. 'She hates you and she hates me!' I cried. 'She revenged herself last night on both of us at once. She saw me leave the ball, and she must have seen you also. She knew how long it would take you to reach home. Then she had but to use her wicked will. Ah, your bruised face is a small thing beside my bruised soul!'

He was struck by my story. That was evident. 'Yes, yes, she watched me out of the room,' he muttered. 'She is capable of it. But is it possible that she has really reduced you to this? What do you intend to do?'

'To stop it!' I cried. 'I am perfectly desperate; I shall give her fair warning today, and the next time will be the last.'

'Do nothing rash,' said he.

'Rash!' I cried. 'The only rash thing is that I should postpone it another hour.' With that I rushed to my room, and here I am on the eve of what may be the great crisis of my life. I shall start at once. I have gained one thing today, for I have made one man, at least, realise the truth of this monstrous experience of mine. And, if the worst should happen, this diary remains as a proof of the goad that has driven me.

Evening. When I came to Wilson's, I was shown up, and found that he was sitting with Miss Penclosa. For half an hour I had to endure his fussy talk about his recent research into the exact nature of the spiritualistic rap, while the creature and I sat in silence looking across the room at each other. I read a sinister amusement in her eyes, and she must have seen hatred and menace in mine. I had almost despaired of having speech with her when he was called from the room, and we were left for a few moments together.

'Well, Professor Gilroy—or is it Mr Gilroy?' said she, with that bitter smile of hers. 'How is your friend Mr Charles Sadler after the ball?'

'You fiend!' I cried. 'You have come to the end of your tricks now. I will have no more of them. Listen to what I say.' I strode across and shook her roughly by the shoulder. 'As sure as there is a God in heaven, I swear that if you try another of your deviltries upon me I will have your life for it. Come what may, I will have your life. I have come to the end of what a man can endure.'

'Accounts are not quite settled between us,' said she, with a passion that equalled my own. 'I can love, and I can hate. You had your choice. You chose to spurn the first; now you must test the other. It will take a little more to break your spirit, I see, but broken it shall be. Miss Marden comes back tomorrow, as I understand.'

'What has that to do with you?' I cried. 'It is a pollution that you should dare even to think of her. If I thought that you would harm her—'

She was frightened, I could see, though she tried to brazen it out. She read the black thought in my mind, and cowered away from me.

'She is fortunate in having such a champion,' said she. 'He actually dares to threaten a lonely woman. I must really congratulate Miss Marden upon her protector.'

The words were bitter, but the voice and manner were more acid still.

'There is no use talking,' said I. 'I only came here to tell you,—and to tell you most solemnly,—that your next outrage upon me will be your last.' With that, as I heard Wilson's step upon the stair, I walked from the room. Ay, she may look venomous and deadly, but, for all that, she is beginning to see now that she has as much to fear from me as I can have from her. Murder! It has an ugly sound. But you don't talk of murdering a snake or of murdering a tiger. Let her have a care now.

May 5. I met Agatha and her mother at the station at eleven o'clock. She is looking so bright, so happy, so beautiful. And she was so overjoyed to see me. What have I done to deserve such love? I went back home with them, and we lunched together. All the troubles seem in a moment to have been shredded back from my life. She tells me that I am looking pale and worried and ill. The dear child puts it down to my loneliness and the perfunctory attentions of a housekeeper. I pray that she may never know the truth! May the shadow, if shadow there must be, lie ever black across my life and leave hers in the sunshine. I have just come back from them, feeling a new man. With her by my side I think that I could show a bold face to any thing which life might send.

5 p.m. Now, let me try to be accurate. Let me try to say exactly how it occurred. It is fresh in my mind, and I can set it down correctly, though it is not likely that the time will ever come when I shall forget the doings of today.

I had returned from the Mardens' after lunch, and was cutting some microscopic sections in my freezing microtome, when in an instant I lost consciousness in the sudden hateful fashion which has become only too familiar to me of late.

When my senses came back to me I was sitting in a small chamber, very different from the one in which I had been working. It was cosy and bright, with chintz-covered settees, coloured hangings, and a thousand pretty little trifles upon the wall. A small ornamental clock ticked in front of me, and the hands pointed to half-past three. It was all quite familiar to me, and yet I stared about for a moment in a half-dazed way until my eyes fell upon a cabinet photograph of myself upon the top of the piano. On the other side stood one of Mrs Marden. Then, of course, I remembered where I was. It was Agatha's boudoir.

But how came I there, and what did I want? A horrible sinking came to my heart. Had I been sent here on some devilish errand? Had that errand already been done? Surely it must; otherwise, why should I be allowed to come back to consciousness? Oh, the agony of that moment! What had I done? I sprang to my feet in my despair, and as I did so a small glass bottle fell from my knees on to the carpet.

It was unbroken, and I picked it up. Outside was written 'Sulphuric Acid. Fort.' When I drew the round glass stopper, a thick fume rose slowly up, and a pungent, choking smell pervaded the room. I recognised it as one which I kept for chemical testing in my chambers. But why had I brought a bottle of vitriol into Agatha's chamber? Was it not this thick, reeking liquid with which jealous women had been known to mar the beauty of their rivals? My heart stood still as I held the bottle to the light. Thank God, it was full! No mischief had been done as yet. But had Agatha come in a minute sooner, was it not certain that the hellish parasite within me would have dashed the stuff into her— Ah, it will not bear to be thought of! But it must have been for that. Why else should I have brought it? At the thought of what I might have done my worn nerves broke down, and I sat shivering and twitching, the pitiable wreck of a man.

It was the sound of Agatha's voice and the rustle of her dress which restored me. I looked up, and saw her blue eyes, so full of tenderness and pity, gazing down at me.

'We must take you away to the country, Austin,' she said. 'You want rest and quiet. You look wretchedly ill.'

'Oh, it is nothing!' said I, trying to smile. 'It was only a momentary weakness. I am all right again now.'

'I am so sorry to keep you waiting. Poor boy, you must have been here quite half an hour! The vicar was in the drawing-room, and, as I knew that you did not care for him, I thought it better that Jane should show you up here. I thought the man would never go!'

'Thank God he stayed! Thank God he stayed!' I cried hysterically.

'Why, what is the matter with you, Austin?' she asked, holding my arm as I staggered up from the chair. 'Why are you glad that the vicar stayed? And what is this little bottle in your hand?'

'Nothing,' I cried, thrusting it into my pocket. 'But I must go. I have something important to do.'

'How stern you look, Austin! I have never seen your face like that. You are angry?'

'Yes, I am angry.'

'But not with me?'

'No, no, my darling! You would not understand.'

'But you have not told me why you came.'

'I came to ask you whether you would always love me—no matter what I did, or what shadow might fall on my name. Would you believe in me and trust me however black appearances might be against me?'

'You know that I would, Austin.'

'Yes, I know that you would. What I do I shall do for you. I am driven to it. There is no other way out, my darling!' I kissed her and rushed from the room.

The time for indecision was at an end. As long as the creature threatened my own prospects and my honour there might be a question as to what I should do. But now, when Agatha—my innocent

Agatha—was endangered, my duty lay before me like a turnpike road. I had no weapon, but I never paused for that. What weapon should I need, when I felt every muscle quivering with the strength of a frenzied man? I ran through the streets, so set upon what I had to do that I was only dimly conscious of the faces of friends whom I met—dimly conscious also that Professor Wilson met me, running with equal precipitance in the opposite direction. Breathless but resolute I reached the house and rang the bell. A white-cheeked maid opened the door, and turned whiter yet when she saw the face that looked in at her.

'Show me up at once to Miss Penclosa,' I demanded.

'Sir,' she gasped, 'Miss Penclosa died this afternoon at half-past three!'

THE STORY OF THE BROWN HAND

EVERYONE knows that Sir Dominick Holden, the famous Indian surgeon, made me his heir, and that his death changed me in an hour from a hard-working and impecunious medical man to a well-to-do landed proprietor. Many know also that there were at least five people between the inheritance and me, and that Sir Dominick's selection appeared to be altogether arbitrary and whimsical. I can assure them, however, that they are quite mistaken, and that, although I only knew Sir Dominick in the closing years of his life, there were, none the less, very real reasons why he should show his goodwill towards me. As a matter of fact, though I say it myself, no man ever did more for another than I did for my Indian uncle. I cannot expect the story to be believed, but it is so singular that I should feel that it was a breach of duty if I did not put it upon record—so here it is, and your belief or incredulity is your own affair.

Sir Dominick Holden, CB, KCSI, and I don't know what besides, was the most distinguished Indian surgeon of his day. In the Army originally, he afterwards settled down into civil practice in Bombay, and visited, as a consultant, every part of India. His name is best remembered in connection with the Oriental Hospital which he founded and supported. The time came, however, when his iron constitution began to show signs of the long strain to which he had subjected it, and his brother practitioners (who were not, perhaps, entirely disinterested upon the point) were unanimous in recommending him to return to England. He held on as long as he could, but at last he developed nervous symptoms of a very pronounced character, and so came back, a broken man, to his native county of Wiltshire. He bought a considerable estate with an ancient manor-house upon the edge of Salisbury Plain, and devoted his old age to the study of Comparative Pathology, which had been his learned hobby all his life, and in which he was a foremost authority.

We of the family were, as may be imagined, much excited by the news of the return of this rich and childless uncle to England. On his part, although by no means exuberant in his hospitality, he showed some sense of his duty to his relations, and each of us in turn had an invitation to visit him. From the accounts of my cousins it appeared to be a melancholy business, and it was with mixed feelings that I at last received my own summons to appear at Rodenhurst. My wife was so carefully excluded in the invitation that my first impulse was to refuse it, but the interests of the children had to be considered, and so, with her consent, I set out one October afternoon upon my visit to Wiltshire, with little thought of what that visit was to entail.

My uncle's estate was situated where the arable land of the plains begins to swell upwards into the rounded chalk hills which are characteristic of the county. As I drove from Dinton Station in the waning light of that autumn day, I was impressed by the weird nature of the scenery. The few scattered cottages of the peasants were so dwarfed by the huge evidences of prehistoric life, that the present appeared to be a dream and the past to be the obtrusive and masterful reality. The road wound through the valleys, formed by a succession of grassy hills, and the summit of each was cut and carved into the most elaborate fortifications, some circular, and some square, but all on a scale which has defied the winds and the rains of many centuries. Some call them Roman and some British, but their true origin and the reasons for this particular tract of country being so interlaced with entrenchments have never been finally made clear. Here and there on the long, smooth, olive-coloured slopes there rose small, rounded barrows or tumuli. Beneath them lie the cremated ashes of the race which cut so deeply into the hills, but their graves tell us nothing save that a jar full of dust represents the man who once laboured under the sun.

It was through this weird country that I approached my uncle's residence of Rodenhurst, and the house was, as I found, in due keeping with its surroundings. Two broken and weather-stained pillars, each surmounted by a mutilated heraldic emblem, flanked the entrance to a neglected drive. A cold wind whistled through the elms which lined it, and the air was full of the drifting leaves. At the far end, under the gloomy arch of trees, a single yellow lamp burned steadily. In the dim half-light of the coming night I saw a long, low building stretching out two irregular wings, with deep eaves, a sloping gambrel roof, and walls which were criss-crossed with timber balks in the fashion of the Tudors. The cheery light of a fire flickered in the broad, latticed window to the left of the low-porched door, and this, as it proved, marked the study of my uncle, for it was thither that I was led by his butler in order to make my host's acquaintance.

He was cowering over his fire, for the moist chill of an English autumn had set him shivering. His lamp was unlit, and I only saw the red glow of the embers beating upon a huge, craggy face, with a Red Indian nose and cheek, and deep furrows and seams from eye to chin, the sinister marks of hidden volcanic fires. He sprang up at my entrance with something of an old-world courtesy and welcomed me warmly to Rodenhurst. At the same time I was conscious, as the lamp was carried in, that it was a very critical pair of light-blue eyes which looked out at me from under shaggy eyebrows, like scouts beneath a bush, and that this outlandish uncle of mine was carefully reading off my character with all the ease of a practised observer and an experienced man of the world.

For my part I looked at him, and looked again, for I had never seen a man whose appearance was more fitted to hold one's attention. His figure was the framework of a giant, but he had fallen away until his coat dangled straight down in a shocking fashion from a pair of broad and bony shoulders. All his limbs were huge and yet emaciated, and I could not take my gaze from his knobby wrists, and long, gnarled hands. But his eyes—those peering, light-blue eyes—they were the most arrestive of any of his peculiarities. It was not their colour alone, nor was it the ambush of hair in which they lurked; but it was the expression which I read in them. For the appearance and bearing of the man were masterful, and one expected a certain corresponding arrogance in his eyes, but instead of that I read the look which tells of a spirit cowed and crushed, the furtive, expectant look of the dog whose master has taken the whip from the rack. I formed my own medical diagnosis upon one glance at those critical and yet appealing eyes. I believed that he was stricken with some mortal ailment, that he knew himself to be exposed to sudden death, and that he lived in terror of it. Such was my judgement—a false one, as the event showed; but I mention it that it may help you to realise the look which I read in his eyes.

My uncle's welcome was, as I have said, a courteous one, and in an hour or so I found myself seated between him and his wife at a comfortable dinner, with curious, pungent delicacies upon the table, and a stealthy, quick-eyed Oriental waiter behind his chair. The old couple had come round to that tragic imitation of the dawn of life when husband and wife, having lost or scattered all those who were their intimates, find themselves face to face and alone once more, their work done, and the end nearing fast. Those who have reached that stage in sweetness and love, who can change their winter into a gentle, Indian summer, have come as victors through the ordeal of life. Lady Holden was a small, alert woman with a kindly eye, and her expression as she glanced at him was a certificate of character to her husband. And yet, though I read a mutual love in their glances, I read also mutual horror, and recognised in her face some reflection of that stealthy fear which I had detected in his. Their talk was sometimes merry and sometimes sad, but there was a forced note in their merriment and a naturalness in their sadness which told me that a heavy heart beat upon either side of me.

We were sitting over our first glass of wine, and the servants had left the room, when the conversation took a turn which produced a remarkable effect upon my host and hostess. I cannot recall what it was which started the topic of the supernatural, but it ended in my showing them that the abnormal in psychical experiences was a subject to which I had, like many neurologists, devoted a great deal of attention. I concluded by narrating my experiences when, as a member of the Psychical Research Society, I had formed one of a committee of three who spent the night in a haunted house. Our adventures were neither exciting nor convincing, but, such as it was, the story appeared to interest my auditors in a remarkable degree. They listened with an eager silence, and I caught a look of intelligence between them which I could not understand. Lady Holden immediately afterwards rose and left the room.

Sir Dominick pushed the cigar-box over to me, and we smoked for some little time in silence. That huge, bony hand of his was twitching as he raised it with his cheroot to his lips, and I felt that the man's nerves were vibrating like fiddle-strings. My instincts told me that he was on the verge of some intimate confidence, and I feared to speak lest I should interrupt it. At last he turned towards me with a spasmodic gesture like a man who throws his last scruple to the winds.

'From the little that I have seen of you it appears to me, Dr Hardacre,' said he, 'that you are the very man I have wanted to meet.'

'I am delighted to hear it, sir.'

'Your head seems to be cool and steady. You will acquit me of any desire to flatter you, for the circumstances are too serious to permit of insincerities. You have some special knowledge upon these subjects, and you evidently view them from that philosophical stand-point which robs them of all vulgar terror. I presume that the sight of an apparition would not seriously discompose you?'

'I think not, sir.'

'Would even interest you, perhaps?'

'Most intensely.'

'As a psychical observer, you would probably investigate it in as impersonal a fashion as an astronomer investigates a wandering comet?'

'Precisely.'

He gave a heavy sigh.

'Believe me, Dr Hardacre, there was a time when I could have spoken as you do now. My nerve was a byword in India. Even the Mutiny never shook it for an instant. And yet you see what I am reduced to—the most timorous man, perhaps, in all this county of Wiltshire. Do not speak too bravely upon this subject, or you may find yourself subjected to as long-drawn a test as I am—a test which can only end in the madhouse or the grave.'

I waited patiently until he should see fit to go farther in his confidence. His preamble had, I need not say, filled me with interest and expectation.

'For some years, Dr Hardacre,' he continued, 'my life and that of my wife have been made miserable by a cause which is so grotesque that it borders upon the ludicrous. And yet familiarity has never made it more easy to bear—on the contrary, as time passes my nerves become more worn and shattered by the constant attrition. If you have no physical fears, Dr Hardacre, I should very much value your opinion upon this phenomenon which troubles us so.'

'For what it is worth my opinion is entirely at your service. May I ask the nature of the phenomenon?'

'I think that your experiences will have a higher evidential value if you are not told in advance what you may expect to encounter. You are yourself aware of the quibbles of unconscious cerebration and subjective impressions with which a scientific sceptic may throw a doubt upon your statement. It would be as well to guard against them in advance.'

'What shall I do, then?'

'I will tell you. Would you mind following me this way?' He led me out of the dining-room and down a long passage until we came to a terminal door. Inside there was a large, bare room fitted as a laboratory, with numerous scientific instruments and bottles. A shelf ran along one side, upon which there stood a long line of glass jars containing pathological and anatomical specimens.

'You see that I still dabble in some of my old studies,' said Sir Dominick. 'These jars are the remains of what was once a most excellent collection, but unfortunately I lost the greater part of them when my house was burned down in Bombay in '92. It was a most unfortunate affair for me—in more ways than one. I had examples of many rare conditions, and my splenic collection was probably unique. These are the survivors.'

I glanced over them, and saw that they really were of a very great value and rarity from a pathological point of view: bloated organs, gaping cysts, distorted bones, odious parasites—a singular exhibition of the products of India.

'There is, as you see, a small settee here,' said my host. 'It was far from our intention to offer a guest so meagre an accommodation, but since affairs have taken this turn, it would be a great kindness upon your part if you would consent to spend the night in this apartment. I beg that you will not hesitate to let me know if the idea should be at all repugnant to you.'

'On the contrary,' I said, 'it is most acceptable.'

'My own room is the second on the left, so that if you should feel that you are in need of company a call would always bring me to your side.'

'I trust that I shall not be compelled to disturb you.'

'It is unlikely that I shall be asleep. I do not sleep much. Do not hesitate to summon me.'

And so with this agreement we joined Lady Holden in the drawing-room and talked of lighter things.

It was no affectation upon my part to say that the prospect of my night's adventure was an agreeable one. I have no pretence to greater physical courage than my neighbours, but familiarity with a subject robs it of those vague and undefined terrors which are the most appalling to the imaginative mind. The human brain is capable of only one strong emotion at a time, and if it be filled with curiosity or scientific enthusiasm, there is no room for fear. It is true that I had my uncle's assurance that he had himself originally taken this point of view, but I reflected that the break-down of his nervous system might be due to his forty years in India as much as to any psychical experiences which had befallen him. I at least was sound in nerve and brain, and it was with something of the pleasurable thrill of anticipation with which the sportsman takes his position beside the haunt of his game that I shut the laboratory door behind me, and partially undressing, lay down upon the rug-covered settee.

It was not an ideal atmosphere for a bedroom. The air was heavy with many chemical odours, that of methylated spirit predominating. Nor were the decorations of my chamber very sedative. The odious line of glass jars with their relics of disease and suffering stretched in front of my very eyes. There was no blind to the window, and a three-quarter moon streamed its white light into the room, tracing a silver square with filigree lattices upon the opposite wall. When I had extinguished my candle this one bright patch in the midst of the general gloom had certainly an eerie and discomposing aspect. A rigid and absolute silence reigned throughout the old house, so that the low swish of the branches in the garden came softly and smoothly to my ears. It may have been the hypnotic lullaby of this gentle susurrus, or it may have been the result of my tiring day, but after many dozings and many efforts to regain my clearness of perception, I fell at last into a deep and dreamless sleep.

I was awakened by some sound in the room, and I instantly raised myself upon my elbow on the couch. Some hours had passed, for the square patch upon the wall had slid downwards and sideways until it lay obliquely at the end of my bed. The rest of the room was in deep shadow. At first I could see nothing, presently, as my eyes became accustomed to the faint light, I was aware, with a thrill which all my scientific absorption could not entirely prevent, that something was moving slowly along the line of the wall. A gentle, shuffling sound, as of soft slippers, came to my ears, and I dimly discerned a human figure walking stealthily from the direction of the door. As it emerged into the patch of moonlight I saw very clearly what it was and how it was employed. It was a man, short and squat, dressed in some sort of dark-grey gown, which hung straight from his shoulders to his feet. The moon shone upon the side of his face, and I saw that it was chocolate-brown in colour, with a ball of black hair like a woman's at the back of his head. He walked slowly, and his eyes were cast upwards towards the line of bottles which contained those gruesome remnants of humanity. He seemed to examine each jar with attention, and then to pass on to the next. When he had come to the end of the line, immediately opposite my bed, he stopped, faced me, threw up his hands with a gesture of despair, and vanished from my sight.

I have said that he threw up his hands, but I should have said his arms, for as he assumed that attitude of despair I observed a singular peculiarity about his appearance. He had only one hand! As the sleeves drooped down from the upflung arms I saw the left plainly, but the right ended in a knobby and unsightly stump. In every other way his appearance was so natural, and I had both seen and heard him so clearly, that I could easily have believed that he was an Indian servant of Sir Dominick's who had come into my room in search of something. It was only his sudden disappearance which suggested anything more sinister to me. As it was I sprang from my couch, lit a candle, and examined the whole room carefully. There were no signs of my visitor, and I was forced to conclude that there had really been something outside the normal laws of Nature in his appearance. I lay awake for the remainder of the night, but nothing else occurred to disturb me.

I am an early riser, but my uncle was an even earlier one, for I found him pacing up and down the lawn at the side of the house. He ran towards me in his eagerness when he saw me come out from the door.

'Well, well!' he cried. 'Did you see him?'

'An Indian with one hand?'

'Precisely.'

'Yes, I saw him'—and I told him all that occurred. When I had finished, he led the way into his study.

'We have a little time before breakfast,' said he. 'It will suffice to give you an explanation of this extraordinary affair—so far as I can explain that which is essentially inexplicable. In the first place, when I tell you that for four years I have never passed one single night, either in Bombay, aboard ship, or here in England without my sleep being broken by this fellow, you will understand why it is that I am a wreck of my former self. His programme is always the same. He appears by my bedside, shakes me roughly by the shoulder, passes from my room into the laboratory, walks slowly along the line of my bottles, and then vanishes. For more than a thousand times he has gone through the same routine.'

'What does he want?'

'He wants his hand.'

'His hand?'

'Yes, it came about in this way. I was summoned to Peshawur for a consultation some ten years ago, and while there I was asked to look at the hand of a native who was passing through with an Afghan caravan. The fellow came from some mountain tribe living away at the back of beyond somewhere on the other side of Kaffiristan. He talked a bastard Pushtoo, and it was all I could do to understand him. He was suffering from a soft sarcomatous swelling of one of the metacarpal joints, and I made him realise that it was only by losing his hand that he could hope to save his life. After much persuasion he consented to the operation, and he asked me, when it was over, what fee I demanded. The poor fellow was almost a beggar, so that the idea of a fee was absurd, but I answered in jest that my fee should be his hand, and that I proposed to add it to my pathological collection.

'To my surprise he demurred very much to the suggestion, and he explained that according to his religion it was an all-important matter that the body should be reunited after death, and so make a perfect dwelling for the spirit. The belief is, of course, an old one, and the mummies of the Egyptians arose from an analogous superstition. I answered him that his hand was already off, and asked him how he intended to preserve it. He replied that he would pickle it in salt and carry it about with him. I suggested that it might be safer in my keeping than his, and that I had better means than salt for preserving it. On realising that I really intended to carefully keep it, his opposition vanished instantly. "But remember, sahib," said he, "I shall want it back when I am dead." I laughed at the remark, and so the matter ended. I returned to my practice, and he no doubt in the course of time was able to continue his journey to Afghanistan.

'Well, as I told you last night, I had a bad fire in my house at Bombay. Half of it was burned down, and, among other things, my pathological collection was largely destroyed. What you see are the poor remains of it. The hand of the hillman went with the rest, but I gave the matter no particular thought at the time. That was six years ago.

'Four years ago—two years after the fire—I was awakened one night by a furious tugging at my sleeve. I sat up under the impression that my favourite mastiff was trying to arouse me. Instead of this, I saw my Indian patient of long ago, dressed in the long, grey gown which was the badge of his people. He was holding up his stump and looking reproachfully at me. He then went over to my bottles, which at that time I kept in my room, and he examined them carefully, after which he gave a gesture of anger and vanished. I realised that he had just died, and that he had come to claim my promise that I should keep his limb in safety for him.

'Well, there you have it all, Dr Hardacre. Every night at the same hour for four years this performance has been repeated. It is a simple thing in itself, but it has worn me out like water dropping on a stone.

It has brought a vile insomnia with it, for I cannot sleep now for the expectation of his coming. It has poisoned my old age and that of my wife, who has been the sharer in this great trouble. But there is the breakfast gong, and she will be waiting impatiently to know how it fared with you last night. We are both much indebted to you for your gallantry, for it takes something from the weight of our misfortune when we share it, even for a single night, with a friend, and it reassures us to our sanity, which we are sometimes driven to question.'

This was the curious narrative which Sir Dominick confided to me—a story which to many would have appeared to be a grotesque impossibility, but which, after my experience of the night before, and my previous knowledge of such things, I was prepared to accept as an absolute fact. I thought deeply over the matter, and brought the whole range of my reading and experience to bear upon it. After breakfast, I surprised my host and hostess by announcing that I was returning to London by the next train.

'My dear doctor,' cried Sir Dominick in great distress, 'you make me feel that I have been guilty of a gross breach of hospitality in intruding this unfortunate matter upon you. I should have borne my own burden.'

'It is, indeed, that matter which is taking me to London,' I answered; 'but you are mistaken, I assure you, if you think that my experience of last night was an unpleasant one to me. On the contrary, I am about to ask your permission to return in the evening and spend one more night in your laboratory. I am very eager to see this visitor once again.'

My uncle was exceedingly anxious to know what I was about to do, but my fears of raising false hopes prevented me from telling him. I was back in my own consulting-room a little after luncheon, and was confirming my memory of a passage in a recent book upon occultism which had arrested my attention when I read it.

'In the case of earth-bound spirits,' said my authority, 'some one dominant idea obsessing them at the hour of death is sufficient to hold them in this material world. They are the amphibia of this life and of the next, capable of passing from one to the other as the turtle passes from land to water. The causes which may bind a soul so strongly to a life which its body has abandoned are any violent emotion. Avarice, revenge, anxiety, love and pity have all been known to have this effect. As a rule it springs from some unfulfilled wish, and when the wish has been fulfilled the material bond relaxes. There are many cases upon record which show the singular persistence of these visitors, and also their disappearance when their wishes have been fulfilled, or in some cases when a reasonable compromise has been effected.'

'*A reasonable compromise effected*'—those were the words which I had brooded over all the morning, and which I now verified in the original. No actual atonement could be made here—but a reasonable compromise! I made my way as fast as a train could take me to the Shadwell Seamen's Hospital, where my old friend Jack Hewett was house-surgeon. Without explaining the situation I made him understand what it was that I wanted.

'A brown man's hand!' said he, in amazement. 'What in the world do you want that for?'

'Never mind. I'll tell you some day. I know that your wards are full of Indians.'

'I should think so. But a hand—' He thought a little and then struck a bell.

'Travers,' said he to a student-dresser, 'what became of the hands of the Lascar which we took off yesterday? I mean the fellow from the East India Dock who got caught in the steam winch.'

'They are in the *post-mortem* room, sir.'

'Just pack one of them in antiseptics and give it to Dr Hardacre.'

And so I found myself back at Rodenhurst before dinner with this curious outcome of my day in town. I still said nothing to Sir Dominick, but I slept that night in the laboratory, and I placed the Lascar's hand in one of the glass jars at the end of my couch.

So interested was I in the result of my experiment that sleep was out of the question. I sat with a shaded lamp beside me and waited patiently for my visitor. This time I saw him clearly from the first. He appeared beside the door, nebulous for an instant, and then hardening into as distinct an outline as any living man. The slippers beneath his grey gown were red and heelless, which accounted for the low, shuffling sound which he made as he walked. As on the previous night he passed slowly along the line of bottles until he paused before that which contained the hand. He reached up to it, his whole figure quivering with expectation, took it down, examined it eagerly, and then, with a face which was convulsed with fury and disappointment, he hurled it down on the floor. There was a crash which resounded through the house, and when I looked up the mutilated Indian had disappeared. A moment later my door flew open and Sir Dominick rushed in.

'You are not hurt?' he cried.

'No—but deeply disappointed.'

He looked in astonishment at the splinters of glass, and the brown hand lying upon the floor.

'Good God!' he cried. 'What is this?'

I told him my idea and its wretched sequel. He listened intently, but shook his head.

'It was well thought of,' said he, 'but I fear that there is no such easy end to my sufferings. But one thing I now insist upon. It is that you shall never again upon any pretext occupy this room. My fears that something might have happened to you—when I heard that crash—have been the most acute of all the agonies which I have undergone. I will not expose myself to a repetition of it.'

He allowed me, however, to spend the remainder of that night where I was, and I lay there worrying over the problem and lamenting my own failure. With the first light of morning there was the Lascar's hand still lying upon the floor to remind me of my fiasco. I lay looking at it—and as I lay suddenly an idea flew like a bullet through my head and brought me quivering with excitement out of my couch. I raised the grim relic from where it had fallen. Yes, it was indeed so. The hand was the *left* hand of the Lascar.

By the first train I was on my way to town, and hurried at once to the Seamen's Hospital. I remembered that both hands of the Lascar had been amputated, but I was terrified lest the precious organ which I was in search of might have been already consumed in the crematory. My suspense was soon ended. It had still been preserved in the *post-mortem* room. And so I returned to Rodenhurst in the evening with my mission accomplished and the material for a fresh experiment.

But Sir Dominick Holden would not hear of my occupying the laboratory again. To all my entreaties he turned a deaf ear. It offended his sense of hospitality, and he could no longer permit it. I left the hand, therefore, as I had done its fellow the night before, and I occupied a comfortable bedroom in another portion of the house, some distance from the scene of my adventures.

But in spite of that my sleep was not destined to be uninterrupted. In the dead of night my host burst into my room, a lamp in his hand. His huge, gaunt figure was enveloped in a loose dressing-gown, and his whole appearance might certainly have seemed more formidable to a weak-nerved man than that of the Indian of the night before. But it was not his entrance so much as his expression which amazed me. He had turned suddenly younger by twenty years at the least. His eyes were shining, his features radiant, and he waved one hand in triumph over his head. I sat up astounded, staring sleepily at this extraordinary visitor. But his words soon drove the sleep from my eyes.

'We have done it! We have succeeded!' he shouted. 'My dear Hardacre, how can I ever in this world repay you?'

'You don't mean to say that it is all right?'

'Indeed I do. I was sure that you would not mind being awakened to hear such blessed news.'

'Mind! I should think not indeed. But is it really certain?'

'I have no doubt whatever upon the point. I owe you such a debt, my dear nephew, as I have never owed a man before, and never expected to. What can I possibly do for you that is commensurate? Providence must have sent you to my rescue. You have saved both my reason and my life, for another six months of this must have seen me either in a cell or a coffin. And my wife—it was wearing her out before my eyes. Never could I have believed that any human being could have lifted this burden off me.' He seized my hand and wrung it in his bony grip.

'It was only an experiment—a forlorn hope—but I am delighted from my heart that it has succeeded. But how do you know that it is all right? Have you seen something?'

He seated himself at the foot of my bed.

'I have seen enough,' said he. 'It satisfies me that I shall be troubled no more. What has passed is easily told. You know that at a certain hour this creature always comes to me. Tonight he arrived at the usual time, and aroused me with even more violence than is his custom. I can only surmise that his disappointment of last night increased the bitterness of his anger against me. He looked angrily at me, and then went on his usual round. But in a few minutes I saw him, for the first time since this persecution began, return to my chamber. He was smiling. I saw the gleam of his white teeth through the dim light. He stood facing me at the end of my bed, and three times he made the low, Eastern salaam which is their solemn leave-taking. And the third time that he bowed he raised his arms over his head, and I saw his *two* hands outstretched in the air. So he vanished, and, as I believe, for ever.'

*

So that is the curious experience which won me the affection and the gratitude of my celebrated uncle, the famous Indian surgeon. His anticipations were realised, and never again was he disturbed by the visits of the restless hillman in search of his lost member. Sir Dominick and Lady Holden spent a very happy old age, unclouded, so far as I know, by any trouble, and they finally died during the great influenza epidemic within a few weeks of each other. In his lifetime he always turned to me for advice in everything which concerned that English life of which he knew so little; and I aided him also in the purchase and development of his estates. It was no great surprise to me, therefore, that I found myself eventually promoted over the heads of five exasperated cousins, and changed in a single day from a hard-working country doctor into the head of an important Wiltshire family. I, at least, have reason to bless the memory of the man with the brown hand, and the day when I was fortunate enough to relieve Rodenhurst of his unwelcome presence.

PLAYING WITH FIRE

I CANNOT pretend to say what occurred on the 14th of April last at No. 17, Badderly Gardens. Put down in black and white, my surmise might seem too crude, too grotesque, for serious consideration. And yet that something did occur, and that it was of a nature which will leave its mark upon every one of us for the rest of our lives, is as certain as the unanimous testimony of five witnesses can make it. I will not enter into any argument or speculation. I will only give a plain statement, which will be submitted to John Moir, Harvey Deacon, and Mrs Delamere, and withheld from publication unless they are prepared to corroborate every detail. I cannot obtain the sanction of Paul Le Duc, for he appears to have left the country.

It was John Moir (the well-known senior partner of Moir, Moir, and Sanderson) who had originally turned our attention to occult subjects. He had, like many very hard and practical men of business, a mystic side to his nature, which had led him to the examination, and eventually to the acceptance, of those elusive phenomena which are grouped together with much that is foolish, and much that is fraudulent, under the common heading of spiritualism. His researches, which had begun with an open mind, ended unhappily in dogma, and he became as positive and fanatical as any other bigot. He represented in our little group the body of men who have turned these singular phenomena into a new religion.

Mrs Delamere, our medium, was his sister, the wife of Delamere, the rising sculptor. Our experience had shown us that to work on these subjects without a medium was as futile as for an astronomer to make observations without a telescope. On the other hand, the introduction of a paid medium was hateful to all of us. Was it not obvious that he or she would feel bound to return some result for money received, and that the temptation to fraud would be an overpowering one? No phenomena could be relied upon which were produced at a guinea an hour. But, fortunately, Moir had discovered that his sister was mediumistic—in other words, that she was a battery of that animal magnetic force which is the only form of energy which is subtle enough to be acted upon from the spiritual plane as well as from our own material one. Of course, when I say this, I do not mean to beg the question; but I am simply indicating the theories upon which we were ourselves, rightly or wrongly, explaining what we saw. The lady came, not altogether with the approval of her husband, and though she never gave indications of any very great psychic force, we were able, at least, to obtain those usual phenomena of message-tilting which are at the same time so puerile and so inexplicable. Every Sunday evening we met in Harvey Deacon's studio at Badderly Gardens, the next house to the corner of Merton Park Road.

Harvey Deacon's imaginative work in art would prepare anyone to find that he was an ardent lover of everything which was *outré* and sensational. A certain picturesqueness in the study of the occult had been the quality which had originally attracted him to it, but his attention was speedily arrested by some of those phenomena to which I have referred, and he was coming rapidly to the conclusion that what he had looked upon as an amusing romance and an after-dinner entertainment was really a very formidable reality. He is a man with a remarkably clear and logical brain—a true descendant of his ancestor, the well-known Scotch professor—and he represented in our small circle the critical element, the man who has no prejudices, is prepared to follow facts as far as he can see them, and refuses to theorise in advance of his data. His caution annoyed Moir as much as the latter's robust faith amused Deacon, but each in his own way was equally keen upon the matter.

And I? What am I to say that I represented? I was not the devotee. I was not the scientific critic. Perhaps the best that I can claim for myself is that I was the dilettante man about town, anxious to be in the swim of every fresh movement, thankful for any new sensation which would take me out of myself and open up fresh possibilities of existence. I am not an enthusiast myself, but I like the company of those who are. Moir's talk, which made me feel as if we had a private pass-key through the door of death, filled me with a vague contentment. The soothing atmosphere of the séance with the darkened lights was delightful to me. In a word, the thing amused me, and so I was there.

It was, as I have said, upon the 14th of April last that the very singular event which I am about to put upon record took place. I was the first of the men to arrive at the studio, but Mrs Delamere was already there, having had afternoon tea with Mrs Harvey Deacon. The two ladies and Deacon himself were standing in front of an unfinished picture of his upon the easel. I am not an expert in art, and I have never professed to understand what Harvey Deacon meant by his pictures; but I could see in this instance that it was all very clever and imaginative, fairies and animals and allegorical figures of all sorts. The ladies were loud in their praises, and indeed the colour effect was a remarkable one.

'What do you think of it, Markham?' he asked.

'Well, it's above me,' said I. 'These beasts—what are they?'

'Mythical monsters, imaginary creatures, heraldic emblems—a sort of weird, bizarre procession of them.'

'With a white horse in front!'

'It's not a horse,' said he, rather testily—which was surprising, for he was a very good-humoured fellow as a rule, and hardly ever took himself seriously.

'What is it, then?'

'Can't you see the horn in front? It's a unicorn. I told you they were heraldic beasts. Can't you recognise one?'

'Very sorry, Deacon,' said I, for he really seemed to be annoyed.

He laughed at his own irritation.

'Excuse me, Markham!' said he; 'the fact is that I have had an awful job over the beast. All day I have been painting him in and painting him out, and trying to imagine what a real live, ramping unicorn would look like. At last I got him, as I hoped; so when you failed to recognise it, it took me on the raw.'

'Why, of course it's a unicorn,' said I, for he was evidently depressed at my obtuseness. 'I can see the horn quite plainly, but I never saw a unicorn except beside the Royal Arms, and so I never thought of the creature. And these others are griffins and cockatrices, and dragons of sorts?'

'Yes, I had no difficulty with them. It was the unicorn which bothered me. However, there's an end of it until tomorrow.' He turned the picture round upon the easel, and we all chatted about other subjects.

Moir was late that evening, and when he did arrive he brought with him, rather to our surprise, a small, stout Frenchman, whom he introduced as Monsieur Paul Le Duc. I say to our surprise, for we held a theory that any intrusion into our spiritual circle deranged the conditions, and introduced an element of suspicion. We knew that we could trust each other, but all our results were vitiated by the presence of an outsider. However, Moir soon reconciled us to the innovation. Monsieur Paul Le Duc was a famous student of occultism, a seer, a medium, and a mystic. He was travelling in England with a letter of introduction to Moir from the President of the Parisian brothers of the Rosy Cross. What more natural than that he should bring him to our little séance, or that we should feel honoured by his presence?

He was, as I have said, a small, stout man, undistinguished in appearance, with a broad, smooth, clean-shaven face, remarkable only for a pair of large, brown, velvety eyes, staring vaguely out in front of him. He was well dressed, with the manners of a gentleman, and his curious little turns of English speech set the ladies smiling. Mrs Deacon had a prejudice against our researches and left the room, upon which we lowered the lights, as was our custom, and drew up our chairs to the square mahogany table which stood in the centre of the studio. The light was subdued, but sufficient to allow us to see each other quite plainly. I remember that I could even observe the curious, podgy little square-topped hands which the Frenchman laid upon the table.

'What a fun!' said he. 'It is many years since I have sat in this fashion, and it is to me amusing. Madame is medium. Does madame make the trance?'

'Well, hardly that,' said Mrs Delamere. 'But I am always conscious of extreme sleepiness.'

'It is the first stage. Then you encourage it, and there comes the trance. When the trance comes, then out jumps your little spirit and in jumps another little spirit, and so you have direct talking or writing. You leave your machine to be worked by another. *Hein?* But what have unicorns to do with it?'

Harvey Deacon started in his chair. The Frenchman was moving his head slowly round and staring into the shadows which draped the walls.

'What a fun!' said he. 'Always unicorns. Who has been thinking so hard upon a subject so bizarre?'

'This is wonderful!' cried Deacon. 'I have been trying to paint one all day. But how could you know it?'

'You have been thinking of them in this room.'

'Certainly.'

'But thoughts are things, my friend. When you imagine a thing you make a thing. You did not know it, *hein*? But I can see your unicorns because it is not only with my eye that I can see.'

'Do you mean to say that I create a thing which has never existed by merely thinking of it?'

'But certainly. It is the fact which lies under all other facts. That is why an evil thought is also a danger.'

'They are, I suppose, upon the astral plane?' said Moir.

'Ah, well, these are but words, my friends. They are there—somewhere—everywhere—I cannot tell myself. I see them. I could touch them.'

'You could not make *us* see them.'

'It is to materialise them. Hold! It is an experiment. But the power is wanting. Let us see what power we have, and then arrange what we shall do. May I place you as I wish?'

'You evidently know a great deal more about it than we do,' said Harvey Deacon; 'I wish that you would take complete control.'

'It may be that the conditions are not good. But we will try what we can do. Madame will sit where she is, I next, and this gentleman beside me. Meester Moir will sit next to madame, because it is well to have blacks and blondes in turn. So! And now with your permission I will turn the lights all out.'

'What is the advantage of the dark?' I asked.

'Because the force with which we deal is a vibration of ether and so also is light. We have the wires all for ourselves now—*hein*? You will not be frightened in the darkness, madame? What a fun is such a séance!'

At first the darkness appeared to be absolutely pitchy, but in a few minutes our eyes became so far accustomed to it that we could just make out each other's presence—very dimly and vaguely, it is true. I could see nothing else in the room—only the black loom of the motionless figures. We were all taking the matter much more seriously than we had ever done before.

'You will place your hands in front. It is hopeless that we touch, since we are so few round so large a table. You will compose yourself, madame, and if sleep should come to you you will not fight against it. And now we sit in silence and we expect—*hein?*'

So we sat in silence and expected, staring out into the blackness in front of us. A clock ticked in the passage. A dog barked intermittently far away. Once or twice a cab rattled past in the street, and the gleam of its lamps through the chink in the curtains was a cheerful break in that gloomy vigil. I felt those physical symptoms with which previous séances had made me familiar—the coldness of the feet, the tingling in the hands, the glow of the palms, the feeling of a cold wind upon the back. Strange little shooting pains came in my forearms, especially as it seemed to me in my left one, which was nearest to our visitor—due no doubt to disturbance of the vascular system, but worthy of some attention all the same. At the same time I was conscious of a strained feeling of expectancy which was almost painful. From the rigid, absolute silence of my companions I gathered that their nerves were as tense as my own.

And then suddenly a sound came out of the darkness—a low, sibilant sound, the quick, thin breathing of a woman. Quicker and thinner yet it came, as between clenched teeth, to end in a loud gasp with a dull rustle of cloth.

'What's that? Is all right?' someone asked in the darkness.

'Yes, all is right,' said the Frenchman. 'It is madame. She is in her trance. Now, gentlemen, if you will wait quiet you will see something, I think, which will interest you much.'

Still the ticking in the hall. Still the breathing, deeper and fuller now, from the medium. Still the occasional flash, more welcome than ever, of the passing lights of the hansoms. What a gap we were bridging, the half-raised veil of the eternal on the one side and the cabs of London on the other. The table was throbbing with a mighty pulse. It swayed steadily, rhythmically, with an easy swooping, scooping motion under our fingers. Sharp little raps and cracks came from its substance, file-firing, volley-firing, the sounds of a fagot burning briskly on a frosty night.

'There is much power,' said the Frenchman. 'See it on the table!'

I had thought it was some delusion of my own, but all could see it now. There was a greenish-yellow phosphorescent light—or I should say a luminous vapour rather than a light—which lay over the surface of the table. It rolled and wreathed and undulated in dim glimmering folds, turning and swirling like clouds of smoke. I could see the white, square-ended hands of the French medium in this baleful light. 'What a fun!' he cried. 'It is splendid!'

'Shall we call the alphabet?' asked Moir.

'But no—for we can do much better,' said our visitor. 'It is but a clumsy thing to tilt the table for every letter of the alphabet, and with such a medium as madame we should do better than that.'

'Yes, you will do better,' said a voice.

'Who was that? Who spoke? Was that you, Markham?'

'No, I did not speak.'

'It was madame who spoke.'

'But it was not her voice.'

'Is that you, Mrs Delamere?'

'It is not the medium, but it is the power which uses the organs of the medium,' said the strange, deep voice.

'Where is Mrs Delamere? It will not hurt her, I trust.'

'The medium is happy in another plane of existence. She has taken my place, as I have taken hers.'

'Who are you?'

'It cannot matter to you who I am. I am one who has lived as you are living, and who has died as you will die.'

We heard the creak and grate of a cab pulling up next door. There was an argument about the fare, and the cabman grumbled hoarsely down the street. The green-yellow cloud still swirled faintly over the table, dull elsewhere, but glowing into a dim luminosity in the direction of the medium. It seemed to be piling itself up in front of her. A sense of fear and cold struck into my heart. It seemed to me that lightly and flippantly we had approached the most real and august of sacraments, that communion with the dead of which the fathers of the Church had spoken.

'Don't you think we are going too far? Should we not break up this séance?' I cried.

But the others were all earnest to see the end of it. They laughed at my scruples.

'All the powers are made for use,' said Harvey Deacon. 'If we *can* do this, we *should* do this. Every new departure of knowledge has been called unlawful in its inception. It is right and proper that we should inquire into the nature of death.'

'It is right and proper,' said the voice.

'There, what more could you ask?' cried Moir, who was much excited. 'Let us have a test. Will you give us a test that you are really there?'

'What test do you demand?'

'Well, now—I have some coins in my pocket. Will you tell me how many?'

'We come back in the hope of teaching and of elevating, and not to guess childish riddles.'

'Ha, ha, Meester Moir, you catch it that time,' cried the Frenchman. 'But surely this is very good sense what the Control is saying.'

'It is a religion, not a game,' said the cold, hard voice.

'Exactly—the very view I take of it,' cried Moir, 'I am sure I am very sorry if I have asked a foolish question. You will not tell me who you are?'

'What does it matter?'

'Have you been a spirit long?'

'Yes.'

'How long?'

'We cannot reckon time as you do. Our conditions are different.'

'Are you happy?'

'Yes.'

'You would not wish to come back to life?'

'No—certainly not.'

'Are you busy?'

'We could not be happy if we were not busy.'

'What do you do?'

'I have said that the conditions are entirely different.'

'Can you give us no idea of your work?'

'We labour for our own improvement and for the advancement of others.'

'Do you like coming here tonight?'

'I am glad to come if I can do any good by coming.'

'Then to do good is your object?'

'It is the object of all life on every plane.'

'You see, Markham, that should answer your scruples.'

It did, for my doubts had passed and only interest remained.

'Have you pain in your life?' I asked.

'No; pain is a thing of the body.'

'Have you mental pain?'

'Yes; one may always be sad or anxious.'

'Do you meet the friends whom you have known on earth?'

'Some of them.'

'Why only some of them?'

'Only those who are sympathetic.'

'Do husbands meet wives?'

'Those who have truly loved.'

'And the others?'

'They are nothing to each other.'

'There must be a spiritual connection?'

'Of course.'

'Is what we are doing right?'

'If done in the right spirit.'

'What is the wrong spirit?'

'Curiosity and levity.'

'May harm come of that?'

'Very serious harm.'

'What sort of harm?'

'You may call up forces over which you have no control.'

'Evil forces?'

'Undeveloped forces.'

'You say they are dangerous. Dangerous to body or mind?'

'Sometimes to both.'

There was a pause, and the blackness seemed to grow blacker still, while the yellow-green fog swirled and smoked upon the table.

'Any questions you would like to ask, Moir?' said Harvey Deacon.

'Only this—do you pray in your world?'

'One should pray in every world.'

'Why?'

'Because it is the acknowledgement of forces outside ourselves.'

'What religion do you hold over there?'

'We differ exactly as you do.'

'You have no certain knowledge?'

'We have only faith.'

'These questions of religion,' said the Frenchman, 'they are of interest to you serious English people, but they are not so much fun. It seems to me that with this power here we might be able to have some great experience—*hein*? Something of which we could talk.'

'But nothing could be more interesting than this,' said Moir.

'Well, if you think so, that is very well,' the Frenchman answered, peevishly. 'For my part, it seems to me that I have heard all this before, and that tonight I should weesh to try some experiment with all this force which is given to us. But if you have other questions, then ask them, and when you are finish we can try something more.'

But the spell was broken. We asked and asked, but the medium sat silent in her chair. Only her deep, regular breathing showed that she was there. The mist still swirled upon the table.

'You have disturbed the harmony. She will not answer.'

'But we have learned already all that she can tell—*hein*? For my part I wish to see something that I have never seen before.'

'What then?'

'You will let me try?'

'What would you do?'

'I have said to you that thoughts are things. Now I wish to *prove* it to you, and to show you that which is only a thought. Yes, yes, I can do it and you will see. Now I ask you only to sit still and say nothing, and keep ever your hands quiet upon the table.'

The room was blacker and more silent than ever. The same feeling of apprehension which had lain heavily upon me at the beginning of the séance was back at my heart once more. The roots of my hair were tingling.

'It is working! It is working!' cried the Frenchman, and there was a crack in his voice as he spoke which told me that he also was strung to his tightest.

The luminous fog drifted slowly off the table, and wavered and flickered across the room. There in the farther and darkest corner it gathered and glowed, hardening down into a shining core—a strange, shifty, luminous, and yet non-illuminating patch of radiance, bright itself, but throwing no rays into the darkness. It had changed from a greenish-yellow to a dusky sullen red. Then round this centre there coiled a dark, smoky substance, thickening, hardening, growing denser and blacker. And then the light went out, smothered in that which had grown round it.

'It has gone.'

'Hush—there's something in the room.'

We heard it in the corner where the light had been, something which breathed deeply and fidgeted in the darkness.

'What is it? Le Duc, what have you done?'

'It is all right. No harm will come.' The Frenchman's voice was treble with agitation.

'Good heavens, Moir, there's a large animal in the room. Here it is, close by my chair! Go away! Go away!'

It was Harvey Deacon's voice, and then came the sound of a blow upon some hard object. And then... And then... how can I tell you what happened then?

Some huge thing hurtled against us in the darkness, rearing, stamping, smashing, springing, snorting. The table was splintered. We were scattered in every direction. It clattered and scrambled amongst us, rushing with horrible energy from one corner of the room to another. We were all screaming with fear, grovelling upon our hands and knees to get away from it. Something trod upon my left hand, and I felt the bones splinter under the weight.

'A light! A light!' someone yelled.

'Moir, you have matches, matches!'

'No, I have none. Deacon, where are the matches? For God's sake, the matches!'

'I can't find them. Here, you Frenchman, stop it!'

'It is beyond me. Oh, *mon Dieu,* I cannot stop it. The door! Where is the door?'

My hand, by good luck, lit upon the handle as I groped about in the darkness. The hard-breathing, snorting, rushing creature tore past me and butted with a fearful crash against the oaken partition. The instant that it had passed I turned the handle, and next moment we were all outside, and the door shut behind us. From within came a horrible crashing and rending and stamping.

'What is it? In Heaven's name, what is it?'

'A horse. I saw it when the door opened. But Mrs Delamere—?'

'We must fetch her out. Come on, Markham; the longer we wait the less we shall like it.'

He flung open the door and we rushed in. She was there on the ground amidst the splinters of her chair. We seized her and dragged her swiftly out, and as we gained the door I looked over my shoulder into the darkness. There were two strange eyes glowing at us, a rattle of hoofs, and I had just time to slam the door when there came a crash upon it which split it from top to bottom.

'It's coming through! It's coming!'

'Run, run for your lives!' cried the Frenchman.

Another crash, and something shot through the riven door. It was a long white spike, gleaming in the lamp-light. For a moment it shone before us, and then with a snap it disappeared again.

'Quick! Quick! This way!' Harvey Deacon shouted. 'Carry her in! Here! Quick!'

We had taken refuge in the dining-room, and shut the heavy oak door. We laid the senseless woman upon the sofa, and as we did so, Moir, the hard man of business, drooped and fainted across the hearthrug. Harvey Deacon was as white as a corpse, jerking and twitching like an epileptic. With a crash we heard the studio door fly to pieces, and the snorting and stamping were in the passage, up and down, up and down, shaking the house with their fury. The Frenchman had sunk his face on his hands, and sobbed like a frightened child.

'What shall we do?' I shook him roughly by the shoulder. 'Is a gun any use?'

'No, no. The power will pass. Then it will end.'

'You might have killed us all—you unspeakable fool—with your infernal experiments.'

'I did not know. How could I tell that it would be frightened? It is mad with terror. It was his fault. He struck it.'

Harvey Deacon sprang up. 'Good heavens!' he cried.

A terrible scream sounded through the house.

'It's my wife! Here, I'm going out. If it's the Evil One himself I am going out!'

He had thrown open the door and rushed out into the passage. At the end of it, at the foot of the stairs, Mrs Deacon was lying senseless, struck down by the sight which she had seen. But there was nothing else.

With eyes of horror we looked about us, but all was perfectly quiet and still. I approached the black square of the studio door, expecting with every slow step that some atrocious shape would hurl itself out of it. But nothing came, and all was silent inside the room. Peeping and peering, our hearts in our mouths, we came to the very threshold, and stared into the darkness. There was still no sound, but in one direction there was also no darkness. A luminous, glowing cloud, with an incandescent centre, hovered in the corner of the room. Slowly it dimmed and faded, growing thinner and fainter, until at last the same dense, velvety blackness filled the whole studio. And with the last flickering gleam of that baleful light the Frenchman broke into a shout of joy.

'What a fun!' he cried. 'No one is hurt, and only the door broken, and the ladies frightened. But, my friends, we have done what has never been done before.'

'And as far as I can help,' said Harvey Deacon, 'it will certainly never be done again.'

And that was what befell on the 14th of April last at No. 17 Badderly Gardens. I began by saying that it would seem too grotesque to dogmatise as to what it was which actually did occur; but I give my impressions, *our* impressions (since they are corroborated by Harvey Deacon and John Moir), for what they are worth. You may, if it pleases you, imagine that we were the victims of an elaborate and extraordinary hoax. Or you may think with us that we underwent a very real and a very terrible experience. Or perhaps you may know more than we do of such occult matters, and can inform us of some similar occurrence. In this latter case a letter to William Markham, 146M, The Albany, would help to throw a light upon that which is very dark to us.

THE LEATHER FUNNEL

My friend, Lionel Dacre, lived in the Avenue de Wagram, Paris. His house was that small one, with the iron railings and grass plot in front of it, on the left-hand side as you pass down from the Arc de Triomphe. I fancy that it had been there long before the avenue was constructed, for the grey tiles were stained with lichens, and the walls were mildewed and discoloured with age. It looked a small house from the street, five windows in front, if I remember right, but it deepened into a single long chamber at the back. It was here that Dacre had that singular library of occult literature, and the fantastic curiosities which served as a hobby for himself, and an amusement for his friends. A wealthy man of refined and eccentric tastes, he had spent much of his life and fortune in gathering together what was said to be a unique private collection of Talmudic, cabalistic, and magical works, many of them of great rarity and value. His tastes leaned toward the marvellous and the monstrous, and I have heard that his experiments in the direction of the unknown have passed all the bounds of civilisation and of decorum. To his English friends he never alluded to such matters, and took the tone of the student and *virtuoso*; but a Frenchman whose tastes were of the same nature has assured me that the worst excesses of the black mass have been perpetrated in that large and lofty hall, which is lined with the shelves of his books, and the cases of his museum.

Dacre's appearance was enough to show that his deep interest in these psychic matters was intellectual rather than spiritual. There was no trace of asceticism upon his heavy face, but there was much mental force in his huge, dome-like skull, which curved upward from amongst his thinning locks, like a snow-peak above its fringe of fir trees. His knowledge was greater than his wisdom, and his powers were far superior to his character. The small bright eyes, buried deeply in his fleshy face, twinkled with intelligence and an unabated curiosity of life, but they were the eyes of a sensualist and an egotist. Enough of the man, for he is dead now, poor devil, dead at the very time that he had made sure that he had at last discovered the elixir of life. It is not with his complex character that I have to deal, but with the very strange and inexplicable incident which had its rise in my visit to him in the early spring of the year '82.

I had known Dacre in England, for my researches in the Assyrian Room of the British Museum had been conducted at the time when he was endeavouring to establish a mystic and esoteric meaning in the Babylonian tablets, and this community of interests had brought us together. Chance remarks had led to daily conversation, and that to something verging upon friendship. I had promised him that on my next visit to Paris I would call upon him. At the time when I was able to fulfil my compact I was living in a cottage at Fontainebleau, and as the evening trains were inconvenient, he asked me to spend the night in his house.

'I have only that one spare couch,' said he, pointing to a broad sofa in his large salon; 'I hope that you will manage to be comfortable there.'

It was a singular bedroom, with its high walls of brown volumes, but there could be no more agreeable furniture to a bookworm like myself, and there is no scent so pleasant to my nostrils as that faint, subtle reek which comes from an ancient book. I assured him that I could desire no more charming chamber, and no more congenial surroundings.

'If the fittings are neither convenient nor conventional, they are at least costly,' said he, looking round at his shelves. 'I have expended nearly a quarter of a million of money upon these objects which surround you. Books, weapons, gems, carvings, tapestries, images—there is hardly a thing here which has not its history, and it is generally one worth telling.'

He was seated as he spoke at one side of the open fireplace, and I at the other. His reading-table was on his right, and the strong lamp above it ringed it with a very vivid circle of golden light. A half-rolled palimpsest lay in the centre, and around it were many quaint articles of bric-à-brac. One of these was a large funnel, such as is used for filling wine casks. It appeared to be made of black wood, and to be rimmed with discoloured brass.

'That is a curious thing,' I remarked. 'What is the history of that?'

'Ah!' said he, 'it is the very question which I have had occasion to ask myself. I would give a good deal to know. Take it in your hands and examine it.'

I did so, and found that what I had imagined to be wood was in reality leather, though age had dried it into an extreme hardness. It was a large funnel, and might hold a quart when full. The brass rim encircled the wide end, but the narrow was also tipped with metal.

'What do you make of it?' asked Dacre.

'I should imagine that it belonged to some vintner or maltster in the Middle Ages,' said I. 'I have seen in England leathern drinking flagons of the seventeenth century—"black jacks" as they were called—which were of the same colour and hardness as this filler.'

'I dare say the date would be about the same,' said Dacre, 'and, no doubt, also, it was used for filling a vessel with liquid. If my suspicions are correct, however, it was a queer vintner who used it, and a very singular cask which was filled. Do you observe nothing strange at the spout end of the funnel.'

As I held it to the light I observed that at a spot some five inches above the brass tip the narrow neck of the leather funnel was all haggled and scored, as if someone had notched it round with a blunt knife. Only at that point was there any roughening of the dead black surface.

'Someone has tried to cut off the neck.'

'Would you call it a cut?'

'It is torn and lacerated. It must have taken some strength to leave these marks on such tough material, whatever the instrument may have been. But what do you think of it? I can tell that you know more than you say.'

Dacre smiled, and his little eyes twinkled with knowledge.

'Have you included the psychology of dreams among your learned studies?' he asked.

'I did not even know that there was such a psychology.'

'My dear sir, that shelf above the gem case is filled with volumes, from Albertus Magnus onward, which deal with no other subject. It is a science in itself.'

'A science of charlatans.'

'The charlatan is always the pioneer. From the astrologer came the astronomer, from the alchemist the chemist, from the mesmerist the experimental psychologist. The quack of yesterday is the professor of tomorrow. Even such subtle and elusive things as dreams will in time be reduced to system and order. When that time comes the researches of our friends on the bookshelf yonder will no longer be the amusement of the mystic, but the foundations of a science.'

'Supposing that is so, what has the science of dreams to do with a large, black, brass-rimmed funnel?'

'I will tell you. You know that I have an agent who is always on the lookout for rarities and curiosities for my collection. Some days ago he heard of a dealer upon one of the Quais who had acquired some old rubbish found in a cupboard in an ancient house at the back of the Rue Mathurin, in the Quartier Latin. The dining-room of this old house is decorated with a coat of arms, chevrons, and bars rouge upon a field argent, which prove, upon inquiry, to be the shield of Nicholas de la Reynie, a high official of King Louis XIV. There can be no doubt that the other articles in the cupboard date back to the early days of that king. The inference is, therefore, that they were all the property of this Nicholas de la Reynie, who was, as I understand, the gentleman specially concerned with the maintenance and execution of the Draconic laws of that epoch.'

'What then?'

'I would ask you now to take the funnel into your hands once more and to examine the upper brass rim. Can you make out any lettering upon it?'

There were certainly some scratches upon it, almost obliterated by time. The general effect was of several letters, the last of which bore some resemblance to a B.

'You make it a B?'

'Yes, I do.'

'So do I. In fact, I have no doubt whatever that it is a B.'

'But the nobleman you mentioned would have had R for his initial.'

'Exactly! That's the beauty of it. He owned this curious object, and yet he had someone else's initials upon it. Why did he do this?'

'I can't imagine; can you?'

'Well, I might, perhaps, guess. Do you observe something drawn a little farther along the rim?'

'I should say it was a crown.'

'It is undoubtedly a crown; but if you examine it in a good light, you will convince yourself that it is not an ordinary crown. It is a heraldic crown—a badge of rank, and it consists of an alternation of four pearls and strawberry leaves, the proper badge of a marquis. We may infer, therefore, that the person whose initials end in B was entitled to wear that coronet.'

'Then this common leather filler belonged to a marquis?'

Dacre gave a peculiar smile.

'Or to some member of the family of a marquis,' said he. 'So much we have clearly gathered from this engraved rim.'

'But what has all this to do with dreams?' I do not know whether it was from a look upon Dacre's face, or from some subtle suggestion in his manner, but a feeling of repulsion, of unreasoning horror, came upon me as I looked at the gnarled old lump of leather.

'I have more than once received important information through my dreams,' said my companion in the didactic manner which he loved to affect. 'I make it a rule now when I am in doubt upon any material point to place the article in question beside me as I sleep, and to hope for some enlightenment. The process does not appear to me to be very obscure, though it has not yet received the blessing of orthodox science. According to my theory, any object which has been intimately associated with any supreme paroxysm of human emotion, whether it be joy or pain, will retain a certain atmosphere or association which it is capable of communicating to a sensitive mind. By a sensitive mind I do not mean an abnormal one, but such a trained and educated mind as you or I possess.'

'You mean, for example, that if I slept beside that old sword upon the wall, I might dream of some bloody incident in which that very sword took part?'

'An excellent example, for, as a matter of fact, that sword was used in that fashion by me, and I saw in my sleep the death of its owner, who perished in a brisk skirmish, which I have been unable to identify, but which occurred at the time of the wars of the Frondists. If you think of it, some of our popular observances show that the fact has already been recognised by our ancestors, although we, in our wisdom, have classed it among superstitions.'

'For example?'

'Well, the placing of the bride's cake beneath the pillow in order that the sleeper may have pleasant dreams. That is one of several instances which you will find set forth in a small *brochure* which I am myself writing upon the subject. But to come back to the point, I slept one night with this funnel beside me, and I had a dream which certainly throws a curious light upon its use and origin.'

'What did you dream?'

'I dreamed—' He paused, and an intent look of interest came over his massive face. 'By Jove, that's well thought of,' said he. 'This really will be an exceedingly interesting experiment. You are yourself a psychic subject—with nerves which respond readily to any impression.'

'I have never tested myself in that direction.'

'Then we shall test you tonight. Might I ask you as a very great favour, when you occupy that couch tonight, to sleep with this old funnel placed by the side of your pillow?'

The request seemed to me a grotesque one; but I have myself, in my complex nature, a hunger after all which is bizarre and fantastic. I had not the faintest belief in Dacre's theory, nor any hopes for success in such an experiment; yet it amused me that the experiment should be made. Dacre, with great gravity, drew a small stand to the head of my settee, and placed the funnel upon it. Then, after a short conversation, he wished me good night and left me.

*

I sat for some little time smoking by the smouldering fire, and turning over in my mind the curious incident which had occurred, and the strange experience which might lie before me. Sceptical as I was, there was something impressive in the assurance of Dacre's manner, and my extraordinary surroundings, the huge room with the strange and often sinister objects which were hung round it, struck solemnity into my soul. Finally I undressed, and turning out the lamp, I lay down. After long tossing I fell asleep. Let me try to describe as accurately as I can the scene which came to me in my dreams. It stands out now in my memory more clearly than anything which I have seen with my waking eyes.

There was a room which bore the appearance of a vault. Four spandrels from the corners ran up to join a sharp, cup-shaped roof. The architecture was rough, but very strong. It was evidently part of a great building.

Three men in black, with curious, top-heavy, black velvet hats, sat in a line upon a red-carpeted dais. Their faces were very solemn and sad. On the left stood two long-gowned men with portfolios in their hands, which seemed to be stuffed with papers. Upon the right, looking toward me, was a small woman with blonde hair and singular, light-blue eyes—the eyes of a child. She was past her first youth, but could not yet be called middle-aged. Her figure was inclined to stoutness and her bearing was proud and confident. Her face was pale, but serene. It was a curious face, comely and yet feline, with a subtle suggestion of cruelty about the straight, strong little mouth and chubby jaw. She was draped in some sort of loose, white gown. Beside her stood a thin, eager priest, who whispered in her ear, and continually raised a crucifix before her eyes. She turned her head and looked fixedly past the crucifix at the three men in black, who were, I felt, her judges.

As I gazed the three men stood up and said something, but I could distinguish no words, though I was aware that it was the central one who was speaking. They then swept out of the room, followed by the two men with the papers. At the same instant several rough-looking fellows in stout jerkins came bustling in and removed first the red carpet, and then the boards which formed the dais, so as to entirely clear the room. When this screen was removed I saw some singular articles of furniture behind it. One looked like a bed with wooden rollers at each end, and a winch handle to regulate its length. Another was a wooden horse. There were several other curious objects, and a number of swinging cords which played over pulleys. It was not unlike a modern gymnasium.

When the room had been cleared there appeared a new figure upon the scene. This was a tall, thin person clad in black, with a gaunt and austere face. The aspect of the man made me shudder. His clothes were all shining with grease and mottled with stains. He bore himself with a slow and impressive dignity, as if he took command of all things from the instant of his entrance. In spite of his rude appearance and sordid dress, it was now *his* business, *his* room, his to command. He carried a coil of light ropes over his left forearm. The lady looked him up and down with a searching glance, but her expression was unchanged. It was confident—even defiant. But it was very different with the priest. His face was ghastly white, and I saw the moisture glisten and run on his high, sloping forehead. He threw up his hands in prayer and he stooped continually to mutter frantic words in the lady's ear.

The man in black now advanced, and taking one of the cords from his left arm, he bound the woman's hands together. She held them meekly toward him as he did so. Then he took her arm with a rough grip and led her toward the wooden horse, which was little higher than her waist. On to this she was lifted and laid, with her back upon it, and her face to the ceiling, while the priest, quivering with horror, had rushed out of the room. The woman's lips were moving rapidly, and though I could hear nothing I knew that she was praying. Her feet hung down on either side of the horse, and I saw that the rough varlets in attendance had fastened cords to her ankles and secured the other ends to iron rings in the stone floor.

My heart sank within me as I saw these ominous preparations, and yet I was held by the fascination of horror, and I could not take my eyes from the strange spectacle. A man had entered the room with a bucket of water in either hand. Another followed with a third bucket. They were laid beside the wooden horse. The second man had a wooden dipper—a bowl with a straight handle—in his other hand. This he gave to the man in black. At the same moment one of the varlets approached with a dark object in his hand, which even in my dream filled me with a vague feeling of familiarity. It was a leathern filler. With horrible energy he thrust it—but I could stand no more. My hair stood on end with horror. I writhed, I struggled, I broke through the bonds of sleep, and I burst with a shriek into my own life, and found myself lying shivering with terror in the huge library, with the moonlight flooding through the window and throwing strange silver and black traceries upon the opposite wall. Oh, what a blessed relief to feel that I was back in the nineteenth century—back out of that mediæval vault into a world where men had human hearts within their bosoms. I sat up on my couch, trembling in every limb, my mind divided between thankfulness and horror. To think that such things were ever done—that they *could* be done without God striking the villains dead. Was it all a fantasy, or did it really stand for something which had happened in the black, cruel days of the world's history? I sank my throbbing head upon my shaking hands. And then, suddenly, my heart seemed to stand still in my bosom, and I could not even scream, so great was my terror. Something was advancing toward me through the darkness of the room.

It is a horror coming upon a horror which breaks a man's spirit. I could not reason, I could not pray; I could only sit like a frozen image, and glare at the dark figure which was coming down the great room. And then it moved out into the white lane of moonlight, and I breathed once more. It was Dacre, and his face showed that he was as frightened as myself.

'Was that you? For God's sake what's the matter?' he asked in a husky voice.

'Oh, Dacre, I am glad to see you! I have been down into hell. It was dreadful.'

'Then it was you who screamed?'

'I dare say it was.'

'It rang through the house. The servants are all terrified.' He struck a match and lit the lamp. 'I think we may get the fire to burn up again,' he added, throwing some logs upon the embers. 'Good God, my dear chap, how white you are! You look as if you had seen a ghost.'

'So I have—several ghosts.'

'The leather funnel has acted, then?'

'I wouldn't sleep near the infernal thing again for all the money you could offer me.'

Dacre chuckled.

'I expected that you would have a lively night of it,' said he. 'You took it out of me in return, for that scream of yours wasn't a very pleasant sound at two in the morning. I suppose from what you say that you have seen the whole dreadful business.'

'What dreadful business?'

'The torture of the water—the "Extraordinary Question," as it was called in the genial days of "Le Roi Soleil." Did you stand it out to the end?'

'No, thank God, I awoke before it really began.'

'Ah! it is just as well for you. I held out till the third bucket. Well, it is an old story, and they are all in their graves now anyhow, so what does it matter how they got there? I suppose that you have no idea what it was that you have seen?'

'The torture of some criminal. She must have been a terrible malefactor indeed if her crimes are in proportion to her penalty.'

'Well, we have that small consolation,' said Dacre, wrapping his dressing-gown round him and crouching closer to the fire. 'They *were* in proportion to her penalty. That is to say, if I am correct in the lady's identity.'

'How could you possibly know her identity?'

For answer Dacre took down an old vellum-covered volume from the shelf.

'Just listen to this,' said he; 'it is in the French of the seventeenth century, but I will give a rough translation as I go. You will judge for yourself whether I have solved the riddle or not.

'"The prisoner was brought before the Grand Chambers and Tournelles of Parliament, sitting as a court of justice, charged with the murder of Master Dreux d'Aubray, her father, and of her two brothers, MM d'Aubray, one being civil lieutenant, and the other a counsellor of Parliament. In person it seemed hard to believe that she had really done such wicked deeds, for she was of a mild appearance, and of short stature, with a fair skin and blue eyes. Yet the Court, having found her guilty, condemned her to the ordinary and to the extraordinary question in order that she might be forced to name her accomplices, after which she should be carried in a cart to the Place de Grève, there to have her head cut off, her body being afterwards burned and her ashes scattered to the winds."

'The date of this entry is July 16, 1676.'

'It is interesting,' said I, 'but not convincing. How do you prove the two women to be the same?'

'I am coming to that. The narrative goes on to tell of the woman's behaviour when questioned. "When the executioner approached her she recognised him by the cords which he held in his hands, and she at once held out her own hands to him, looking at him from head to foot without uttering a word." How's that?'

'Yes, it was so.'

'"She gazed without wincing upon the wooden horse and rings which had twisted so many limbs and caused so many shrieks of agony. When her eyes fell upon the three pails of water, which were all ready for her, she said with a smile, 'All that water must have been brought here for the purpose of drowning me, Monsieur. You have no idea, I trust, of making a person of my small stature swallow it all.'" Shall I read the details of the torture?'

'No, for Heaven's sake, don't.'

'Here is a sentence which must surely show you that what is here recorded is the very scene which you have gazed upon tonight: "The good Abbé Pirot, unable to contemplate the agonies which were suffered by his penitent, had hurried from the room." Does that convince you?'

'It does entirely. There can be no question that it is indeed the same event. But who, then, is this lady whose appearance was so attractive and whose end was so horrible?'

For answer Dacre came across to me, and placed the small lamp upon the table which stood by my bed. Lifting up the ill-omened filler, he turned the brass rim so that the light fell full upon it. Seen in this way the engraving seemed clearer than on the night before.

'We have already agreed that this is the badge of a marquis or of a marquise,' said he. 'We have also settled that the last letter is B.'

'It is undoubtedly so.'

'I now suggest to you that the other letters from left to right are, M, M, a small d, A, a small d, and then the final B.'

'Yes, I am sure that you are right. I can make out the two small d's quite plainly.'

'What I have read to you tonight,' said Dacre, 'is the official record of the trial of Marie Madeleine d'Aubray, Marquise de Brinvilliers, one of the most famous poisoners and murderers of all time.'

I sat in silence, overwhelmed at the extraordinary nature of the incident, and at the completeness of the proof with which Dacre had exposed its real meaning. In a vague way I remembered some details of the woman's career, her unbridled debauchery, the cold-blooded and protracted torture of her sick father, the murder of her brothers for motives of petty gain. I recollected also that the bravery of her end had done something to atone for the horror of her life, and that all Paris had sympathised with her last moments, and blessed her as a martyr within a few days of the time when they had cursed her as a murderess. One objection, and one only, occurred to my mind.

'How came her initials and her badge of rank upon the filler? Surely they did not carry their mediæval homage to the nobility to the point of decorating instruments of torture with their titles?'

'I was puzzled with the same point,' said Dacre, 'but it admits of a simple explanation. The case excited extraordinary interest at the time, and nothing could be more natural than that La Reynie, the head of the police, should retain this filler as a grim souvenir. It was not often that a marchioness of France underwent the extraordinary question. That he should engrave her initials upon it for the information of others was surely a very ordinary proceeding upon his part.'

'And this?' I asked, pointing to the marks upon the leathern neck.

'She was a cruel tigress,' said Dacre, as he turned away. 'I think it is evident that like other tigresses her teeth were both strong and sharp.'

THE TERROR OF BLUE JOHN GAP

THE following narrative was found among the papers of Dr James Hardcastle, who died of phthisis on February 4, 1908, at 36, Upper Coventry Flats, South Kensington. Those who knew him best, while refusing to express an opinion upon this particular statement, are unanimous in asserting that he was a man of a sober and scientific turn of mind, absolutely devoid of imagination, and most unlikely to invent any abnormal series of events. The paper was contained in an envelope, which was docketed, 'A Short Account of the Circumstances which occurred near Miss Allerton's Farm in North-West Derbyshire in the Spring of Last Year.' The envelope was sealed, and on the other side was written in pencil—

'Dear Seaton,—

'It may interest, and perhaps pain you, to know that the incredulity with which you met my story has prevented me from ever opening my mouth upon the subject again. I leave this record after my death, and perhaps strangers may be found to have more confidence in me than my friend.'

Inquiry has failed to elicit who this Seaton may have been. I may add that the visit of the deceased to Allerton's Farm, and the general nature of the alarm there, apart from his particular explanation, have been absolutely established. With this foreword I append his account exactly as he left it. It is in the form of a diary, some entries in which have been expanded, while a few have been erased.

*

April 17.—Already I feel the benefit of this wonderful upland air. The farm of the Allertons lies fourteen hundred and twenty feet above sea-level, so it may well be a bracing climate. Beyond the usual morning cough I have very little discomfort, and, what with the fresh milk and the home-grown mutton, I have every chance of putting on weight. I think Saunderson will be pleased.

The two Miss Allertons are charmingly quaint and kind, two dear little hard-working old maids, who are ready to lavish all the heart which might have gone out to husband and to children upon an invalid stranger. Truly, the old maid is a most useful person, one of the reserve forces of the community. They talk of the superfluous woman, but what would the poor superfluous man do without her kindly presence? By the way, in their simplicity they very quickly let out the reason why Saunderson recommended their farm. The Professor rose from the ranks himself, and I believe that in his youth he was not above scaring crows in these very fields.

It is a most lonely spot, and the walks are picturesque in the extreme. The farm consists of grazing land lying at the bottom of an irregular valley. On each side are the fantastic limestone hills, formed of rock so soft that you can break it away with your hands. All this country is hollow. Could you strike it with some gigantic hammer it would boom like a drum, or possibly cave in altogether and expose some huge subterranean sea. A great sea there must surely be, for on all sides the streams run into the mountain itself, never to reappear. There are gaps everywhere amid the rocks, and when you pass through them you find yourself in great caverns, which wind down into the bowels of the earth. I have a small bicycle lamp, and it is a perpetual joy to me to carry it into these weird solitudes, and to see the wonderful silver and black effects when I throw its light upon the stalactites which drape the lofty roofs. Shut off the lamp, and you are in the blackest darkness. Turn it on, and it is a scene from the Arabian Nights.

But there is one of these strange openings in the earth which has a special interest, for it is the handiwork, not of nature, but of man. I had never heard of Blue John when I came to these parts. It is the name given to a peculiar mineral of a beautiful purple shade, which is only found at one or two places in the world. It is so rare that an ordinary vase of Blue John would be valued at a great price. The Romans, with that extraordinary instinct of theirs, discovered that it was to be found in this valley, and sank a horizontal shaft deep into the mountain side. The opening of their mine has been called Blue John Gap, a clean-cut arch in the rock, the mouth all overgrown with bushes. It is a goodly passage which the Roman miners have cut, and it intersects some of the great water-worn caves, so that if you enter Blue John Gap you would do well to mark your steps and to have a good store of candles, or you may never make your way back to the daylight again. I have not yet gone deeply into it, but this very day I stood at the mouth of the arched tunnel, and peering down into the black recesses beyond, I vowed that when my health returned I would devote some holiday to exploring those mysterious depths and finding out for myself how far the Roman had penetrated into the Derbyshire hills.

Strange how superstitious these countrymen are! I should have thought better of young Armitage, for he is a man of some education and character, and a very fine fellow for his station in life. I was standing at the Blue John Gap when he came across the field to me.

'Well, doctor,' said he, 'you're not afraid, anyhow.'

'Afraid!' I answered. 'Afraid of what?'

'Of it,' said he, with a jerk of his thumb towards the black vault, 'of the Terror that lives in the Blue John Cave.'

How absurdly easy it is for a legend to arise in a lonely countryside! I examined him as to the reasons for his weird belief. It seems that from time to time sheep have been missing from the fields, carried bodily away, according to Armitage. That they could have wandered away of their own accord and disappeared among the mountains was an explanation to which he would not listen. On one occasion a pool of blood had been found, and some tufts of wool. That also, I pointed out, could be explained in a perfectly natural way. Further, the nights upon which sheep disappeared were invariably very dark, cloudy nights with no moon. This I met with the obvious retort that those were the nights which a commonplace sheep-stealer would naturally choose for his work. On one occasion a gap had been made in a wall, and some of the stones scattered for a considerable distance. Human agency again, in my opinion. Finally, Armitage clinched all his arguments by telling me that he had actually heard the Creature—indeed, that anyone could hear it who remained long enough at the Gap. It was a distant roaring of an immense volume. I could not but smile at this, knowing, as I do, the strange reverberations which come out of an underground water system running amid the chasms of a limestone formation. My incredulity annoyed Armitage so that he turned and left me with some abruptness.

And now comes the queer point about the whole business. I was still standing near the mouth of the cave turning over in my mind the various statements of Armitage, and reflecting how readily they could be explained away, when suddenly, from the depth of the tunnel beside me, there issued a most extraordinary sound. How shall I describe it? First of all, it seemed to be a great distance away, far down in the bowels of the earth. Secondly, in spite of this suggestion of distance, it was very loud. Lastly, it was not a boom nor a crash, such as one would associate with falling water or tumbling rock, but it was a high whine, tremulous and vibrating, almost like the whinnying of a horse. It was certainly a most remarkable experience, and one which for a moment, I must admit, gave a new significance to Armitage's words. I waited by the Blue John Gap for half an hour or more, but there was no return of the sound, so at last I wandered back to the farmhouse, rather mystified by what had occurred. Decidedly I shall explore that cavern when my strength is restored. Of course, Armitage's explanation is too absurd for discussion, and yet that sound was certainly very strange. It still rings in my ears as I write.

April 20.—In the last three days I have made several expeditions to the Blue John Gap, and have even penetrated some short distance, but my bicycle lantern is so small and weak that I dare not trust myself very far. I shall do the thing more systematically. I have heard no sound at all, and could almost believe that I had been the victim of some hallucination suggested, perhaps, by Armitage's conversation. Of course, the whole idea is absurd, and yet I must confess that those bushes at the entrance of the cave do present an appearance as if some heavy creature had forced its way through them. I begin to be keenly interested. I have said nothing to the Miss Allertons, for they are quite superstitious enough already, but I have bought some candles, and mean to investigate for myself.

I observed this morning that among the numerous tufts of sheep's wool which lay among the bushes near the cavern there was one which was smeared with blood. Of course, my reason tells me that if sheep wander into such rocky places they are likely to injure themselves, and yet somehow that splash of crimson gave me a sudden shock, and for a moment I found myself shrinking back in horror from the old Roman arch. A fetid breath seemed to ooze from the black depths into which I peered. Could it indeed be possible that some nameless thing, some dreadful presence, was lurking down yonder? I should have been incapable of such feelings in the days of my strength, but one grows more nervous and fanciful when one's health is shaken.

For the moment I weakened in my resolution, and was ready to leave the secret of the old mine, if one exists, for ever unsolved. But tonight my interest has returned and my nerves grown more steady. Tomorrow I trust that I shall have gone more deeply into this matter.

April 22.—Let me try and set down as accurately as I can my extraordinary experience of yesterday. I started in the afternoon, and made my way to the Blue John Gap. I confess that my misgivings returned as I gazed into its depths, and I wished that I had brought a companion to share my exploration. Finally, with a return of resolution, I lit my candle, pushed my way through the briars, and descended into the rocky shaft.

It went down at an acute angle for some fifty feet, the floor being covered with broken stone. Thence there extended a long, straight passage cut in the solid rock. I am no geologist, but the lining of this corridor was certainly of some harder material than limestone, for there were points where I could actually see the tool-marks which the old miners had left in their excavation, as fresh as if they had been done yesterday. Down this strange, old-world corridor I stumbled, my feeble flame throwing a dim circle of light around me, which made the shadows beyond the more threatening and obscure. Finally, I came to a spot where the Roman tunnel opened into a water-worn cavern—a huge hall, hung with long white icicles of lime deposit. From this central chamber I could dimly perceive that a number of passages worn by the subterranean streams wound away into the depths of the earth. I was standing there wondering whether I had better return, or whether I dare venture farther into this dangerous labyrinth, when my eyes fell upon something at my feet which strongly arrested my attention.

The greater part of the floor of the cavern was covered with boulders of rock or with hard incrustations of lime, but at this particular point there had been a drip from the distant roof, which had left a patch of soft mud. In the very centre of this there was a huge mark—an ill-defined blotch, deep, broad and irregular, as if a great boulder had fallen upon it. No loose stone lay near, however, nor was there anything to account for the impression. It was far too large to be caused by any possible animal, and besides, there was only the one, and the patch of mud was of such a size that no reasonable stride could have covered it. As I rose from the examination of that singular mark and then looked round into the black shadows which hemmed me in, I must confess that I felt for a moment a most unpleasant sinking of my heart, and that, do what I could, the candle trembled in my outstretched hand.

I soon recovered my nerve, however, when I reflected how absurd it was to associate so huge and shapeless a mark with the track of any known animal. Even an elephant could not have produced it. I determined, therefore, that I would not be scared by vague and senseless fears from carrying out my exploration. Before proceeding, I took good note of a curious rock formation in the wall by which I could recognise the entrance of the Roman tunnel. The precaution was very necessary, for the great cave, so far as I could see it, was intersected by passages. Having made sure of my position, and reassured myself by examining my spare candles and my matches, I advanced slowly over the rocky and uneven surface of the cavern.

And now I come to the point where I met with such sudden and desperate disaster. A stream, some twenty feet broad, ran across my path, and I walked for some little distance along the bank to find a spot where I could cross dry-shod. Finally, I came to a place where a single flat boulder lay near the centre, which I could reach in a stride. As it chanced, however, the rock had been cut away and made top-heavy by the rush of the stream, so that it tilted over as I landed on it and shot me into the ice-cold water. My candle went out, and I found myself floundering about in utter and absolute darkness.

I staggered to my feet again, more amused than alarmed by my adventure. The candle had fallen from my hand, and was lost in the stream, but I had two others in my pocket, so that it was of no importance. I got one of them ready, and drew out my box of matches to light it. Only then did I realise my position. The box had been soaked in my fall into the river. It was impossible to strike the matches.

A cold hand seemed to close round my heart as I realised my position. The darkness was opaque and horrible. It was so utter that one put one's hand up to one's face as if to press off something solid. I stood still, and by an effort I steadied myself. I tried to reconstruct in my mind a map of the floor of the cavern as I had last seen it. Alas! the bearings which had impressed themselves upon my mind were high on the wall, and not to be found by touch. Still, I remembered in a general way how the sides were situated, and I hoped that by groping my way along them I should at last come to the opening of the Roman tunnel. Moving very slowly, and continually striking against the rocks, I set out on this desperate quest.

But I very soon realised how impossible it was. In that black, velvety darkness one lost all one's bearings in an instant. Before I had made a dozen paces, I was utterly bewildered as to my whereabouts. The rippling of the stream, which was the one sound audible, showed me where it lay, but the moment that I left its bank I was utterly lost. The idea of finding my way back in absolute darkness through that limestone labyrinth was clearly an impossible one.

I sat down upon a boulder and reflected upon my unfortunate plight. I had not told anyone that I proposed to come to the Blue John mine, and it was unlikely that a search party would come after me. Therefore I must trust to my own resources to get clear of the danger. There was only one hope, and that was that the matches might dry. When I fell into the river, only half of me had got thoroughly wet. My left shoulder had remained above the water. I took the box of matches, therefore, and put it into my left armpit. The moist air of the cavern might possibly be counteracted by the heat of my body, but even so, I knew that I could not hope to get a light for many hours. Meanwhile there was nothing for it but to wait.

By good luck I had slipped several biscuits into my pocket before I left the farm-house. These I now devoured, and washed them down with a draught from that wretched stream which had been the cause of all my misfortunes. Then I felt about for a comfortable seat among the rocks, and, having discovered a place where I could get a support for my back, I stretched out my legs and settled myself down to wait. I was wretchedly damp and cold, but I tried to cheer myself with the reflection that modern science prescribed open windows and walks in all weather for my disease. Gradually, lulled by the monotonous gurgle of the stream, and by the absolute darkness, I sank into an uneasy slumber.

How long this lasted I cannot say. It may have been for an hour, it may have been for several. Suddenly I sat up on my rock couch, with every nerve thrilling and every sense acutely on the alert. Beyond all doubt I had heard a sound—some sound very distinct from the gurgling of the waters. It had passed, but the reverberation of it still lingered in my ear. Was it a search party? They would most certainly have shouted, and vague as this sound was which had wakened me, it was very distinct from the human voice. I sat palpitating and hardly daring to breathe. There it was again! And again! Now it had become continuous. It was a tread—yes, surely it was the tread of some living creature. But what a tread it was! It gave one the impression of enormous weight carried upon sponge-like feet, which gave forth a muffled but ear-filling sound. The darkness was as complete as ever, but the tread was regular and decisive. And it was coming beyond all question in my direction.

My skin grew cold, and my hair stood on end as I listened to that steady and ponderous footfall. There was some creature there, and surely by the speed of its advance, it was one which could see in the dark. I crouched low on my rock and tried to blend myself into it. The steps grew nearer still, then stopped, and presently I was aware of a loud lapping and gurgling. The creature was drinking at the stream. Then again there was silence, broken by a succession of long sniffs and snorts of tremendous volume and energy. Had it caught the scent of me? My own nostrils were filled by a low fetid odour, mephitic and abominable. Then I heard the steps again. They were on my side of the stream now. The stones rattled within a few yards of where I lay. Hardly daring to breathe, I crouched upon my rock. Then the steps drew away. I heard the splash as it returned across the river, and the sound died away into the distance in the direction from which it had come.

For a long time I lay upon the rock, too much horrified to move. I thought of the sound which I had heard coming from the depths of the cave, of Armitage's fears, of the strange impression in the mud, and now came this final and absolute proof that there was indeed some inconceivable monster, something utterly unearthly and dreadful, which lurked in the hollow of the mountain. Of its nature or form I could frame no conception, save that it was both light-footed and gigantic. The combat between my reason, which told me that such things could not be, and my senses, which told me that they were, raged within me as I lay. Finally, I was almost ready to persuade myself that this experience had been part of some evil dream, and that my abnormal condition might have conjured up an hallucination. But there remained one final experience which removed the last possibility of doubt from my mind.

I had taken my matches from my armpit and felt them. They seemed perfectly hard and dry. Stooping down into a crevice of the rocks, I tried one of them. To my delight it took fire at once. I lit the candle, and, with a terrified backward glance into the obscure depths of the cavern, I hurried in the direction of the Roman passage. As I did so I passed the patch of mud on which I had seen the huge imprint. Now I stood astonished before it, for there were three similar imprints upon its surface, enormous in size, irregular in outline, of a depth which indicated the ponderous weight which had left them. Then a great terror surged over me. Stooping and shading my candle with my hand, I ran in a frenzy of fear to the rocky archway, hastened up it, and never stopped until, with weary feet and panting lungs, I rushed up the final slope of stones, broke through the tangle of briars, and flung myself exhausted upon the soft grass under the peaceful light of the stars. It was three in the morning when I reached the farm-house, and today I am all unstrung and quivering after my terrific adventure. As yet I have told no one. I must move warily in the matter. What would the poor lonely women, or the uneducated yokels here think of it if I were to tell them my experience? Let me go to someone who can understand and advise.

April 25.—I was laid up in bed for two days after my incredible adventure in the cavern. I use the adjective with a very definite meaning, for I have had an experience since which has shocked me almost as much as the other. I have said that I was looking round for someone who could advise me. There is a Dr Mark Johnson who practises some few miles away, to whom I had a note of recommendation from Professor Saunderson. To him I drove, when I was strong enough to get about, and I recounted to him my whole strange experience. He listened intently, and then carefully examined me, paying special attention to my reflexes and to the pupils of my eyes. When he had finished, he refused to discuss my adventure, saying that it was entirely beyond him, but he gave me the card of a Mr Picton at Castleton, with the advice that I should instantly go to him and tell him the story exactly as I had done to himself. He was, according to my adviser, the very man who was pre-eminently suited to help me. I went on to the station, therefore, and made my way to the little town, which is some ten miles away. Mr Picton appeared to be a man of importance, as his brass plate was displayed upon the door of a considerable building on the outskirts of the town. I was about to ring his bell, when some misgiving came into my mind, and, crossing to a neighbouring shop, I asked the man behind the counter if he could tell me anything of Mr Picton. 'Why,' said he, 'he is the best mad doctor in Derbyshire, and yonder is his asylum.' You can imagine that it was not long before I had shaken the dust of Castleton from my feet and returned to the farm, cursing all unimaginative pedants who cannot conceive that there may be things in creation which have never yet chanced to come across their mole's vision. After all, now that I am cooler, I can afford to admit that I have been no more sympathetic to Armitage than Dr Johnson has been to me.

April 27.—When I was a student I had the reputation of being a man of courage and enterprise. I remember that when there was a ghost-hunt at Coltbridge it was I who sat up in the haunted house. Is it advancing years (after all, I am only thirty-five), or is it this physical malady which has caused degeneration? Certainly my heart quails when I think of that horrible cavern in the hill, and the certainty that it has some monstrous occupant. What shall I do? There is not an hour in the day that I do not debate the question. If I say nothing, then the mystery remains unsolved. If I do say anything, then I have the alternative of mad alarm over the whole countryside, or of absolute incredulity which may end in consigning me to an asylum. On the whole, I think that my best course is to wait, and to prepare for some expedition which shall be more deliberate and better thought out than the last. As a first step I have been to Castleton and obtained a few essentials—a large acetylene lantern for one thing, and a good double-barrelled sporting rifle for another. The latter I have hired, but I have bought a dozen heavy game cartridges, which would bring down a rhinoceros. Now I am ready for my troglodyte friend. Give me better health and a little spate of energy, and I shall try conclusions with him yet. But who and what is he? Ah! there is the question which stands between me and my sleep. How many theories do I form, only to discard each in turn! It is all so utterly unthinkable. And yet the cry, the footmark, the tread in the cavern—no reasoning can get past these. I think of the old-world legends of dragons and of other monsters. Were they, perhaps, not such fairy-tales as we have thought? Can it be that there is some fact which underlies them, and am I, of all mortals, the one who is chosen to expose it?

May 3.—For several days I have been laid up by the vagaries of an English spring, and during those days there have been developments, the true and sinister meaning of which no one can appreciate save myself. I may say that we have had cloudy and moonless nights of late, which according to my information were the seasons upon which sheep disappeared. Well, sheep *have* disappeared. Two of Miss Allerton's, one of old Pearson's of the Cat Walk, and one of Mrs Moulton's. Four in all during three nights. No trace is left of them at all, and the countryside is buzzing with rumours of gipsies and of sheep-stealers.

But there is something more serious than that. Young Armitage has disappeared also. He left his moorland cottage early on Wednesday night and has never been heard of since. He was an unattached man, so there is less sensation than would otherwise be the case. The popular explanation is that he owes money, and has found a situation in some other part of the country, whence he will presently write for his belongings. But I have grave misgivings. Is it not much more likely that the recent tragedy of the sheep has caused him to take some steps which may have ended in his own destruction? He may, for example, have lain in wait for the creature and been carried off by it into the recesses of the mountains. What an inconceivable fate for a civilised Englishman of the twentieth century! And yet I feel that it is possible and even probable. But in that case, how far am I answerable both for his death and for any other mishap which may occur? Surely with the knowledge I already possess it must be my duty to see that something is done, or if necessary to do it myself. It must be the latter, for this morning I went down to the local police-station and told my story. The inspector entered it all in a large book and bowed me out with commendable gravity, but I heard a burst of laughter before I had got down his garden path. No doubt he was recounting my adventure to his family.

June 10.—I am writing this, propped up in bed, six weeks after my last entry in this journal. I have gone through a terrible shock both to mind and body, arising from such an experience as has seldom befallen a human being before. But I have attained my end. The danger from the Terror which dwells in the Blue John Gap has passed never to return. Thus much at least I, a broken invalid, have done for the common good. Let me now recount what occurred as clearly as I may.

The night of Friday, May 3, was dark and cloudy—the very night for the monster to walk. About eleven o'clock I went from the farm-house with my lantern and my rifle, having first left a note upon the table of my bedroom in which I said that, if I were missing, search should be made for me in the direction of the Gap. I made my way to the mouth of the Roman shaft, and, having perched myself among the rocks close to the opening, I shut off my lantern and waited patiently with my loaded rifle ready to my hand.

It was a melancholy vigil. All down the winding valley I could see the scattered lights of the farm-houses, and the church clock of Chapel-le-Dale tolling the hours came faintly to my ears. These tokens of my fellow-men served only to make my own position seem the more lonely, and to call for a greater effort to overcome the terror which tempted me continually to get back to the farm, and abandon for ever this dangerous quest. And yet there lies deep in every man a rooted self-respect which makes it hard for him to turn back from that which he has once undertaken. This feeling of personal pride was my salvation now, and it was that alone which held me fast when every instinct of my nature was dragging me away. I am glad now that I had the strength. In spite of all that it has cost me, my manhood is at least above reproach.

Twelve o'clock struck in the distant church, then one, then two. It was the darkest hour of the night. The clouds were drifting low, and there was not a star in the sky. An owl was hooting somewhere among the rocks, but no other sound, save the gentle sough of the wind, came to my ears. And then suddenly I heard it! From far away down the tunnel came those muffled steps, so soft and yet so ponderous. I heard also the rattle of stones as they gave way under that giant tread. They drew nearer. They were close upon me. I heard the crashing of the bushes round the entrance, and then dimly through the darkness I was conscious of the loom of some enormous shape, some monstrous inchoate creature, passing swiftly and very silently out from the tunnel. I was paralysed with fear and amazement. Long as I had waited, now that it had actually come I was unprepared for the shock. I lay motionless and breathless, whilst the great dark mass whisked by me and was swallowed up in the night.

But now I nerved myself for its return. No sound came from the sleeping countryside to tell of the horror which was loose. In no way could I judge how far off it was, what it was doing, or when it might be back. But not a second time should my nerve fail me, not a second time should it pass unchallenged. I swore it between my clenched teeth as I laid my cocked rifle across the rock.

And yet it nearly happened. There was no warning of approach now as the creature passed over the grass. Suddenly, like a dark, drifting shadow, the huge bulk loomed up once more before me, making for the entrance of the cave. Again came that paralysis of volition which held my crooked forefinger impotent upon the trigger. But with a desperate effort I shook it off. Even as the brushwood rustled, and the monstrous beast blended with the shadow of the Gap, I fired at the retreating form. In the blaze of the gun I caught a glimpse of a great shaggy mass, something with rough and bristling hair of a withered grey colour, fading away to white in its lower parts, the huge body supported upon short, thick, curving legs. I had just that glance, and then I heard the rattle of the stones as the creature tore down into its burrow. In an instant, with a triumphant revulsion of feeling, I had cast my fears to the wind, and uncovering my powerful lantern, with my rifle in my hand, I sprang down from my rock and rushed after the monster down the old Roman shaft.

My splendid lamp cast a brilliant flood of vivid light in front of me, very different from the yellow glimmer which had aided me down the same passage only twelve days before. As I ran, I saw the great beast lurching along before me, its huge bulk filling up the whole space from wall to wall. Its hair looked like coarse faded oakum, and hung down in long, dense masses which swayed as it moved. It was like an enormous unclipped sheep in its fleece, but in size it was far larger than the largest elephant, and its breadth seemed to be nearly as great as its height. It fills me with amazement now to think that I should have dared to follow such a horror into the bowels of the earth, but when one's blood is up, and when one's quarry seems to be flying, the old primeval hunting-spirit awakes and prudence is cast to the wind. Rifle in hand, I ran at the top of my speed upon the trail of the monster.

I had seen that the creature was swift. Now I was to find out to my cost that it was also very cunning. I had imagined that it was in panic flight, and that I had only to pursue it. The idea that it might turn upon me never entered my excited brain. I have already explained that the passage down which I was racing opened into a great central cave. Into this I rushed, fearful lest I should lose all trace of the beast. But he had turned upon his own traces, and in a moment we were face to face.

That picture, seen in the brilliant white light of the lantern, is etched for ever upon my brain. He had reared up on his hind legs as a bear would do, and stood above me, enormous, menacing—such a creature as no nightmare had ever brought to my imagination. I have said that he reared like a bear, and there was something bear-like—if one could conceive a bear which was tenfold the bulk of any bear seen upon earth—in his whole pose and attitude, in his great crooked forelegs with their ivory-white claws, in his rugged skin, and in his red, gaping mouth, fringed with monstrous fangs. Only in one point did he differ from the bear, or from any other creature which walks the earth, and even at that supreme moment a shudder of horror passed over me as I observed that the eyes which glistened in the glow of my lantern were huge, projecting bulbs, white and sightless. For a moment his great paws swung over my head. The next he fell forward upon me, I and my broken lantern crashed to the earth, and I remember no more.

*

When I came to myself I was back in the farm-house of the Allertons. Two days had passed since my terrible adventure in the Blue John Gap. It seems that I had lain all night in the cave insensible from concussion of the brain, with my left arm and two ribs badly fractured. In the morning my note had been found, a search party of a dozen farmers assembled, and I had been tracked down and carried back to my bedroom, where I had lain in high delirium ever since. There was, it seems, no sign of the creature, and no bloodstain which would show that my bullet had found him as he passed. Save for my own plight and the marks upon the mud, there was nothing to prove that what I said was true.

Six weeks have now elapsed, and I am able to sit out once more in the sunshine. Just opposite me is the steep hillside, grey with shaly rock, and yonder on its flank is the dark cleft which marks the opening of the Blue John Gap. But it is no longer a source of terror. Never again through that ill-omened tunnel shall any strange shape flit out into the world of men. The educated and the scientific, the Dr Johnsons and the like, may smile at my narrative, but the poorer folk of the countryside had never a doubt as to its truth. On the day after my recovering consciousness they assembled in their hundreds round the Blue John Gap. As the *Castleton Courier* said:

> 'It was useless for our correspondent, or for any of the adventurous gentlemen who had come from Matlock, Buxton, and other parts, to offer to descend, to explore the cave to the end, and to finally test the

extraordinary narrative of Dr James Hardcastle. The country people had taken the matter into their own hands, and from an early hour of the morning they had worked hard in stopping up the entrance of the tunnel. There is a sharp slope where the shaft begins, and great boulders, rolled along by many willing hands, were thrust down it until the Gap was absolutely sealed. So ends the episode which has caused such excitement throughout the country. Local opinion is fiercely divided upon the subject. On the one hand are those who point to Dr Hardcastle's impaired health, and to the possibility of cerebral lesions of tubercular origin giving rise to strange hallucinations. Some *idée fixe*, according to these gentlemen, caused the doctor to wander down the tunnel, and a fall among the rocks was sufficient to account for his injuries. On the other hand, a legend of a strange creature in the Gap has existed for some months back, and the farmers look upon Dr Hardcastle's narrative and his personal injuries as a final corroboration. So the matter stands, and so the matter will continue to stand, for no definite solution seems to us to be now possible. It transcends human wit to give any scientific explanation which could cover the alleged facts.'

Perhaps before the *Courier* published these words they would have been wise to send their representative to me. I have thought the matter out, as no one else has occasion to do, and it is possible that I might have removed some of the more obvious difficulties of the narrative and brought it one degree nearer to scientific acceptance. Let me then write down the only explanation which seems to me to elucidate what I know to my cost to have been a series of facts. My theory may seem to be wildly improbable, but at least no one can venture to say that it is impossible.

My view is—and it was formed, as is shown by my diary, before my personal adventure—that in this part of England there is a vast subterranean lake or sea, which is fed by the great number of streams which pass down through the limestone. Where there is a large collection of water there must also be some evaporation, mists or rain, and a possibility of vegetation. This in turn suggests that there may be animal life, arising, as the vegetable life would also do, from those seeds and types which had been introduced at an early period of the world's history, when communication with the outer air was more easy. This place had then developed a fauna and flora of its own, including such monsters as the one which I had seen, which may well have been the old cave-bear, enormously enlarged and modified by its new environment. For countless æons the internal and the external creation had kept apart, growing steadily away from each other. Then there had come some rift in the depths of the mountain which had enabled one creature to wander up and, by means of the Roman tunnel, to reach the open air. Like all subterranean life, it had lost the power of sight, but this had no doubt been compensated for by nature in other directions. Certainly it had some means of finding its way about, and of hunting down the sheep upon the hillside. As to its choice of dark nights, it is part of my theory that light was painful to those great white eyeballs, and that it was only a pitch-black world which it could tolerate. Perhaps, indeed, it was the glare of my lantern which saved my life at that awful moment when we were face to face. So I read the riddle. I leave these facts behind me, and if you can explain them, do so; or if you choose to doubt them, do so. Neither your belief nor your incredulity can alter them, nor affect one whose task is nearly over.

*

So ended the strange narrative of Dr James Hardcastle.

HOW IT HAPPENED

SHE was a writing medium. This is what she wrote:—

I can remember some things upon that evening most distinctly, and others are like some vague, broken dreams. That is what makes it so difficult to tell a connected story. I have no idea now what it was that had taken me to London and brought me back so late. It just merges into all my other visits to London. But from the time that I got out at the little country station everything is extraordinarily clear. I can live it again—every instant of it.

I remember so well walking down the platform and looking at the illuminated clock at the end which told me that it was half-past eleven. I remember also my wondering whether I could get home before midnight. Then I remember the big motor, with its glaring headlights and glitter of polished brass, waiting for me outside. It was my new thirty-horse-power Robur, which had only been delivered that day. I remember also asking Perkins, my chauffeur, how she had gone, and his saying that he thought she was excellent.

'I'll try her myself,' said I, and I climbed into the driver's seat.

'The gears are not the same,' said he. 'Perhaps, sir, I had better drive.'

'No; I should like to try her,' said I.

And so we started on the five-mile drive for home.

My old car had the gears as they used always to be in notches on a bar. In this car you passed the gear-lever through a gate to get on the higher ones. It was not difficult to master, and soon I thought that I understood it. It was foolish, no doubt, to begin to learn a new system in the dark, but one often does foolish things, and one has not always to pay the full price for them. I got along very well until I came to Claystall Hill. It is one of the worst hills in England, a mile and a half long and one in six in places, with three fairly sharp curves. My park gate stands at the very foot of it upon the main London road.

We were just over the brow of this hill, where the grade is steepest, when the trouble began. I had been on the top speed, and wanted to get her on the free; but she stuck between gears, and I had to get her back on the top again. By this time she was going at a great rate, so I clapped on both brakes, and one after the other they gave way. I didn't mind so much when I felt my footbrake snap, but when I put all my weight on my side-brake, and the lever clanged to its full limit without a catch, it brought a cold sweat out of me. By this time we were fairly tearing down the slope. The lights were brilliant, and I brought her round the first curve all right. Then we did the second one, though it was a close shave for the ditch. There was a mile of straight then with the third curve beneath it, and after that the gate of the park. If I could shoot into that harbour all would be well, for the slope up to the house would bring her to a stand.

Perkins behaved splendidly. I should like that to be known. He was perfectly cool and alert. I had thought at the very beginning of taking the bank, and he read my intention.

'I wouldn't do it, sir,' said he. 'At this pace it must go over and we should have it on the top of us.'

Of course he was right. He got to the electric switch and had it off, so we were in the free; but we were still running at a fearful pace. He laid his hands on the wheel.

'I'll keep her steady,' said he, 'if you care to jump and chance it. We can never get round that curve. Better jump, sir.'

'No,' said I; 'I'll stick it out. You can jump if you like.'

'I'll stick it with you, sir,' said he.

If it had been the old car I should have jammed the gear-lever into the reverse, and seen what would happen. I expect she would have stripped her gears or smashed up somehow, but it would have been a chance. As it was, I was helpless. Perkins tried to climb across, but you couldn't do it going at that pace. The wheels were whirring like a high wind and the big body creaking and groaning with the strain. But the lights were brilliant, and one could steer to an inch. I remember thinking what an awful and yet majestic sight we should appear to anyone who met us. It was a narrow road, and we were just a great, roaring, golden death to anyone who came in our path.

We got round the corner with one wheel three feet high upon the bank. I thought we were surely over, but after staggering for a moment she righted and darted onwards. That was the third corner and the last one. There was only the park gate now. It was facing us, but, as luck would have it, not facing us directly. It was about twenty yards to the left up the main road into which we ran. Perhaps I could have done it, but I expect that the steering-gear had been jarred when we ran on the bank. The wheel did not turn easily. We shot out of the lane. I saw the open gate on the left. I whirled round my wheel with all the strength of my wrists. Perkins and I threw our bodies across, and then the next instant, going at fifty miles an hour, my right wheel struck full on the right-hand pillar of my own gate. I heard the crash. I was conscious of flying through the air, and then—and then—!

When I became aware of my own existence once more I was among some brushwood in the shadow of the oaks upon the lodge side of the drive. A man was standing beside me. I imagined at first that it was Perkins, but when I looked again I saw that it was Stanley, a man whom I had known at college some years before, and for whom I had a really genuine affection. There was always something peculiarly sympathetic to me in Stanley's personality; and I was proud to think that I had some similar influence upon him. At the present moment I was surprised to see him, but I was like a man in a dream, giddy and shaken and quite prepared to take things as I found them without questioning them.

'What a smash!' I said. 'Good Lord, what an awful smash!'

He nodded his head, and even in the gloom I could see that he was smiling the gentle, wistful smile which I connected with him.

I was quite unable to move. Indeed, I had not any desire to try to move. But my senses were exceedingly alert. I saw the wreck of the motor lit up by the moving lanterns. I saw the little group of people and heard the hushed voices. There were the lodge-keeper and his wife, and one or two more. They were taking no notice of me, but were very busy round the car. Then suddenly I heard a cry of pain.

'The weight is on him. Lift it easy,' cried a voice.

'It's only my leg!' said another one, which I recognised as Perkins's. 'Where's master?' he cried.

'Here I am,' I answered, but they did not seem to hear me. They were all bending over something which lay in front of the car.

Stanley laid his hand upon my shoulder, and his touch was inexpressibly soothing. I felt light and happy, in spite of all.

'No pain, of course?' said he.

'None,' said I.

'There never is,' said he.

And then suddenly a wave of amazement passed over me. Stanley! Stanley! Why, Stanley had surely died of enteric at Bloemfontein in the Boer War!

'Stanley!' I cried, and the words seemed to choke my throat—'Stanley, you are dead.'

He looked at me with the same old gentle, wistful smile.

'So are you,' he answered.

THE HORROR OF THE HEIGHTS

(Which Includes the Manuscript Known as the Joyce-Armstrong Fragment)

THE idea that the extraordinary narrative which has been called the Joyce-Armstrong Fragment is an elaborate practical joke evolved by some unknown person, cursed by a perverted and sinister sense of humour, has now been abandoned by all who have examined the matter. The most *macabre* and imaginative of plotters would hesitate before linking his morbid fancies with the unquestioned and tragic facts which reinforce the statement. Though the assertions contained in it are amazing and even monstrous, it is none the less forcing itself upon the general intelligence that they are true, and that we must readjust our ideas to the new situation. This world of ours appears to be separated by a slight and precarious margin of safety from a most singular and unexpected danger. I will endeavour in this narrative, which reproduces the original document in its necessarily somewhat fragmentary form, to lay before the reader the whole of the facts up to date, prefacing my statement by saying that, if there be any who doubt the narrative of Joyce-Armstrong, there can be no question at all as to the facts concerning Lieutenant Myrtle, RN, and Mr Hay Connor, who undoubtedly met their end in the manner described.

The Joyce-Armstrong Fragment was found in the field which is called Lower Haycock, lying one mile to the westward of the village of Withyham, upon the Kent and Sussex border. It was on the fifteenth of September last that an agricultural labourer, James Flynn, in the employment of Mathew Dodd, farmer, of the Chauntry Farm, Withyham, perceived a briar pipe lying near the footpath which skirts the hedge in Lower Haycock. A few paces farther on he picked up a pair of broken binocular glasses. Finally, among some nettles in the ditch, he caught sight of a flat, canvas-backed book, which proved to be a note-book with detachable leaves, some of which had come loose and were fluttering along the base of the hedge. These he collected, but some, including the first, were never recovered, and leave a deplorable hiatus in this all-important statement. The note-book was taken by the labourer to his master, who in turn showed it to Dr J. H. Atherton, of Hartfield. This gentleman at once recognised the need for an expert examination, and the manuscript was forwarded to the Aero Club in London, where it now lies.

The first two pages of the manuscript are missing. There is also one torn away at the end of the narrative, though none of these affect the general coherence of the story. It is conjectured that the missing opening is concerned with the record of Mr Joyce-Armstrong's qualifications as an aeronaut, which can be gathered from other sources and are admitted to be unsurpassed among the air-pilots of England. For many years he has been looked upon as among the most daring and the most intellectual of flying men, a combination which has enabled him to both invent and test several new devices, including the common gyroscopic attachment which is known by his name. The main body of the manuscript is written neatly in ink, but the last few lines are in pencil and are so ragged as to be hardly legible—exactly, in fact, as they might be expected to appear if they were scribbled off hurriedly from the seat of a moving aeroplane. There are, it may be added, several stains, both on the last page and on the outside cover which have been pronounced by the Home Office experts to be blood—probably human and certainly mammalian. The fact that something closely resembling the organism of malaria was discovered in this blood, and that Joyce-Armstrong is known to have suffered from intermittent fever, is a remarkable example of the new weapons which modern science has placed in the hands of our detectives.

And now a word as to the personality of the author of this epoch-making statement. Joyce-Armstrong, according to the few friends who really knew something of the man, was a poet and a dreamer, as well as a mechanic and an inventor. He was a man of considerable wealth, much of which he had spent in the pursuit of his aeronautical hobby. He had four private aeroplanes in his hangars near Devizes, and is said to have made no fewer than one hundred and seventy ascents in the course of last year. He was a retiring man with dark moods, in which he would avoid the society of his fellows. Captain Dangerfield, who knew him better than anyone, says that there were times when his eccentricity threatened to develop into something more serious. His habit of carrying a shot-gun with him in his aeroplane was one manifestation of it.

Another was the morbid effect which the fall of Lieutenant Myrtle had upon his mind. Myrtle, who was attempting the height record, fell from an altitude of something over thirty thousand feet. Horrible to narrate, his head was entirely obliterated, though his body and limbs preserved their configuration. At every gathering of airmen, Joyce-Armstrong, according to Dangerfield, would ask, with an enigmatic smile: 'And where, pray, is Myrtle's head?'

On another occasion after dinner, at the mess of the Flying School on Salisbury Plain, he started a debate as to what will be the most permanent danger which airmen will have to encounter. Having listened to successive opinions as to air-pockets, faulty construction, and overbanking, he ended by shrugging his shoulders and refusing to put forward his own views, though he gave the impression that they differed from any advanced by his companions.

It is worth remarking that after his own complete disappearance it was found that his private affairs were arranged with a precision which may show that he had a strong premonition of disaster. With these essential explanations I will now give the narrative exactly as it stands, beginning at page three of the blood-soaked notebook:—

'Nevertheless, when I dined at Rheims with Coselli and Gustav Raymond I found that neither of them was aware of any particular danger in the higher layers of the atmosphere. I did not actually say what was in my thoughts, but I got so near to it that if they had any corresponding idea they could not have failed to express it. But then they are two empty, vainglorious fellows with no thought beyond seeing their silly names in the newspaper. It is interesting to note that neither of them had ever been much beyond the twenty-thousand-foot level. Of course, men have been higher than this both in balloons and in the ascent of mountains. It must be well above that point that the aeroplane enters the danger zone—always presuming that my premonitions are correct.

'Aeroplaning has been with us now for more than twenty years, and one might well ask: Why should this peril be only revealing itself in our day? The answer is obvious. In the old days of weak engines, when a hundred horse-power Gnome or Green was considered ample for every need, the flights were very restricted. Now that three hundred horse-power is the rule rather than the exception, visits to the upper layers have become easier and more common. Some of us can remember how, in our youth, Garros made a world-wide reputation by attaining nineteen thousand feet, and it was considered a remarkable achievement to fly over the Alps. Our standard now has been immeasurably raised, and there are twenty high flights for one in former years. Many of them have been undertaken with impunity. The thirty-thousand-foot level has been reached time after time with no discomfort beyond cold and asthma. What does this prove? A visitor might descend upon this planet a thousand times and never see a tiger. Yet tigers exist, and if he chanced to come down into a jungle he might be devoured. There are jungles of the upper air, and there are worse things than tigers which inhabit them. I believe in time they will map these jungles accurately out. Even at the present moment I could name two of them. One of them lies over the Pau-Biarritz district of France. Another is just over my head as I write here in my house in Wiltshire. I rather think there is a third in the Homburg-Wiesbaden district.

'It was the disappearance of the airmen that first set me thinking. Of course, everyone said that they had fallen into the sea, but that did not satisfy me at all. First, there was Verrier in France; his machine was found near Bayonne, but they never got his body. There was the case of Baxter also, who vanished, though his engine and some of the iron fixings were found in a wood in Leicestershire. In that case, Dr Middleton, of Amesbury, who was watching the flight with a telescope, declares that just before the clouds obscured the view he saw the machine, which was at an enormous height, suddenly rise perpendicularly upwards in a succession of jerks in a manner that he would have thought to be impossible. That was the last seen of Baxter. There was a correspondence in the papers, but it never led to anything. There were several other similar cases, and then there was the death of Hay

Connor. What a cackle there was about an unsolved mystery of the air, and what columns in the halfpenny papers, and yet how little was ever done to get to the bottom of the business! He came down in a tremendous vol-plané from an unknown height. He never got off his machine and died in his pilot's seat. Died of what? "Heart disease," said the doctors. Rubbish! Hay Connor's heart was as sound as mine is. What did Venables say? Venables was the only man who was at his side when he died. He said that he was shivering and looked like a man who had been badly scared. "Died of fright," said Venables, but could not imagine what he was frightened about. Only said one word to Venables, which sounded like "Monstrous." They could make nothing of that at the inquest. But I could make something of it. Monsters! That was the last word of poor Harry Hay Connor. And he *did* die of fright, just as Venables thought.

'And then there was Myrtle's head. Do you really believe—does anybody really believe—that a man's head could be driven clean into his body by the force of a fall? Well, perhaps it may be possible, but I, for one, have never believed that it was so with Myrtle. And the grease upon his clothes—"all slimy with grease," said somebody at the inquest. Queer that nobody got thinking after that! I did—but, then, I had been thinking for a good long time. I've made three ascents—how Dangerfield used to chaff me about my shot-gun—but I've never been high enough. Now, with this new, light Paul Veroner machine and its one hundred and seventy-five Robur, I should easily touch the thirty thousand tomorrow. I'll have a shot at the record. Maybe I shall have a shot at something else as well. Of course, it's dangerous. If a fellow wants to avoid danger he had best keep out of flying altogether and subside finally into flannel slippers and a dressing-gown. But I'll visit the air-jungle tomorrow—and if there's anything there I shall know it. If I return, I'll find myself a bit of a celebrity. If I don't, this note-book may explain what I am trying to do, and how I lost my life in doing it. But no drivel about accidents or mysteries, if *you* please.

'I chose my Paul Veroner monoplane for the job. There's nothing like a monoplane when real work is to be done. Beaumont found that out in very early days. For one thing it doesn't mind damp, and the weather looks as if we should be in the clouds all the time. It's a bonny little model and answers my hand like a tender-mouthed horse. The engine is a ten-cylinder rotary Robur working up to one hundred and seventy-five. It has all the modern improvements—enclosed fuselage, high-curved landing skids, brakes, gyroscopic steadiers, and three speeds, worked by an alteration of the angle of the planes upon the Venetian-blind principle. I took a shot-gun with me and a dozen cartridges filled with buck-shot. You should have seen the face of Perkins, my old mechanic, when I directed him to put them in. I was dressed like an Arctic explorer, with two jerseys under my overalls, thick socks inside my padded boots, a storm-cap with flaps, and my talc goggles. It was stifling outside the hangars, but I was going for the summit of the Himalayas, and had to dress for the part. Perkins knew there was something on and implored me to take him with me. Perhaps I should if I were using the biplane, but a monoplane is a one-man show—if you want to get the last foot of lift out of it. Of course, I took an oxygen bag; the man who goes for the altitude record without one will either be frozen or smothered—or both.

'I had a good look at the planes, the rudder-bar, and the elevating lever before I got in. Everything was in order so far as I could see. Then I switched on my engine and found that she was running sweetly. When they let her go she rose almost at once upon the lowest speed. I circled my home field once or twice just to warm her up, and then, with a wave to Perkins and the others, I flattened out my planes and put her on her highest. She skimmed like a swallow down wind for eight or ten miles until I turned her nose up a little and she began to climb in a great spiral for the cloud-bank above me. It's all-important to rise slowly and adapt yourself to the pressure as you go.

'It was a close, warm day for an English September, and there was the hush and heaviness of impending rain. Now and then there came sudden puffs of wind from the south-west—one of them so gusty and unexpected that it caught me napping and turned me half-round for an instant. I remember the time when gusts and whirls and air-pockets used to be things of danger—before we learned to put an overmastering power into our engines. Just as I reached the cloud-banks, with the altimeter marking three thousand, down came the rain. My word, how it poured! It drummed upon my wings and lashed against my face, blurring my glasses so that I could hardly see. I got down on to a low speed, for it was painful to travel against it. As I got higher it became hail, and I had to turn tail to it. One of my cylinders was out of action—a dirty plug, I should imagine, but still I was rising steadily with plenty of power. After a bit the trouble passed, whatever it was, and I heard the full, deep-throated purr—the ten singing as one. That's where the beauty of our modern silencers comes in. We can at last control our engines by ear. How they squeal and squeak and sob when they are in trouble! All those cries for help were wasted in the old days, when every sound was swallowed up by the monstrous racket of the machine. If only the early aviators could come back to see the beauty and perfection of the mechanism which have been bought at the cost of their lives!

'About nine-thirty I was nearing the clouds. Down below me, all blurred and shadowed with rain, lay the vast expanse of Salisbury Plain. Half a dozen flying machines were doing hackwork at the thousand-foot level, looking like little black swallows against the green background. I dare say they were wondering what I was doing up in cloud-land. Suddenly a grey curtain drew across beneath me and the wet folds of vapours were swirling round my face. It was clammily cold and miserable. But I was above the hail-storm, and that was something gained. The cloud was as dark and thick as a London fog. In my anxiety to get clear, I cocked her nose up until the automatic alarm-bell rang, and I actually began to slide backwards. My sopped and dripping wings had made me heavier than I thought, but presently I was in lighter cloud, and soon had cleared the first layer. There was a second—opal-coloured and fleecy—at a great height above my head, a white, unbroken ceiling above, and a dark, unbroken floor below, with the monoplane labouring upwards upon a vast spiral between them. It is deadly lonely in these cloud-spaces. Once a great flight of some small water-birds went past me, flying very fast to the westwards. The quick whir of their wings and their musical cry were cheery to my ear. I fancy that they were teal, but I am a wretched zoologist. Now that we humans have become birds we must really learn to know our brethren by sight.

'The wind down beneath me whirled and swayed the broad cloud-plain. Once a great eddy formed in it, a whirlpool of vapour, and through it, as down a funnel, I caught sight of the distant world. A large white biplane was passing at a vast depth beneath me. I fancy it was the morning mail service betwixt Bristol and London. Then the drift swirled inwards again and the great solitude was unbroken.

'Just after ten I touched the lower edge of the upper cloud-stratum. It consisted of fine diaphanous vapour drifting swiftly from the westward. The wind had been steadily rising all this time and it was now blowing a sharp breeze—twenty-eight an hour by my gauge. Already it was very cold, though my altimeter only marked nine thousand. The engines were working beautifully, and we went droning steadily upwards. The cloud-bank was thicker than I had expected, but at last it thinned out into a golden mist before me, and then in an instant I had shot out from it, and there was an unclouded sky and a brilliant sun above my head—all blue and gold above, all shining silver below, one vast, glimmering plain as far as my eyes could reach. It was a quarter past ten o'clock, and the barograph needle pointed to twelve thousand eight hundred. Up I went and up, my ears concentrated upon the deep purring of my motor, my eyes busy always with the watch, the revolution indicator, the petrol lever, and the oil pump. No wonder aviators are said to be a fearless race. With so many things to think of there is no time to trouble about oneself. About this time I noted how unreliable is the compass when above a certain height from earth. At fifteen thousand feet mine was pointing east and a point south. The sun and the wind gave me my true bearings.

'I had hoped to reach an eternal stillness in these high altitudes, but with every thousand feet of ascent the gale grew stronger. My machine groaned and trembled in every joint and rivet as she faced it, and swept away like a sheet of paper when I banked her on the turn, skimming down wind at a greater pace, perhaps, than ever mortal man has moved. Yet I had always to turn again and tack up in the wind's eye, for it was not merely a height record that I was after. By all my calculations it was above little Wiltshire that my air-jungle lay, and all my labour might be lost if I struck the outer layers at some farther point.

'When I reached the nineteen-thousand-foot level, which was about midday, the wind was so severe that I looked with some anxiety to the stays of my wings, expecting momentarily to see them snap or slacken. I even cast loose the parachute behind me, and fastened its hook into the ring of my leathern belt, so as to be ready for the worst. Now was the time when a bit of scamped work by the mechanic is paid for by the life of the aeronaut. But she held together bravely. Every cord and strut was humming and vibrating like so many harp-strings, but it was glorious to see how, for all the beating and the buffeting, she was still the conqueror of Nature and the mistress of the sky. There is surely something divine in man himself that he should rise so superior to the limitations which Creation seemed to impose—rise, too, by such unselfish, heroic devotion as this air-conquest has shown. Talk of human degeneration! When has such a story as this been written in the annals of our race?

'These were the thoughts in my head as I climbed that monstrous, inclined plane with the wind sometimes beating in my face and sometimes whistling behind my ears, while the cloud-land beneath me fell away to such a distance that the folds and hummocks of silver had all smoothed out into one flat, shining plain. But suddenly I had a horrible and unprecedented experience. I have known before what it is to be in what our neighbours have called a *tourbillon*, but never on such a scale as this. That huge, sweeping river of wind of which I have spoken had, as it appears, whirlpools within it which were as monstrous as itself. Without a moment's warning I was dragged suddenly into the heart of one. I spun round for a minute or two with such velocity that I almost lost my senses, and then fell suddenly, left wing foremost, down the vacuum funnel in the centre. I dropped like a stone, and lost nearly a thousand feet. It was only my belt that kept me in my seat, and the shock and breathlessness left me hanging half-insensible over the side of the fuselage. But I am always capable of a supreme effort—it is my one great merit as an aviator. I was conscious that the descent was slower. The whirlpool was a cone rather than a funnel, and I had come to the apex. With a terrific wrench, throwing my weight all to one side, I levelled my planes and brought her head away from the wind. In an instant I had shot out of the eddies and was skimming down the sky. Then, shaken but victorious, I turned her nose up and began once more my steady grind on the upward spiral. I took a large sweep to avoid the danger-spot of the whirlpool, and soon I was safely above it. Just after one o'clock I was twenty-one thousand feet above the sea-level. To my great joy I had topped the gale, and with every hundred feet of ascent the air grew stiller. On the other hand, it was very cold, and I was conscious of that peculiar nausea which goes with rarefaction of the air. For the first time I unscrewed the mouth of my oxygen bag and took an occasional whiff of the glorious gas. I could feel it running like a cordial through my veins, and I was exhilarated almost to the point of drunkenness. I shouted and sang as I soared upwards into the cold, still outer world.

'It is very clear to me that the insensibility which came upon Glaisher, and in a lesser degree upon Coxwell when, in 1862, they ascended in a balloon to the height of thirty thousand feet, was due to the extreme speed with which a perpendicular ascent is made. Doing it at an easy gradient and accustoming oneself to the lessened barometric pressure by slow degrees, there are no such dreadful symptoms. At the same great height I found that even without my oxygen inhaler I could breathe without undue distress. It was bitterly cold, however, and my thermometer was at zero, Fahrenheit. At one-thirty I was nearly seven miles above the surface of the earth, and still ascending steadily. I found, however, that the rarefied air was giving markedly less support to my planes, and that my angle of ascent had to be considerably lowered in consequence. It was already clear that even with my light weight and strong engine-power there was a point in front of me where I should be held. To make matters worse, one of my sparking-plugs was in trouble again and there was intermittent misfiring in the engine. My heart was heavy with the fear of failure.

'It was about that time that I had a most extraordinary experience. Something whizzed past me in a trail of smoke and exploded with a loud, hissing sound, sending forth a cloud of steam. For the instant

I could not imagine what had happened. Then I remembered that the earth is for ever being bombarded by meteor stones, and would be hardly inhabitable were they not in nearly every case turned to vapour in the outer layers of the atmosphere. Here is a new danger for the high-altitude man, for two others passed me when I was nearing the forty-thousand-foot mark. I cannot doubt that at the edge of the earth's envelope the risk would be a very real one.

'My barograph needle marked forty-one thousand three hundred when I became aware that I could go no farther. Physically, the strain was not as yet greater than I could bear, but my machine had reached its limit. The attenuated air gave no firm support to the wings, and the least tilt developed into side-slip, while she seemed sluggish on her controls. Possibly, had the engine been at its best, another thousand feet might have been within our capacity, but it was still misfiring, and two out of the ten cylinders appeared to be out of action. If I had not already reached the zone for which I was searching then I should never see it upon this journey. But was it not possible that I had attained it? Soaring in circles like a monstrous hawk upon the forty-thousand-foot level I let the monoplane guide herself, and with my Mannheim glass I made a careful observation of my surroundings. The heavens were perfectly clear; there was no indication of those dangers which I had imagined.

'I have said that I was soaring in circles. It struck me suddenly that I would do well to take a wider sweep and open up a new air-tract. If the hunter entered an earth-jungle he would drive through it if he wished to find his game. My reasoning had led me to believe that the air-jungle which I had imagined lay somewhere over Wiltshire. This should be to the south and west of me. I took my bearings from the sun, for the compass was hopeless and no trace of earth was to be seen—nothing but the distant, silver cloud-plain. However, I got my direction as best

I might and kept her head straight to the mark. I reckoned that my petrol supply would not last for more than another hour or so, but I could afford to use it to the last drop, since a single magnificent vol-plané could at any time take me to the earth.

'Suddenly I was aware of something new. The air in front of me had lost its crystal clearness. It was full of long, ragged wisps of something which I can only compare to very fine cigarette-smoke. It hung about in wreaths and coils, turning and twisting slowly in the sunlight. As the monoplane shot through it, I was aware of a faint taste of oil upon my lips, and there was a greasy scum upon the woodwork of the machine. Some infinitely fine organic matter appeared to be suspended in the atmosphere. There was no life there. It was inchoate and diffuse, extending for many square acres and then fringing on into the void. No, it was not life. But might it not be the remains of life? Above all, might it not be the food of life, of monstrous life, even as the humble grease of the ocean is the food for the mighty whale? The thought was in my mind when my eyes looked upwards and I saw the most wonderful vision that ever man has seen. Can I hope to convey it to you even as I saw it myself last Thursday?

'Conceive a jelly-fish such as sails in our summer seas, bell-shaped and of enormous size—far larger, I should judge, than the dome of St Paul's. It was of a light pink colour veined with a delicate green, but the whole huge fabric so tenuous that it was but a fairy outline against the dark blue sky. It pulsated with a delicate and regular rhythm. From it there depended two long, drooping, green tentacles, which swayed slowly backwards and forwards. This gorgeous vision passed gently with noiseless dignity over my head, as light and fragile as a soap-bubble, and drifted upon its stately way.

'I had half-turned my monoplane, that I might look after this beautiful creature, when, in a moment, I found myself amidst a perfect fleet of them, of all sizes, but none so large as the first. Some were quite small, but the majority about as big as an average balloon, and with much the same curvature at the top. There was in them a delicacy of texture and colouring which reminded me of the finest Venetian glass. Pale shades of pink and green were the prevailing tints, but all had a lovely iridescence where the sun shimmered through their dainty forms. Some hundreds of them drifted past me, a wonderful fairy squadron of strange, unknown argosies of the sky—creatures whose forms and substance were so attuned to these pure heights that one could not conceive anything so delicate within actual sight or sound of earth.

'But soon my attention was drawn to a new phenomenon—the serpents of the outer air. These were long, thin, fantastic coils of vapour-like material, which turned and twisted with great speed, flying round and round at such a pace that the eyes could hardly follow them. Some of these ghost-like creatures were twenty or thirty feet long, but it was difficult to tell their girth, for their outline was so hazy that it seemed to fade away into the air around them. These air-snakes were of a very light grey or smoke colour, with some darker lines within, which gave the impression of a definite organism. One of them whisked past my very face, and I was conscious of a cold, clammy contact, but their composition was so unsubstantial that I could not connect them with any thought of physical danger, any more than the beautiful bell-like creatures which had preceded them. There was no more solidity in their frames than in the floating spume from a broken wave.

'But a more terrible experience was in store for me. Floating downwards from a great height there came a purplish patch of vapour, small as I saw it first, but rapidly enlarging as it approached me, until it appeared to be hundreds of square feet in size. Though fashioned of some transparent, jelly-like substance, it was none the less of much more definite outline and solid consistence than anything which I had seen before. There were more traces, too, of a physical organisation, especially two vast, shadowy, circular plates upon either side, which may have been eyes, and a perfectly solid white projection between them which was as curved and cruel as the beak of a vulture.

'The whole aspect of this monster was formidable and threatening, and it kept changing its colour from a very light mauve to a dark, angry purple so thick that it cast a shadow as it drifted between my monoplane and the sun. On the upper curve of its huge body there were three great projections which I can only describe as enormous bubbles, and I was convinced as I looked at them that they were charged with some extremely light gas which served to buoy up the misshapen and semi-solid mass in the rarefied air. The creature moved swiftly along, keeping pace easily with the monoplane, and for twenty miles or more it formed my horrible escort, hovering over me like a bird of prey which is waiting to pounce, its method of progression—done so swiftly that it was not easy to follow—was to throw out a long, glutinous streamer in front of it, which in turn seemed to draw forward the rest of the writhing body. So elastic and gelatinous was it that never for two successive minutes was it the same shape, and yet each change made it more threatening and loathsome than the last.

'I knew that it meant mischief. Every purple flush of its hideous body told me so. The vague, goggling eyes which were turned always upon me were cold and merciless in their viscid hatred. I dipped the nose of my monoplane downwards to escape it. As I did so, as quick as a flash there shot out a long tentacle from this mass of floating blubber, and it fell as light and sinuous as a whip-lash across the front of my machine. There was a loud hiss as it lay for a moment across the hot engine, and it whisked itself into the air again, while the huge, flat body drew itself together as if in sudden pain. I dipped to a vol-piqué, but again a tentacle fell over the monoplane and was shorn off by the propeller as easily as it might have cut through a smoke wreath. A long, gliding, sticky, serpent-like coil came from behind and caught me round the waist, dragging me out of the fuselage. I tore at it, my fingers sinking into the smooth, glue-like surface, and for an instant I disengaged myself, but only to be caught round the boot by another coil, which gave me a jerk that tilted me almost on to my back.

'As I fell over I blazed off both barrels of my gun, though, indeed, it was like attacking an elephant with a pea-shooter to imagine that any human weapon could cripple that mighty bulk. And yet I aimed better than I knew, for, with a loud report, one of the great blisters upon the creature's back exploded with the puncture of the buck-shot. It was very clear that my conjecture was right, and that these vast, clear bladders were distended with some lifting gas, for in an instant the huge, cloud-like body turned sideways, writhing desperately to find its balance, while the white beak snapped and gaped in horrible fury. But already I had shot away on the steepest glide that I dared to attempt, my engine still full on, the flying propeller and the force of gravity shooting me downwards like an aerolite. Far behind me I saw a dull, purplish smudge growing swiftly smaller and merging into the blue sky behind it. I was safe out of the deadly jungle of the outer air.

'Once out of danger I throttled my engine, for nothing tears a machine to pieces quicker than running on full power from a height. It was a glorious, spiral vol-plané from nearly eight miles of altitude—first, to the level of the silver cloud-bank, then to that of the storm-cloud beneath it, and finally, in beating rain, to the surface of the earth. I saw the Bristol Channel beneath me as I broke from the clouds, but, having still some petrol in my tank, I got twenty miles inland before I found myself stranded in a field half a mile from the village of Ashcombe. There I got three tins of petrol from a passing motor-car, and at ten minutes past six that evening I alighted gently in my own home meadow at Devizes, after such a journey as no mortal upon earth has ever yet taken and lived to tell the tale. I have seen the beauty and I have seen the horror of the heights—and greater beauty or greater horror than that is not within the ken of man.

'And now it is my plan to go once again before I give my results to the world. My reason for this is that I must surely have something to show by way of proof before I lay such a tale before my fellow-men. It is true that others will soon follow and will confirm what I have said, and yet I should wish to carry conviction from the first. Those lovely iridescent bubbles of the air should not be hard to capture. They drift slowly upon their way, and the swift monoplane could intercept their leisurely course. It is likely enough that they would dissolve in the heavier layers of the atmosphere, and that some small heap of amorphous jelly might be all that I should bring to earth with me. And yet something there would surely be by which I could substantiate my story. Yes, I will go, even if I run a risk by doing so. These purple horrors would not seem to be numerous. It is probable that I shall not see one. If I do I shall dive at once. At the worst there is always the shot-gun and my knowledge of...'

Here a page of the manuscript is unfortunately missing. On the next page is written, in large, straggling writing:—

> 'Forty-three thousand feet. I shall never see earth again. They are beneath me, three of them. God help me; it is a dreadful death to die!'

Such in its entirety is the Joyce-Armstrong Statement. Of the man nothing has since been seen. Pieces of his shattered monoplane have been picked up in the preserves of Mr Budd-Lushington upon the borders of Kent and Sussex, within a few miles of the spot where the note-book was discovered. If the unfortunate aviator's theory is correct that this air-jungle, as he called it, existed only over the south-west of England, then it would seem that he had fled from it at the full speed of his monoplane, but had been overtaken and devoured by these horrible creatures at some spot in the outer atmosphere above the place where the grim relics were found. The picture of that monoplane skimming down the sky, with the nameless terrors flying as swiftly beneath it and cutting it off always from the earth while they gradually closed in upon their victim, is one upon which a man who valued his sanity would prefer not to dwell. There are many, as I am aware, who still jeer at the facts which I have here set down, but even they must admit that Joyce-Armstrong has disappeared, and I would commend to them his own words: 'This note-book may explain what I am trying to do, and how I lost my life in doing it. But no drivel about accidents or mysteries, if *you* please.'

THE BULLY OF BROCAS COURT

THAT year—it was in 1878—the South Midland Yeomanry were out near Luton, and the real question which appealed to every man in the great camp was not how to prepare for a possible European war, but the far more vital one how to get a man who could stand up for ten rounds to Farrier-Sergeant Burton. Slogger Burton was a fine upstanding fourteen stone of bone and brawn, with a smack in either hand which would leave any ordinary mortal senseless. A match must be found for him somewhere or his head would outgrow his dragoon helmet. Therefore Sir Fred. Milburn, better known as Mumbles, was dispatched to London to find if among the fancy there was no one who would make a journey in order to take down the number of the bold dragoon.

They were bad days, those, in the prize-ring. The old knuckle-fighting had died out in scandal and disgrace, smothered by the pestilent crowd of betting men and ruffians of all sorts who hung upon the edge of the movement and brought disgrace and ruin upon the decent fighting men, who were often humble heroes whose gallantry has never been surpassed. An honest sportsman who desired to see a fight was usually set upon by villains, against whom he had no redress, since he was himself engaged on what was technically an illegal action. He was stripped in the open street, his purse taken, and his head split open if he ventured to resist. The ringside could only be reached by men who were prepared to fight their way there with cudgels and hunting-crops. No wonder that the classic sport was attended now by those only who had nothing to lose.

On the other hand, the era of the reserved building and the legal glove-fight had not yet arisen, and the cult was in a strange intermediate condition. It was impossible to regulate it, and equally impossible to abolish it, since nothing appeals more directly and powerfully to the average Briton. Therefore there were scrambling contests in stableyards and barns, hurried visits to France, secret meetings at dawn in wild parts of the country, and all manner of evasions and experiments. The men themselves became as unsatisfactory as their surroundings. There could be no honest open contest, and the loudest bragger talked his way to the top of the list. Only across the Atlantic had the huge figure of John Lawrence Sullivan appeared, who was destined to be the last of the earlier system and the first of the later one.

Things being in this condition, the sporting Yeomanry Captain found it no easy matter among the boxing saloons and sporting pubs of London to find a man who could be relied upon to give a good account of the huge Farrier-Sergeant. Heavy-weights were at a premium. Finally his choice fell upon Alf Stevens of Kentish Town, an excellent rising middle-weight who had never yet known defeat and had indeed some claims to the championship. His professional experience and craft would surely make up for the three stone of weight which separated him from the formidable dragoon. It was in this hope that Sir Fred. Milburn engaged him, and proceeded to convey him in his dog-cart behind a pair of spanking greys to the camp of the Yeomen. They were to start one evening, drive up the Great North Road, sleep at St Albans, and finish their journey next day.

The prize-fighter met the sporting Baronet at the Golden Cross, where Bates, the little groom, was standing at the head of the spirited horses. Stevens, a pale-faced, clean-cut young fellow, mounted beside his employer and waved his hand to a little knot of fighting men, rough, collarless, reefer-coated fellows who had gathered to bid their comrade good-bye. 'Good luck, Alf!' came in a hoarse chorus as the boy released the horses' heads and sprang in behind, while the high dog-cart swung swiftly round the curve into Trafalgar Square.

Sir Frederick was so busy steering among the traffic in Oxford Street and the Edgware Road that he had little thought for anything else, but when he got into the edges of the country near Hendon, and the hedges had at last taken the place of that endless panorama of brick dwellings, he let his horses go easy with a loose rein while he turned his attention to the young man at his side. He had found him by correspondence and recommendation, so that he had some curiosity now in looking him over. Twilight was already falling and the light dim, but what the Baronet saw pleased him well. The man was a fighter every inch, clean-cut, deep-chested, with the long straight cheek and deep-set eye which goes with an obstinate courage. Above all, he was a man who had never yet met his master and was still upheld by the deep sustaining confidence which is never quite the same after a single defeat. The Baronet chuckled as he realised what a surprise packet was being carried north for the Farrier-Sergeant.

'I suppose you are in some sort of training, Stevens?' he remarked, turning to his companion.

'Yes, sir; I am fit to fight for my life.'

'So I should judge by the look of you.'

'I live regular all the time, sir, but I was matched against Mike Connor for this last week-end and scaled down to eleven four. Then he paid forfeit, and here I am at the top of my form.'

'That's lucky. You'll need it all against a man who has a pull of three stone and four inches.'

The young man smiled.

'I have given greater odds than that, sir.'

'I dare say. But he's a game man as well.'

'Well, sir, one can but do one's best.'

The Baronet liked the modest but assured tone of the young pugilist. Suddenly an amusing thought struck him, and he burst out laughing.

'By Jove!' he cried. 'What a lark if the Bully is out tonight!'

Alf Stevens pricked up his ears.

'Who might he be, sir?'

'Well, that's what the folk are asking. Some say they've seen him, and some say he's a fairy-tale, but there's good evidence that he is a real man with a pair of rare good fists that leave their marks behind him.'

'And where might he live?'

'On this very road. It's between Finchley and Elstree, as I've heard. There are two chaps, and they come out on nights when the moon is at full and challenge the passers-by to fight in the old style. One fights and the other picks up. By George! the fellow *can* fight, too, by all accounts. Chaps have been found in the morning with their faces all cut to ribbons to show that the Bully had been at work upon them.'

Alf Stevens was full of interest.

'I've always wanted to try an old-style battle, sir, but it never chanced to come my way. I believe it would suit me better than the gloves.'

'Then you won't refuse the Bully?'

'Refuse him! I'd go ten mile to meet him.'

'By George! it would be great!' cried the Baronet. 'Well, the moon is at the full, and the place should be about here.'

'If he's as good as you say,' Stevens remarked, 'he should be known in the ring, unless he is just an amateur who amuses himself like that.'

'Some think he's an ostler, or maybe a racing man from the training stables over yonder. Where there are horses there is boxing. If you can believe the accounts, there is something a bit queer and outlandish about the fellow. Hi! Look out, damn you, look out!'

The Baronet's voice had risen to a sudden screech of surprise and of anger. At this point the road dips down into a hollow, heavily shaded by trees, so that at night it arches across like the mouth of a tunnel. At the foot of the slope there stand two great stone pillars, which, as viewed by daylight, are lichen-stained and weathered, with heraldic devices on each which are so mutilated by time that they are mere protuberances of stone. An iron gate of elegant design, hanging loosely upon rusted hinges, proclaims both the past glories and the present decay of Brocas Old Hall, which lies at the end of the weed-encumbered avenue. It was from the shadow of this ancient gateway that an active figure had sprung suddenly into the centre of the road and had, with great dexterity, held up the horses, who ramped and pawed as they were forced back upon their haunches.

'Here, Rowe, you 'old the tits, will ye?' cried a high strident voice. 'I've a little word to say to this 'ere slap-up Corinthian before 'e goes any farther.'

A second man had emerged from the shadows and without a word took hold of the horses' heads. He was a short, thick fellow, dressed in a curious brown many-caped overcoat, which came to his knees, with gaiters and boots beneath it. He wore no hat, and those in the dog-cart had a view, as he came in front of the side-lamps, of a surly red face with an ill-fitting lower lip clean shaven, and a high black cravat swathed tightly under the chin. As he gripped the leathers his more active comrade sprang forward and rested a bony hand upon the side of the splashboard while he looked keenly up with a pair of fierce blue eyes at the faces of the two travellers, the light beating full upon his own features. He wore a hat low upon his brow, but in spite of its shadow both the Baronet and the pugilist could see enough to shrink from him, for it was an evil face, evil but very formidable, stern, craggy, high-nosed, and fierce, with an inexorable mouth which bespoke a nature which would neither ask for mercy nor grant it. As to his age, one could only say for certain that a man with such a face was young enough to have all his virility and old enough to have experienced all the wickedness of life. The cold, savage eyes took a deliberate survey, first of the Baronet and then of the young man beside him.

'Aye, Rowe, it's a slap-up Corinthian, same as I said,' he remarked over his shoulder to his companion. 'But this other is a likely chap. If 'e isn't a millin' cove 'e ought to be. Any'ow, we'll try 'im out.'

'Look here,' said the Baronet, 'I don't know who you are, except that you are a damned impertinent fellow. I'd put the lash of my whip across your face for two pins!'

'Stow that gammon, gov'nor! It ain't safe to speak to me like that.'

'I've heard of you and your ways!' cried the angry soldier. 'I'll teach you to stop my horses on the Queen's high road! You've got the wrong men this time, my fine fellow, as you will soon learn.'

'That's as it may be,' said the stranger. 'May'ap, master, we may all learn something before we part. One or other of you 'as got to get down and put up your 'ands before you get any farther.'

Stevens had instantly sprung down into the road.

'If you want a fight you've come to the right shop,' said he; 'it's my trade, so don't say I took you unawares.'

The stranger gave a cry of satisfaction.

'Blow my dickey!' he shouted. 'It *is* a millin' cove, Joe, same as I said. No more chaw-bacons for us, but the real thing. Well, young man, you've met your master tonight. Happen you never 'eard what Lord Longmore said o' me? "A man must be made special to beat you," says 'e. That's wot Lord Longmore said.'

'That was before the Bull came along,' growled the man in front, speaking for the first time.

'Stow your chaffing, Joe! A little more about the Bull and you and me will quarrel. 'E bested me once, but it's all betters and no takers that I glut 'im if ever we meet again. Well, young man, what d'ye think of me?'

'I think you've got your share of cheek.'

'Cheek. Wot's that?'

'Impudence, bluff—gas, if you like.'

The last word had a surprising effect upon the stranger. He smote his leg with his hand and broke out into a high neighing laugh, in which he was joined by his gruff companion.

'You've said the right word, my beauty,' cried the latter, '"Gas" is the word and no error. Well, there's a good moon, but the clouds are comin' up. We had best use the light while we can.'

Whilst this conversation had been going on the Baronet had been looking with an ever-growing amazement at the attire of the stranger. A good deal of it confirmed his belief that he was connected with some stables, though making every allowance for this his appearance was very eccentric and old-fashioned. Upon his head he wore a yellowish-white top-hat of long-haired beaver, such as is still affected by some drivers of four-in-hands, with a bell crown and a curling brim. His dress consisted of a short-waisted swallow-tail coat, snuff-coloured, with steel buttons. It opened in front to show a vest of striped silk, while his legs were encased in buff knee-breeches with blue stockings and low shoes. The figure was angular and hard, with a great suggestion of wiry activity. This Bully of Brocas was clearly a very great character, and the young dragoon officer chuckled as he thought what a glorious story he would carry back to the mess of this queer old-world figure and the thrashing which he was about to receive from the famous London boxer.

Billy, the little groom, had taken charge of the horses, who were shivering and sweating.

'This way!' said the stout man, turning towards the gate. It was a sinister place, black and weird, with the crumbling pillars and the heavy arching trees. Neither the Baronet nor the pugilist liked the look of it.

'Where are you going, then?'

'This is no place for a fight,' said the stout man. 'We've got as pretty a place as ever you saw inside the gate here. You couldn't beat it on Molesey Hurst.'

'The road is good enough for me,' said Stevens.

'The road is good enough for two Johnny Raws,' said the man with the beaver hat. 'It ain't good enough for two slap-up millin' coves like you an' me. You ain't afeard, are you?'

'Not of you or ten like you,' said Stevens, stoutly.

'Well, then, come with me and do it as it ought to be done.'

Sir Frederick and Stevens exchanged glances.

'I'm game,' said the pugilist.

'Come on, then.'

The little party of four passed through the gateway. Behind them in the darkness the horses stamped and reared, while the voice of the boy could be heard as he vainly tried to soothe them. After walking fifty yards up the grass-grown drive the guide turned to the right through a thick belt of trees, and they came out upon a circular plot of grass, white and clear in the moonlight. It had a raised bank, and on the farther side was one of those little pillared stone summer-houses beloved by the early Georgians.

'What did I tell you?' cried the stout man, triumphantly. 'Could you do better than this within twenty mile of town? It was made for it. Now, Tom, get to work upon him, and show us what you can do.'

It had all become like an extraordinary dream. The strange men, their odd dress, their queer speech, the moonlit circle of grass, and the pillared summer-house all wove themselves into one fantastic whole. It was only the sight of Alf Stevens's ill-fitting tweed suit, and his homely English face surmounting it, which brought the Baronet back to the workaday world. The thin stranger had taken off his beaver hat, his swallow-tailed coat, his silk waistcoat, and finally his shirt had been drawn over his head by his second. Stevens in a cool and leisurely fashion kept pace with the preparations of his antagonist. Then the two fighting men turned upon each other.

But as they did so Stevens gave an exclamation of surprise and horror. The removal of the beaver hat had disclosed a horrible mutilation of the head of his antagonist. The whole upper forehead had fallen in, and there seemed to be a broad red weal between his close-cropped hair and his heavy brows.

'Good Lord,' cried the young pugilist. 'What's amiss with the man?'

The question seemed to rouse a cold fury in his antagonist.

'You look out for your own head, master,' said he. 'You'll find enough to do, I'm thinkin', without talkin' about mine.'

This retort drew a shout of hoarse laughter from his second. 'Well said, my Tommy!' he cried. 'It's Lombard Street to a China orange on the one and only.'

The man whom he called Tom was standing with his hands up in the centre of the natural ring. He looked a big man in his clothes, but he seemed bigger in the buff, and his barrel chest, sloping shoulders, and loosely-slung muscular arms were all ideal for the game. His grim eyes gleamed fiercely beneath his misshapen brows, and his lips were set in a fixed hard smile, more menacing than a scowl. The pugilist confessed, as he approached him, that he had never seen a more formidable figure. But his bold heart rose to the fact that he had never yet found the man who could master him, and that it was hardly credible that he would appear as an old-fashioned stranger on a country road. Therefore, with an answering smile, he took up his position and raised his hands.

But what followed was entirely beyond his experience. The stranger feinted quickly with his left, and sent in a swinging hit with his right, so quick and hard that Stevens had barely time to avoid it and to counter with a short jab as his opponent rushed in upon him. Next instant the man's bony arms were round him, and the pugilist was hurled into the air in a whirling cross-buttock, coming down with a heavy thud upon the grass. The stranger stood back and folded his arms while Stevens scrambled to his feet with a red flush of anger upon his cheeks.

'Look here,' he cried. 'What sort of game is this?'

'We claim foul!' the Baronet shouted.

'Foul be damned! As clean a throw as ever I saw!' said the stout man. 'What rules do you fight under?'

'Queensberry, of course.'

'I never heard of it. It's London prize-ring with us.'

'Come on, then!' cried Stevens, furiously. 'I can wrestle as well as another. You won't get me napping again.'

Nor did he. The next time that the stranger rushed in Stevens caught him in as strong a grip, and after swinging and swaying they came down together in a dog-fall. Three times this occurred, and each time the stranger walked across to his friend and seated himself upon the grassy bank before he recommenced.

'What d'ye make of him?' the Baronet asked, in one of these pauses.

Stevens was bleeding from the ear, but otherwise showed no sign of damage.

'He knows a lot,' said the pugilist. 'I don't know where he learned it, but he's had a deal of practice somewhere. He's as strong as a lion and as hard as a board, for all his queer face.'

'Keep him at out-fighting. I think you are his master there.'

'I'm not so sure that I'm his master anywhere, but I'll try my best.'

It was a desperate fight, and as round followed round it became clear, even to the amazed Baronet, that the middle-weight champion had met his match. The stranger had a clever draw and a rush which, with his springing hits, made him a most dangerous foe. His head and body seemed insensible to blows, and the horribly malignant smile never for one instant flickered from his lips. He hit very hard with fists like flints, and his blows whizzed up from every angle. He had one particularly deadly lead, an uppercut at the jaw, which again and again nearly came home, until at last it did actually fly past the guard and brought Stevens to the ground. The stout man gave a whoop of triumph.

'The whisker hit, by George! It's a horse to a hen on my Tommy! Another like that, lad, and you have him beat.'

'I say, Stevens, this is going too far,' said the Baronet, as he supported his weary man. 'What will the regiment say if I bring you up all knocked to pieces in a bye-battle! Shake hands with this fellow and give him best, or you'll not be fit for your job.'

'Give him best? Not I!' cried Stevens, angrily. 'I'll knock that damned smile off his ugly mug before I've done.'

'What about the Sergeant?'

'I'd rather go back to London and never see the Sergeant than have my number taken down by this chap.'

'Well, 'ad enough?' his opponent asked, in a sneering voice, as he moved from his seat on the bank.

For answer young Stevens sprang forward and rushed at his man with all the strength that was left to him. By the fury of his onset he drove him back, and for a long minute had all the better of the exchanges. But this iron fighter seemed never to tire. His step was as quick and his blow as hard as ever when this long rally had ended. Stevens had eased up from pure exhaustion. But his opponent did not ease up. He came back on him with a shower of furious blows which beat down the weary guard of the pugilist. Alf Stevens was at the end of his strength and would in another instant have sunk to the ground but for a singular intervention.

It has been said that in their approach to the ring the party had passed through a grove of trees. Out of these there came a peculiar shrill cry, a cry of agony, which might be from a child or from some small woodland creature in distress. It was inarticulate, high-pitched and inexpressibly melancholy. At the sound the stranger, who had knocked Stevens on to his knees, staggered back and looked round him with an expression of helpless horror upon his face. The smile had left his lips and there only remained the loose-lipped weakness of a man in the last extremity of terror.

'It's after me again, mate!' he cried.

'Stick it out, Tom! You have him nearly beat! It can't hurt you.'

'It can 'urt me! It will 'urt me!' screamed the fighting man. 'My God! I can't face it! Ah, I see it! I see it!'

With a scream of fear he turned and bounded off into the brushwood. His companion, swearing loudly, picked up the pile of clothes and darted after him, the dark shadows swallowing up their flying figures.

Stevens, half-senselessly, had staggered back and lay upon the grassy bank, his head pillowed upon the chest of the young Baronet, who was holding his flask of brandy to his lips. As they sat there they were both aware that the cries had become louder and shriller. Then from among the bushes there ran a small white terrier, nosing about as if following a trail and yelping most piteously. It squattered across the grassy sward, taking no notice of the two young men. Then it also vanished into the shadows. As it did so the two spectators sprang to their feet and ran as hard as they could tear for the gateway and the trap. Terror had seized them—a panic terror far above reason or control. Shivering and shaking, they threw themselves into the dog-cart, and it was not until the willing horses had put two good miles between that ill-omened hollow and themselves that they at last ventured to speak.

'Did you ever see such a dog?' asked the Baronet.

'No,' cried Stevens. 'And, please God, I never may again.'

Late that night the two travellers broke their journey at the Swan Inn, near Harpenden Common. The landlord was an old acquaintance of the Baronet's, and gladly joined him in a glass of port after supper. A famous old sport was Mr Joe Horner, of the Swan, and he would talk by the hour of the legends of the ring, whether new or old. The name of Alf Stevens was well known to him, and he looked at him with the deepest interest.

'Why, sir, you have surely been fighting,' said he. 'I hadn't read of any engagement in the papers.'

'Enough said of that,' Stevens answered, in a surly voice.

'Well, no offence! I suppose'—his smiling face became suddenly very serious—'I suppose you didn't, by chance, see anything of him they call the Bully of Brocas as you came north?'

'Well, what if we did?'

The landlord was tense with excitement.

'It was him that nearly killed Bob Meadows. It was at the very gate of Brocas Old Hall that he stopped him. Another man was with him.

Bob was game to the marrow, but he was found hit to pieces on the lawn inside the gate where the summer-house stands.'

The Baronet nodded.

'Ah, you've been there!' cried the landlord.

'Well, we may as well make a clean breast of it,' said the Baronet, looking at Stevens. 'We have been there, and we met the man you speak of—an ugly customer he is, too!'

'Tell me!' said the landlord, in a voice that sank to a whisper. 'Is it true what Bob Meadows says, that the men are dressed like our grandfathers, and that the fighting man has his head all caved in?'

'Well, he was old-fashioned, certainly, and his head was the queerest ever I saw.'

'God in Heaven!' cried the landlord. 'Do you know, sir, that Tom Hickman, the famous prize-fighter, together with his pal, Joe Rowe, a silversmith of the City, met his death at that very point in the year 1822, when he was drunk, and tried to drive on the wrong side of a wagon? Both were killed and the wheel of the wagon crushed in Hickman's forehead.'

'Hickman! Hickman!' said the Baronet. 'Not the gasman?'

'Yes, sir, they called him Gas. He won his fights with what they called the "whisker hit," and no one could stand against him until Neate—him that they called the Bristol Bull—brought him down.'

Stevens had risen from the table as white as cheese.

'Let's get out of this, sir. I want fresh air. Let us get on our way.'

The landlord clapped him on the back.

'Cheer up, lad! You've held him off, anyhow, and that's more than anyone else has ever done. Sit down and have another glass of wine, for if a man in England has earned it this night it is you. There's many a debt you would pay if you gave the Gasman a welting, whether dead or alive. Do you know what he did in this very room?'

The two travellers looked round with startled eyes at the lofty room, stone-flagged and oak-panelled, with great open grate at the farther end.

'Yes, in this very room. I had it from old Squire Scotter, who was here that very night. It was the day when Shelton beat Josh Hudson out St Albans way, and Gas had won a pocketful of money on the fight. He and his pal Rowe came in here upon their way, and he was mad-raging drunk. The folk fairly shrunk into the corners and under the tables, for he was stalkin' round with the great kitchen poker in his hand, and there was murder behind the smile upon his face. He was like that when the drink was in him—cruel, reckless, and a terror to the world. Well, what think you that he did at last with the poker? There was a little dog, a terrier as I've heard, coiled up before the fire, for it was a bitter December night. The Gasman broke its back with one blow of the poker. Then he burst out laughin', flung a curse or two at the folk that shrunk away from him, and so out to his high gig that was waiting outside. The next we heard was that he was carried down to Finchley with his head ground to a jelly by the wagon wheel. Yes, they do say the little dog with its bleeding skin and its broken back has been seen since then, crawlin' and yelpin' about Brocas Corner, as if it were lookin' for the swine that killed it. So you see, Mr Stevens, you were fightin' for more than yourself when you put it across the Gasman.'

'Maybe so,' said the young prize-fighter, 'but I want no more fights like that. The Farrier-Sergeant is good enough for me, sir, and if it is the same to you, we'll take a railway train back to town.'

STORY SOURCES

'The Captain of the "Polestar"' first published in *Temple Bar*, January 1883 and first collected in *The Captain of the 'Polestar'* (Longmans, Green, 1890).

'The Winning Shot' first published in *Bow Bells*, 11 July 1883.

'John Barrington Cowles' first published in *Cassell's Saturday Journal*, 12–19 April 1884 and first collected in *The Captain of the* Polestar (Longmans, Green, 1890).

'*De Profundis*' first published in *The Idler*, March 1892 and first collected in *The Last Galley* (Smith, Elder, 1911).

'The Parasite' first serialised in *Harper's Weekly*, 10 November to 1 December 1894 and published separately as *The Parasite* (Constable, 1894).

'The Story of the Brown Hand' first published in *The Strand*, May 1899 and first collected in *Round the Fire Stories* (Smith, Elder, 1908).

'Playing with Fire' first published in *The Strand*, March 1900 and first collected in *Round the Fire Stories* (Smith, Elder, 1908).

'The Leather Funnel' first published in *McClure's Magazine*, November 1902 and first collected in *Round the Fire Stories* (Smith, Elder, 1908).

'The Terror of Blue John Gap' first published in *The Strand*, August 1910 and first collected in *The Last Galley* (Smith, Elder, 1911).

'How It Happened' first published in *The Strand*, September 1913 and first collected in *Danger! And Other Stories* (John Murray, 1918).

'The Horror of the Heights' first published in *The Strand*, November 1913 and first collected in *Danger! And Other Stories* (John Murray, 1918).

'Stranger Than Fiction' first published in *The Strand,* December 1915.

'The Bully of Brocas Court' first published in *The Strand,* November 1921 and first collected in *Tales of the Ring and Camp* (John Murray, 1922).